The
ANGEL
Falls

Colin Youngman

The Works of Colin Youngman:

The Angel Falls

The Doom Brae Witch

Alley Rat

DEAD Heat

Twists*

*Incorporates:

DEAD Lines
Brittle Justice
The Refugee
A Fall Before Pride
Vicious Circle

All the above are also available separately

This is a work of fiction.

All characters and events are products of the author's imagination.

All locations are real (though some liberties have been taken with architectural design, precise geographic settings, and timelines.)

A SprintS Publication

ISBN: 979-8-6024-9368-9

DEDICATION

For the citizens of the magnificent city of
Newcastle upon Tyne.

Colin Youngman

'Where we begin is neither our end nor where we are now. Yet, our beginning leaves its mark on us; moulds and shapes us into the person we are, and the one we are yet to become. This is my beginning.'

Ryan Jarrod

'The cradle rocks above an abyss, and common sense tells us that our existence is but a brief crack of light between two eternities of darkness.'

Vladimir Nabakov

CHAPTER ONE

The pen torch slipped from between his teeth, rolled to the floor, and extinguished itself. Darkness swallowed him whole. Darkness, and fear.

He waited for the fear to subside. It didn't. His chest rose and fell; short, shallow breaths. His hands shook. Sweat dripped into his eyes. Blinded him.

'Think, man. Think.' But his thought processes receded into the shadows of his mind like rats. 'For fuck's sake, come on. Get a grip.'

Okay. The space was confined. The torch must be nearby. He knew he lay on his back. All he had to do was reach out and feel for it. Except, he held the device in his right hand; the mechanism in his left.

He forced his breath out in spurts. Ever-so-gently, he lowered his right hand to his stomach. Released his grip. The objects stayed there. He exhaled noisily.

The man opened his eyes impossibly wide. Pupils yawned, searching for the faintest of light sources. There was none. Only an interminable blackness within which lurked his greatest fear.

He scrabbled his fingers over the litter-strewn floor, caressing everything they touched. His hand bumped the torch. It rolled further away from him. He swore.

He reached out further. Felt the torch slip into his hand. Rummaged for the switch. When the light came, it was nothing more than a waif-like dribble but, to him, it was as brilliant as a searchlight.

With the torch back between his teeth, he secured the last few wires with tape and tucked them back into the open orifice. With the dexterity latex affords the gloved hand, he screwed the cover into position.

A finger flicked at a wristwatch. The face glowed green in the claustrophobic darkness. The same finger moved onto the face of the clock and pushed hour and minute-hand forward to the desired position.

Finally, with the device taped fast against the skirting board, the hunched figure dragged a pile of disused cardboard boxes in front of it

Job done, the intruder clicked off the torch, retreated into the shadows of the ninth-floor corridor, and pushed open the fire exit door.

**

Just off Whaggs Lane, the fourth-hand Fiat Uno, its rear window etched by Pug nose-art, stood parked in the narrow confines of Cornmoor Road, off-side wheels on the pavement.

The occupant made a guttural noise and stretched until his hands touched the roof. It had been a long night. The driver caught sight of himself in the rear-view mirror. He licked a finger and smoothed down an errant wisp of strawberry blond hair. He also straightened a non-existent crease in his navy-blue jacket. He readjusted himself to get a better view, noticed his tie was off-centre, and quickly corrected it, too.

Ryan Jarrod was not yet eighteen and a half, but he wore his uniform with pride. Chest-swelling, heart-bursting pride. After all, he'd spent the first quarter of his nineteenth year preparing for it and, last night, he'd worn it in anger for the first time.

Not that he was angry. Ryan Jarrod never got angry. Anger dulled the senses. Affected the thought-process. That's what they'd told him during his Special Constable training. They'd laughed when he told them he never got angry. They told him the job would make him angry. He knew it wouldn't.

Ryan Jarrod didn't do anger.

But he did get tired. He closed his eyes and waited.

**

Florence Roadhouse rose early. She prided herself on the fact she functioned better today on five hours sleep than on eight in her prime. 'If Margaret managed so magnificently on four hours, I'm sure I can handle five,' she told herself, referring to the famed staying power of her revered Baroness Thatcher. But it was only ever herself she told, never anyone else.

Not that she was ashamed of her politics. Far from it. Besides, the village of Whickham was somewhat of a Tory enclave in Labour-oriented Tyneside. She'd find plenty like-minded individuals of her generation in her immediate neighbourhood. No, she didn't tell anyone simply there was never anyone to tell.

For a moment, her eyes glassed over as they flicked to the sepia photograph tucked away in a display cabinet. A handsome young man, tall and erect in starched army uniform, smiled back.

She shook her head. 'It's better the way it is,' she chided. 'Folk just get in the way.'

Florence tied her garish dressing gown of maroon, lilac and green tartan tight to her skeletal frame and busied herself preparing breakfast. She caught sight of her reflection mirrored in the kitchen window's pre-dawn blackness and regarded herself critically.

Thin white hair where once there'd been a cascade of raven tresses. The upturned curve of her nose which, in younger days, seemed cute and attractive now appeared to permanently seek out the source of a repugnant smell.

The sound of her gate creaking open brought her out of her melancholy. Her visitor fumbled in a shoulder bag, pulled out a rolled-up object, and pushed it through the letterbox at the same moment Florence Roadhouse reached the hallway.

A cursory glance at the reddish-orange banner of the newspaper on her Welcome mat told her all she needed to know. She flung open the door. Despite the paucity of light from a flickering streetlight at the end of her path, a Pavlovian reaction saw Florence's observation powers switch on instantaneously.

Within seconds she knew everything she needed about the figure retreating from view.

She ticked off the clues in her head, a skill honed over many years observing young nurses under her charge at field hospitals the world over. Battered trainers, laces tucked in rather than tied. Denims baggy to the point of absurdity. Windcheater jacket – grey or fawn – indecipherable slogan on the back. A fluorescent band ran directly from left shoulder to right hip attached to a low-slung bag. The slender shoulders of youth.

She could have been studying the rear view of any of a dozen local youths. But Florence made an instant and correct diagnosis.

'James Jarrod. What a surprise. Thought you'd got away with it again, did you? Well, I wasn't so slow this time, was I? Get back here. This instant.'

His identity betrayed by the shock of orange hair gelled almost vertical until it resembled a Dickensian candle, James didn't break stride, though his whistle took on a discordant vibrato.

Florence Roadhouse took one step over her threshold. Blue-veined skin grabbed tightly at her shin, tibia and fibula standing out like machete blades. She grabbed at her gown to protect her from the morning frost. 'Boy! I said stop. Right there. Are you deaf?'

James Jarrod – Jam Jar to his peers – stood still. Ever so slowly, the fire atop the shaven neck began to turn until Jam Jar caught a glimpse of the tall yet stooped harlequin in the illuminated doorway. 'Sorry, missus. Didn't hear you over the noise of your coat.'

Florence Roadhouse's eyes narrowed. Her reedy voice dropped an octave. It became more composed yet, somehow, more clinical.

'Young man,' she began. 'You know very well I read the local newspaper and the Telegraph, and I really think it's the local paper and the Telegraph I should get, don't you? Every morning for the last thirty years, that's how it's been. Every morning, that is, until you start delivering for Mr Ramesh. Now, be a good boy and hand them over.'

'*I sound like a policeman talking to an armed robber*', she thought. But, as her breath condensed in the morning chill and masked her face in an unholy aura, she saw her words had had an effect.

Jam Jar hesitated but, if there was a GCSE in teenageness, James Jarrod would be top of the class. 'Piss off, you old dyke. Still missing your Page Three girls, are you?'

The instant the words left his mouth, he tried to paw them back in again. But it was too late. He watched Florence turn the predominant colour of her tartan. She said nothing. Just looked. The look which had transformed the stuffiest of surgeons into compliant putty.

The boy's exuberant cockiness withered and died; his confidence crushed like the petals of an orchid in an iron fist. 'Sorry, missus. I was only having a laugh. Honest. Here's your papers. Look, I'll leave them on your path. And you can keep the other one, free of charge, like. There might be a crossword or summat you can do.' He glanced at the old woman. She didn't look appeased. 'My brother's a copper you know. You can't do owt to me...'

The sentence stayed unfinished. Jam Jar was already out of Queen's Drive and half-way along Cornmoor Road to the safety of his brother's car.

Florence chuckled to herself. 'The old girl's still got it in her.'

CHAPTER TWO

'This isn't going to work.'

Ryan Jarrod reached the conclusion as he parked the white Fiat in Four Lane Ends car park and joined the procession of folk making their way along Benton Park Road.

Rain fell. Icy lances speared his face and stung his bare hands. Thick splats drenched his hair as they fell from the Tree House on the corner of Balliol Gardens. But it didn't refresh him nor make him feel any less tired.

He'd finished his first shift, helped his unusually quiet younger brother with his paper round, showered, changed and set off across the Tyne Bridge to his day job. He'd managed to grab a bacon buttie and coffee at a Gregg's but what he hadn't grabbed was sleep.

Of course, his employer assured him he qualified for special leave for constabulary duties. All Government departments did. But, no matter how many mandatory Unconscious Bias training courses management went on, Ryan knew conscious bias remained. He'd still be required to meet targets, explain away his failures at tedious performance meetings, and feel accountable to his colleagues for his absences.

No, he didn't want to go down the 'special leave' route. He'd stick it out. After all, it was only a temporary thing until he joined the force proper.

Then he remembered that's what his dad had said. And he was still there until he retired forty-odd years later.

'Bollocks.'

But he wasn't angry. Ryan Jarrod didn't get angry.

**

Ryan wasn't the only one who was tired. Unless he got a last-minute call, Teddy McGuffie's shift was at an end. It had been a quiet night, which made it seem even longer. But the last fare had made it worthwhile.

Teddy rubbed the note between stubby fingers as if seeking confirmation in Braille of what his eyes scarcely dared believe. For a moment, he'd almost called his fare back to the cab so he could point out the error. He soon thought better of it. If someone could afford to leave a £50 tip, even one unaccustomed to Her Majesty's currency, he decided they wouldn't notice if it went to a more deserving cause.

McGuffie watched as his fare walked purposefully from the cab. Rain teemed onto the windscreen, diffusing the passenger into a myriad of eerie prisms. Only the crisp feel of the note in the palm of his hand convinced Teddy that the spectre had been a living breathing person.

Teddy shrugged, folded the note into the top pocket of his bri-nylon shirt, and began to make plans to share it with his best mate, Jack Daniels.

**

The fingers poised momentarily over the heavy metal casing of the 1960's typewriter. As the gnarled knuckles of its arthritic sister popped and crackled alongside, the good hand clanked out the final words of its message.

'…and as someone who spent the better part of fifty years devoted to the care of others, either our wounded veterans or in the National Health Service, I can assure your readers that the time is ripe for its privatisation. Let's not have any more cries of 'never'. The right time is not never, not even next year or next month. The time is now. Yours,
F Roadhouse (Miss).

With the decisive thump of the last full stop, F Roadhouse (Miss) returned the carriage, scrolled the page from the roller, and read aloud her latest tirade against officialdom, housing grants, immigrants, student grants – any rant will do.

Peering over the rim of her half-moon spectacles, Florence struggled to unscrew the top from the fountain pen with which she'd ink in the 'v' on the top of every 'y' her stubborn typewriter ribbon had refused to recognise.

Satisfied at last, Florence lifted the Victorian lady from the position she'd occupied on her mantelpiece for the last eighteen years, reached for the almost empty book of stamps beneath, then thought better of it.

No, she decided. This one deserves to be delivered by hand. After the fifth read of her letter to the editor, she retreated to her William Morris-inspired living room with a cup of milky Ovaltine.

The tinny chime of her clock signalled the time. Seven-thirty am on the morning of December 1st.

**

'God's pressed the pause button on life.'

It was the only explanation Sonia Hilton could come up with as she hovered three-foot above her desk.

Like her peers, she planned on being up all night. She'd pored over her dissertation, sustained by black coffee and Pot Noodles. She knew this because she could see the congealed mess inside the pot from her position above her desk.

And she knew about the coffee because it was in front of her; the cup in mid-air just out of reach, its contents aimed downwards towards her laptop computer, frozen in time like a scalding icicle.

She knew all these things, yet not the most important: why was she floating above her desk?

She'd seen nothing, heard nothing and felt nothing – yet she found herself in this surreal position; in the early hours, suspended in mid-air staring down at the omnipresent traffic flow along the Central Motorway beneath her, their taillights blinking at as if they were the reflection of her own bloodshot eyes.

Then, God's finger hit fast-forward and she saw, heard and felt everything.

She saw the flare of the explosion; scarlet, crimson and orange.

She heard the blast, so loud her eardrums imploded.

And she felt the plate-glass window slice her open from throat to abdomen as she was catapulted from her ninth-floor student accommodation.

Sonia Hilton was dead ten feet before her eviscerated remains plunged through the roof of a Ford Galaxy onto the lap of the horrified driver.

**

The telephone was already ringing as she approached her desk on the third story of the Mercury offices. Stretching over the desk from the wrong side, a leg with the slim musculature of a tennis player lifted off the floor for balance while its owner lifted the receiver.

'Wolfe,' she said, cradling the handset under her chin. She shrugged her shoulders. Her coat slid down her back until she wriggled her arms free and it fell to the floor.

Looking on from his desk opposite, Raymond Carpenter, News Sub-Editor, saw Megan Wolfe become alert. He heard her say 'Whoa!', watched her grab a pen from an adjacent desk, slip into a chair and propel herself across a gap between desks.

'Ok, that's superb, Bob,' she was saying into the mouthpiece. 'Anyone with you?' There was a delay of a nanosecond, hardly time for a reply to register, before she added, 'We'll get a team down with you. Pronto.'

Raymond watched as she swivelled her monitor through 180 degrees, fingers jabbing at the touch-screen menu; a workstation assessor's nightmare.

'Any casualties?' she asked the disembodied Bob. 'HOW many? Wow! What a story!'

Raymond saw her flick back her tawny hair. Her eyes were alive, sparkling. Raymond deserted his own desk, abandoned the wallpaper of national's festooned across it. By rights, the call should have come through his desk. Everyone knew it didn't work that way. The whole news desk knew who really ran the show.

Megan Wolfe dialled an internal extension. 'Emma? Megan.' She glanced up at the whiteboard above her desk, coloured magnetic tiles stuck to it. She focussed on a blue tile. 'Emma, I need you to get hold of Mike Cash. Tell him and Lee Milton to get down to Northumbria Uni; the City East campus. There's been an explosion. Heavy casualties.'

She glanced at the whiteboard again. Homed in on an orange tile. 'Tell you what, get onto David Woods first. It's not his thing but he's the one on call. Get him on the human angle. Victim's families, that sort of thing, yeah? We'll need his photographic skills there, anyway.'

Wolfe paused for breath for the first time. 'No freelances on this one. I want it contained in-house. And tell the team to wear their headcams. Mobilise our best videographers. This could be the shot in the arm our digital platform needs.'

Wolfe set down the phone. Stretched her long legs in front of her. Extended her arms high above her head and arched her back like a cat in front of a fire.

Carpenter saw the blush rise to her high cheekbones. He didn't need know the details of the story. Her body language told him she was onto a big one. He'd seen the look before. Once when she scooped Fleet Street to the story of the Foreign Secretary's resignation, once more when her expose of a fallen celebrity led to his suicide. And twice in bed after each of the former.

He knew he was in for a long day and an all-too-short night.

He reached her desk and bent across it to look at the scribbled notes made in Pitman script. As he did so, she leant close. Her copper hair fell over one sky-blue eye.

'Raymond,' she purred into his ear. 'I was born for days like this.'

CHAPTER THREE

Blue.

Black.

Blue.

Black.

Blue.

Black.

The shifting patterns flitted across Teddy McGuffie's vision like a bubble-lamp. Except he didn't know how, because his eyes were closed.

With an audible grunt, he forced open the immense heaviness of his eyelids.

Blue.

Then found the effort too great. They snapped back shut with the taught elasticity of a bungee rope.

Black.

Boy, he'd had hangovers aplenty, but never anything like this. His nostrils felt as if they were packed with quick-drying cement. The pressure in his sinuses built up like a geyser about to release its ejaculate. All the time, there was an oppressive weight across his forehead, a nauseous sensation in his stomach; a sense of remoteness from reality.

And his world was spinning as if he were on a carousel from Hell. But the revolutions were different. This time, it spun

Blue.

Black.

Blue.

Black.

He tried to make sense of it. Vague memories drifted back to him. He remembered setting out from his flat. Starting his shift. He remembered picking up a student on her way from Uni to meet her boyfriend. The old lady who'd left a tea-dance. The long, quiet hours of night. A couple of night-club stragglers who'd found something to do for three hours after the clubs shut.

He remembered the foreigner. The fifty-pound tip. His plan to invest it wisely in a Tennessee Jack. And then he remembered…nothing. Occasional images drifted to him but, before he could grasp them, they floated tantalisingly out of reach. Like a fifty-pound note caught on a breeze.

The effort was too much for him, so he gave up trying to remember. Suffice to know it must have been a helluva good sour mash. Instead, he concentrated on something else. Like why everything was

Blue.

Black.

Blue.

Black.

And why he was on the pavement. Teddy knew he was on the pavement because he felt the kerb dig in his ribs like a dagger. It had been many years since he'd been so bladdered he hadn't made it home.

'God. What a state.'

He tried to roll on his side; a precursor to sitting up, then, if his stomach and the revolving

Blue.

Black

allowed, he'd rise to his feet.

But he couldn't. Stiff from a night on the tiles. Literally. But it felt more than that. As if he were somehow restrained.

He became aware of a sound other than the rushing noise in his ears. The sound wasn't clear. Almost unworldly. But it was there.

And still the rain fell. He felt it splatter onto his face, run down his forehead, over his closed lids. With an effort greater than he thought possible, Teddy raised a hand. Drew it across his face. Wiped the rain away. It felt oddly thick. Almost warm. Yet, he was cold. So cold. He shivered violently; great, uncontrollable shudders from toenails to hair root.

Teddy McGuffie tried to open his eyes once more.

Looking into the strange

Blue

Blackness,

Teddy sensed someone crouch over him. He prepared to speak to the figure. He licked his lips. The rain tasted salty, somehow familiar, almost like…and then the recognition was gone; the fifty-pound note once more blown out of reach. McGuffie refocussed his attention on the figure stooped over him. He wanted to ask the stranger what he was doing. Wanted to stop him rifling his pockets. But he hadn't the motivation or the strength.

All he noticed through the

Blackness

was that the figure was dressed in

Blue.

**

The first number 97 of the day was always cold. Cold, and quiet. This morning, the passenger list comprised two shift-workers slumbering fitfully in the rear, a couple of businessmen playing peek-a-boo behind unfurled broadsheets, and a haggard pensioner taking advantage of the off-peak concession simply to kill time before time killed him.

The only other occupant balanced herself precariously by the exit door. She'd noticed 'road closed' and 'diversion' signs but played little heed to them. Like most cities, Newcastle was amid a never-ending evolution which seemed to consist of replacing roundabouts with traffic lights, then back again, for no other reason than to keep unemployment figures down.

Florence Roadhouse sensed this was different. She'd have seen the planning notices if it was routine works. And, besides, this time half the city seemed out-of-bounds. Curiosity piqued, she chose to alight the bus on Grainger Street and walk the eerily deserted streets.

As the bus drew to a halt, she turned to face the driver, clutched the cold steel of the handrail with her good hand and stepped backwards, her feet seeking the sanctuary of each step the way a blind man gropes for a door handle.

Once on terra firma, Florence discovered a surprising spring to her step. In her handbag was the pristine envelope containing the latest in her lengthy line of Letters to the Editor. She glanced at her watch. She was on St John Street and bang on schedule to make the reception desk of the Groat Market office just as it opened. She knew Virginia would be opening the shutters at that very moment. Florence made a point of delivering her letters to Virginia. Despite the overwhelming perfume she wore, Virginia was nice. Not like Moira, the other receptionist.

With her mind still on the office girls, Florence turned into the claustrophobic alleyway of Pudding Chare. The lingering aroma of garlic as she passed Puccini's restaurant brought her head up, and she breasted a ribbon of blue and white tape strung across the lane as if she were an athlete.

Pudding Chare was out of bounds, even to pedestrians.

Florence harrumphed. She had no wish to backtrack. Ever-so-gently, she lifted the tape and stooped beneath the cordon. Until her aging brain clicked into gear. The tape wasn't the yellow and black of the Highway's Agency. It was blue and white. Police blue and white.

Via the reflection in the darkened windows of an unopened store, she saw the dazzling strobe lights of emergency vehicles fly up Grey Street.

**

'Where the bloody hell's the ambulance?', Ryan Jarrod shouted. 'We're losing him'.

His second day as a Special and already he had a potential corpse in his arms. He couldn't see the extent of the man's injuries, but he knew they were bad. The guy's breathing was shallow, urgent rasping breaths. Ryan sensed blood congeal on his pristine uniform, felt dark patches coagulate across his lap in which he cradled the victim's head.

A disembodied voice crackled back at him. 'They should be with you any minute now, boys. All Hell's broke loose at the Campus. All our guys are there; the ambulance and fire service'll be no different. It's taking precedence over everything.'

'What's the latest on that?'

'You just concentrate on your guy. It's not a place for a Special. We'll get you over there if you're needed. Over.'

Ryan ran a palm over his face. 'Jeez. Perhaps I should've stuck to the day job after all.' He looked further down Pudding Chare to his partner, Frank Burrows.

'Frank – any sign of the meat wagon yet?'

Burrows, a world-weary PC whose ambition spread no further than his pension, climbed out of the back of the abandoned cab. 'Nope. You'll hear him before you see him.'

There was no urgency in his voice. No compassion. Ryan wondered what it was about the uniform that seemed to remove all semblance of humanity from those inside it.

He felt the dead weight of Teddy McGuffie in his arms and knew he'd found his answer.

A crowd began to form, jostling for ringside seats. 'Frankie, man. Get these people behind the tape, will you? Give the poor guy some space.'

Frank Burrows ambled down the lane; his bow-legged gait reminiscent of a gunslinger from way out west. Ryan watched as his colleague stepped alongside the patrol car. Silhouetted against the flashing blue light, the gunslinger was now Charlie Chaplin in a flickering silent movie.

'Come on, Frankie boy. Get a move on. I need a hand here.' Burrows didn't hear Ryan's plea. The Doppler effect of the green and yellow checked ambulance's siren drowned him out as it careened around the corner, body swaying violently against the natural camber of the road.

It screeched to a halt, siren wailing, the ferocity of its light mingled with the lesser candescence of the patrol car.

Blue. Blue.

Black.

Blue. Blue.

Black.

Two figures in dark green coveralls, fluorescents thrown loosely over them, leapt from the cab.

Ryan heard the smaller of the two demand, 'Where's he?' A female voice.

Ryan waved to her. 'Here. He's down here. For God's sake, be quick.' He looked up. 'Frank. Howay, man. Get that crowd back.'

The taller of the paramedics unhooked a flashlight from his belt. The beam veered towards Ryan, illuminated the wall above his head, down onto his face – so bright he had to shield his eyes from the glare. Then, lower still. Onto the prostate figure of Teddy McGuffie, and what remained of his face.

All colour drained from Ryan Jarrod. For the first time, he'd seen the full extent of the man's injuries. Unable to comprehend what he saw, Jarrod stumbled backwards, propped himself against the wall, and began to sink down its rough brick surface towards the cobbles of Pudding Chare.

Frank Burrows ran forward. Yes, Ryan noted, Frank was sprinting. Burrows caught his young sidekick in his arms just as Ryan fell. 'Easy, Ryan, lad. I'll take over now. There's a good lad. Easy does it. You've done good so far. Now, just breathe deep, yeah?'

And Frank was true to his word. He took over as Ryan turned from the pitiful scene, retched, and thanked God he'd skipped breakfast.

'Who we got here?' the female paramedic asked, her voice controlled but urgent. She spoke to Frank Burrows, but her eyes never left Teddy McGuffie.

'Edward Frazer McGuffie, cab license number 1-3-ze...'

'How long's he been like this?' she interrupted, not concerned with police detail.

'Found him about twenty minutes ago. Could've been here all night, what with the blast and all; no-one'll have been down here.'

'Okay. Edward – I'm Angelina. I'm here to care for you. Now, if you can hear me, squeeze my hand.'

Nothing.

Angelina Firenze rolled up McGuffie's cheap shirt sleeve. She worked to attach a plastic tube into his arm. When she looked into the eyes of Teddy McGuffie, she saw only her own almond eyes reflected back from McGuffie's glassy stare.

'Can't get a line in, Ross.' Then, more urgently, 'His pulse has gone. We need to shock him.'

Ross Clarke sprinted back to the ambulance, scattering rubberneckers along the way. An old lady in the crowd said she'd been a nurse; asked him if she could help. Ross shook his head, and Florence Roadhouse slinked back into the crowd.

Angelina Firenze clasped her fists together and brought them down on the centre of McGuffie's chest. He didn't even flinch while she pummelled away.

'Still no output here. Get the fibs ready.' Firenze pressed hard against McGuffie's chest. Again, and again.

McGuffie vomited explosively, a fountain of thick red gunge coated Angelina's uniform and her olive skin.

The lack of a breakfast didn't save Ryan Jarod this time.

Ross Clarke ripped open McGuffie's shirt. Buttons popped, ran down the gutter like coins thrown from a wedding car. He pulled the paddles from the portable charger. Applied them to McGuffie's chest.

'Clear?'

'Clear," Firenze confirmed.

There was a brief click, the hiss of an asthmatic robot, followed by a thundering surge of power that lifted McGuffie clean off the ground.

'Nothing. Again. Clear?'

'Clear.'

The click. The hiss. The surge. The jerk.

For an instant, Teddy McGuffie opened his eyes. Everything became clear, the events of last night now ingrained in his memory. He saw blazing neon images; images projected over the figure standing with his back to him down the lane.

The figure of Ryan Jarrod.

Ryan Jarrod, dressed in

Blue.

Then, everything went very, very

Black.

CHAPTER FOUR

Naked save for the towel around her hair, Megan Wolfe stepped from the shower. She hadn't slept well, her mind filled with the events of yesterday.

Overnight, she'd gone through every word she'd committed to print, analysing whether their impact could have been greater with a different word here, another phrase there. Megan Wolfe was never satisfied with her work. She envied her colleagues working the on-line content. They didn't need words: the images captured on headcams and the direct quotes of those interviewed on mic told their own story.

With a yawn, Megan Wolfe padded across to her apartment's picture-window. She tipped the blinds and looked over the expanse of the River Tyne.

Everything looked sharper, clearly defined, in the glimmering silver of a frosty morning. Linear cloud formations streaked a sky stained pink with the blush of a bashful sun. By the river below, the remnants of mist spilled over the banks, enveloping much of the quayside. Only the seven bridges remained visible, the arch of the Millennium Bridge rising like a chrome rainbow above the shroud.

Megan looked up towards the urban sprawl of the city opposite. A dust cloud hung over it; the heights of the Vermont Hotel and St Andrew's Cathedral spire seemed to shimmer like a mirage through a sandstorm. It was so calm, so tranquil.

Unlike last night.

She remembered the tangled wreckage of steel and brick, recalled the blood stains, heard the wails of the bereaved and the screams of the maimed. And she knew she'd got an exceptional story.

Wolfe stretched an arm through the blinds and slid open the window. She closed her eyes against the striking cold, drew in gulps of chilled air, and felt Goosebumps erupt on her skin. She felt her nipples harden.

And that's when she remembered. She glanced at her bed where Raymond Carpenter slumbered like an anaesthetised gorilla.

Megan looked him over the way she viewed empty bottles the morning after a party. Embarrassed, she scratched at the apple-shaped birthmark on her forearm, which her tattooist had transformed into a Hopi sun, and pulled on a man's XL silk shirt. It wasn't Carpenter's, but it hid her nudity.

By the time she returned with two mugs of coffee, black for her, white and sugared for him, Raymond was awake and propped up in bed.

She sat alongside him.

'Morning, gorgeous,' he said.

Megan winced at the endearment. 'Good morning, Raymond.' She replied as if she were welcoming someone to a business meeting.

He smiled as she handed over the mug. 'Sleep well, yeah?'

'Not bad,' she lied. 'You?'

'Like a baby. Listen, what time's Marcus scheduled the editorial meeting? I was wondering if we had time…'

'8.30. And, no; we haven't.' Let's have this coffee, you can use the shower, and we'll head out. I'll drop you off at the office, then loop round and park.'

'Ashamed of me, yeah?'

His habit of turning a statement into a question irritated her, but she hid it. 'No, it's not that. But work's work, and this is...' she searched for a word with no connotations of 'pleasure' and settled on 'Recreation.'

'Ok, ok. I know my place. It's just strange. I mean, last night, and now this morning – it's like we're different people.'

'We ARE different people, Raymond. And always will be. Last night's history. Let's focus on work now. '

He put down his coffee and stretched an arm towards her. 'Yeah, and I'm your boss. So, you do what I say. And now I'm saying...'

'No, Raymond, NO. And I mean it. Besides, when have I ever done anything you've told me to?'

'All right, feisty lady. Only a joke, right?'

'Apology accepted,' she said, not sure whether Raymond had offered one or not. 'But, stop acting like a teenager. It does nothing for you. The world's changed. Move on and get over it. Now, I'm going to work. Let yourself out. Drop the key in the mailbox.'

She left to dress. When she returned, Raymond was still in bed, sheets pulled up to his shoulders like a scolded child.

She shook her head. 'I'm off. See you later.'

'Megan', he asked. 'After work; do you think we could have a drink? We need to talk.'

'No. Not today. Listen, Raymond. You need to understand. I don't drink. I don't do drugs. This,' she motioned at the bed, 'Is what I do. It's my release. If you can't handle it, just say 'no', ok?'

She slammed the door behind her, leaving a shell-shocked Carpenter in awe of her capriciousness, and no wiser about the state of their relationship.

**

Detective Chief Inspector Stephen Danskin studied the face opposite him. He barely recognised it as his own. Unshaven stubble framed his lower jaw. Red streaks, the comet trails of sleeplessness, ran through the sclera of his eyes. His skin was sallow; yellow, even. He rubbed his jaw with one hand, an eye with the other, and groaned.

On a good day, Danskin believed he bore a passing resemblance to Alan Shearer. Today was not a good day. Today, he looked into the shaving mirror and saw Homer Simpson stare back at him.

With another sigh, Danskin reached for the Corsodyl and took a swig. He held it in his mouth, waited until the sting hit, and swallowed. He screwed the top back onto his vodka substitute, ran the cold tap, and doused his face.

'Fuck it.'

Never in his twenty-three years with the City and County Force had he dealt with anything like this. There'd been major incidents before but nothing on this scale. The Raul Moat manhunt was probably the biggest challenge he'd faced. But this; this was different league.

Danskin sprayed shaving foam into his hand, smeared his face until he resembled Santa Claus, then decided against it. He rinsed his face in more ice-cold water.

This morning, he had to face the press. Far better do it as he looked now, rough as fuck, after working the case all night. A freshly groomed face in front of the cameras gave the impression of inertia.

Even if that's precisely where the case stood: inert.

DCI Danskin had nothing to give the piranhas. No leads, no claim of responsibility by ISIS or the New IRA, no motive. All he had was the number of fatalities. Which he'd downplay. Better to drip-feed the figures than cause even greater panic by revealing the scale of the devastation.

Stephen Danskin towelled dry his face.

'Fuck it,' he repeated.

**

They assembled around an ovoid table waiting for His Lordship's arrival. Marcus Vorster, founder, owner, editor-in-chief and financial crutch of the Mercury, was fashionably late.

They looked at their watches, stared out the window, and fingered Surface Pros. They did anything but talk.

A tense silence wasn't unusual prior to the daily editorial meeting. Heads of department kept their powder dry, ready to pitch their story for the highest level of exposure, but today was different.

They all knew the lead story, knew that Megan Wolfe owned it, but they all wanted a role in it.

Megan Wolfe faced the door. She was first to see it bounce open. First to see Marcus Vorster, tall and lean, stride through. First to see the flush of excitement on his face.

Around the table, cleverly designed to replicate Mercury's orbit, his team straightened in their chairs.

Vorster clapped his hands, rubbed them together. 'Okay. Let's get this show on the road, as you guys would say.'

He tossed his head so the foppish fringe cleared his eyes. He looked for all the world like the male half of a husband and wife team of TV presenters.

'No jousting for position, guys,' he continued, 'We're all agreed on today's lead.' He didn't wait for agreement. 'I want all angles covered, and I expect 'exclusives. We were first to the scene so, if we're not ahead of the game, asses will get kicked.'

The profanity came out as 'isses,' though his audience, familiar with the flattened tones of Vorster's Natal accent, no longer noticed it.

'What we got so far, Raymond?'

All eyes turned to Megan Wolfe. They knew she'd take up the baton 'We got our people all across it. Precious little in the way of hard facts. We'll get the official line later this morning. David Woods has done a fantastic job on the families of the dead and the injured. We don't have official numbers but from his work, I'd guess over fifty killed, twice that number hospitalised. There's a pressie later. I'll be there. I'll take the Digi guys with me.'

'That's what I was counting on. You can't beat live feeds on our web portal. Raymond, why weren't we live last night?'

Megan sensed a ticking off. She let Carpenter answer.

'Err. Well, I thought we may infringe privacy rights. Also, the sights were pretty gruesome...'

'Exactly my point. This is what we need, Ray. I set the Mercury up precisely for the 'gory bits' and the privacy invasions. I wanted it to be raw. If it's on camera, and if the words are from the mouths of those affected, no-one can sue. Raymond, for heaven's sake, smell the coffee. A wasted opportunity. It mustn't happen again. Understood?'

Carpenter swallowed. He nodded to the desk, rather than Vorster, but it was accepted.

'Right. Megan. You lead with our print output. Get your team on it flat-out and run the content by me.'

Megan offered a salute in return.

'Now,' Vorster continued, 'Any other stories we're ignoring, Lee?'

Leeward Milton, a Floridian with the complexion of a bruised plum and a voice so deep it belonged to movie trailers, looked at his notes. 'We got a line on the Royal visit in January. I could do a piece on that. Better still, I'd like to put a security twist on it. Link it to the attacks.'

Vorster nodded. 'I like it. Let's focus everything on the bombing'.

An older man, Mike Cash, interjected. 'We need to be careful, don't we? How do we know it was a bomb and not a gas leak?'

Milton growled. 'That ain't no gas explosion. Trust me, that was a bomb.'

Marcus turned to Molly Uzumba. 'Molly, any international news we need pick up?'

The dark-skinned blonde crossed her legs. 'There's always something, but nothing to topple this. How about I pick up on international reaction to the incident? Perhaps see if I can link a Brexit line?'

'No way, 'Marcus said. 'Everyone's done Brexit to death. Let's be different. Go with what the Internationals are saying about the bombing.' He looked at Cash. 'Explosion,' he added.

He paused for a sip of water. 'We'll keep some of our regulars to one page. Crossword, horoscope, Letters to the Ed. One page only. Anything significant on the entertainment front, Sue?'

Suzi Mawhinney, an ex-actress and current drunk, shook her head. 'Not if we want to run a special on the terror attack. Anything else can wait.'

Mike Cash raised an arm.

Marcus acknowledged. 'I know, Mike, I know. An explosion to a bomb to a terrorist attack. Too big a leap, right?'

'A quantum one,' Cash nodded.

Marcus circled the table. 'Stewart, cut the sports down for today. Keep it to the usual transfer rumours, perhaps a brief forward look at the Christmas fixtures. No more. We've only so many pages to fill, and I want to milk this for all it's worth.'

Vorster paused. Took a deep breath. 'Ok, people, let's get busy. I've got the video guys waiting outside. They're up next.' He looked around the conference room. Lowered his voice. 'They could just be the guys who keep us in business.'

His eyes snapped back to the group. As an afterthought, said, 'Any more news we need cover?'

No-one spoke. Megan filled the void. 'Just one. Got reports of a taxi driver seriously injured. Nasty beating. Just around the corner from here, as it happens. Have we room to run it?'

Marcus thought for a moment. 'Is he dead?'

'Don't know. They took him to Cramlington Special Emergency Care hospital. The City ones are full to bursting point. I've not had an opportunity to follow up yet. Thought I'd wait for your say so.'

'Well, if he's not dead, no. We leave it. If he's popped off his mortal, we'll run it on a quieter news day. Now, any questions?'

Megan spoke again. 'Do we know who's running the press conference? I guess it'll be Superintendent Connor?'

Marcus snorted. 'Not likely. He'll not appear until they've solved it. No, I understand Danskin's taking it.'

'Good. I'll push him until he steps in his own shit.'

'Megan,' Marcus concluded, 'I do believe you've still got a future in this industry. Go get him, tiger.'

CHAPTER FIVE

A stiff northerly breeze ruffled Ryan Jarrod's hair. He squinted against the wind and zipped up his coat. It seemed permanently windy on the open grassland adjacent to Whickham High School but, today, Ryan welcomed it.

The chill blew the cobwebs away; cobwebs which trapped visions of Teddy McGuffie spewing his innards over a paramedic, and a transfixed mob of bystanders filming the horrors from beyond the cordon.

'They had it all wrong,' he thought. *'Special leave should be available after the shift, not for it.'* If it was, there'd be no need for him to pull a sickie.

He shivered as he waited for Spud, he of the artistic nose, to finish his business. To his left, windswept fallow land afforded a view across the expansive Derwent Valley, to the village of Rowlands Gill, and beyond. To his right, at two o'clock as he stood, the vista was very different. Just as open, just as clear, but across a different river.

Beyond the sprawl of the MetroCentre, over the Tyne Valley, the view was urban. The grey slab of Newcastle, its Cathedrals and hotels, high-rises and office blocks, even the arc of the Tyne Bridge, stretched skywards as if in salutation.

From his vantage point off Fellside Road, the city looked no different today than it had yesterday, the devastation towards the east of the city invisible. But Ryan Jarrod knew it had changed. The entire city had changed. Irrevocably.

He jerked the leader in his hand, brought the snuffling dog to heel, and swept the horizon with his eyes. Somewhere in his field of vision, Ryan realised, hid the person whose act had changed everything.

'We'll get you,' he muttered.

**

Even as Ryan Jarrod tuned his TV to BBC News, Stephen Danskin stepped behind a pop-up lectern beneath the statue of the River God Tyne outside Newcastle Civic Centre.

With its elongated limbs, right arm pointing skyward, left to the Earth, the statue struck the pose of a forlorn Gollum bereft of his Precious. Forlorn and bereft captured the mood. Danskin took a deep breath and tried not to blink against the battery of flashbulbs. A mob of journalists, TV reporters and cameramen jostled for position in front of the lectern as if they were refugees around a relief convoy.

A smaller, silver-haired man and a taller woman flanked DCI Danskin. The man, Danskin's trusted lieutenant DI Lyall Parker, gave a nod of encouragement.

'Welcome, everyone,' a grim-faced Danskin began. 'For the record, my name is DCI Stephen Danskin, representing Detective Superintendent Connor. I'm sure you'll understand Superintendent Connor is extremely busy leading this investigation.'

Somewhere in the crowd, Megan Wolfe gave an ironic smile.

'I shall release a short statement of the facts as we know them, then I shall take a few questions. Thank you.'

A fresh volley of flashes rained down on him.

'At 4.58am, a serious explosion occurred within the confines of Northumbria University's City East campus. This resulted in eleven people losing their lives, and many more injured. We believe several of those injured are in a critical condition, with others who have injuries described to me as life-changing.'

Danskin paused to allow his words to sink in. When the flashbulbs subsided, he continued. 'We are still in the process of contacting family and next-of-kin so, as a result, we are not in a position to release any further information. Family specialist officers are working with the relatives as I speak.'

The hush around Danskin was noticeable. He'd expected a rabble-rousing mob, but the press remained respectful. He sought to keep them that way.

'All of our thoughts are with the families of those injured and deceased. It is especially painful for them in the run up to Christmas. We would ask you to respect their privacy at this challenging time, and also ask the general public's understanding whilst roads around the area remain closed pending our investigations.'

Danskin felt Parker's arm touch the small of his back. He knew the tricky part approached.

'You will appreciate our investigations are at an early stage. Facts are sketchy but I can tell you this.' He looked up from his notes and prepared for the onslaught. 'This was not an accident. This was a deliberate act.'

Danskin had broken the spell. Flashbulbs exploded like fireworks. Journalists shouted their questions, demanded to be heard. DCI Stephen Danskin stood impassive and waited for the mob to calm themselves. His eyes scanned the journalists. Finally, he pointed out one man in the crowd. 'I'll take your question.'

'Donald Nixon,' the man said, 'BBC News. You say it was a deliberate act. Are you telling us this was an act of terrorism?'

Danskin was prepared. 'At this stage of the investigation, we have no reason to believe this to be the case. We are, however, keeping an entirely open mind.'

Another arm shot up. 'Sally Freeman, Sky News. DCI Danskin, was there a warning? Did the police fail to act on information?'

'No, Miss Freeman. There were no warnings. Next question.'

He pointed to a man at the edge of the crowd. The man's name was lost in the general hubbub. 'Has anyone claimed responsibility for the outrage?'

Danskin tried not to show his irritation. 'No. If they had, we would know it was a terrorist act. I've already put on record we are not following that line of enquiry at this stage. I'll take one more question, then if you excuse me, I've an operation to run.'

'Have you a message for the public at large?' a man from the Press Association asked.

'We are trawling through CCTV as we speak but if the public have any information whatsoever, if they've seen a friend or family member, colleague or associate who has acted out of character, I'd ask them to get in touch. Immediately. We have no reason to believe this is anything other than a heinous but isolated act. We do not believe there is any danger to the rest of the public, but we ask that everyone remains vigilant and report anything they see as suspicious. We have an information hotline and I will share that number with you. I implore anyone with information to call us. Thank you.'

Stephen Danskin pulled his papers together. Prepared to leave. Reporters began dispersing, keen to file their story. Lyall Parker congratulated Danskin who, in turn, puffed out his cheeks and wished he'd brought his Corsodyl.

He stepped from the lectern towards a waiting car. A woman collided with him. 'Sorry, madam', he said.

'That's no problem, DCI Danskin,' Megan Wolfe replied. 'I was just wondering, though, why you said there were eleven deaths? My colleagues have already spoken to thirty sets of bereaved parents. And there'll be more, I have no doubt.'

Danskin felt a chill run down his spine. 'And you are?'

'Megan Wolfe. Mercury. Inspector Danskin, how many fatalities are we looking at here?'

'Like I said, we know of eleven.' He continued through the crowd, wished the conference had been held somewhere more accessible to his car.

The woman stayed at the DCI's shoulder, shrugging off the attempts of Parker and the female police officer to waylay her.

'DCI Danskin, we have the family's interviews caught on camera. They will be on-line in less than ten minutes. Why won't you tell me how many deaths we're looking at?'

Sweat trickled down Danskin's back. He was a copper, not a diplomat.

'Listen,' he snarled, 'I don't give a rat's arse what you put on-line on your tacky tabloid shite. 'I'll stick to eleven for now. If you want to tell the world fifty-one people died, that's up to you.'

Megan smirked. 'Fifty-one. Thank you, Detective Chief Inspector.'

'No. It's eleven. If you say fifty-one, I'll deny it. I'll tell them you're scaremongering. Say that I'll provide an update when it's right and proper to do so. Who are they going to believe – me or you? Now, fuck off out of my way.'

He brushed Megan Wolfe aside, stepped into his car, and was gone.

'Get all that?', Megan asked. The guy with a camera belt and hidden microphone nodded.

CHAPTER SIX

The door opened with a creak lifted from a Hammer movie.

'Only me, Gran. Do you want a cuppa?'

'Yes please, Ernest.'

Ryan's heart sank. He said nothing and went straight to the pokey kitchen of the ex-council house. Three cups of stone-cold tea stood on the bench. He tipped the contents down the sink and prepared two fresh cups.

'Here we are.'

'Thank you. What would I do without a husband like you?'

Ryan placed the cup on a table and sat opposite Doris Jarrod. 'It's me, Gran. Ryan. Do you remember?'

'Of course, I do. Where's your Grandad, have you seen him?'

'He's not here,' Ryan replied.

'Never mind.' She began to rise. 'Can I make you a cup of tea, James?'

'No thank you, Gran. You've some tea there. And, I'm Ryan.'

The old woman's empty eyes seemed to look through him. 'Oh.'

She fell into silence, her eyelids drooped, and within seconds Doris was back in a world where everything made sense.

Ryan reached across for the TV remote and pressed the mute button. He checked his watch. If Gran was still asleep by the time he'd finished his drink, he'd let himself out.

On the screen, he watched an angry looking TV host thrust a microphone at a couple of tattooed women with greasy hair who were about to wash their dirty linen in public. He flicked channels. Someone who'd bought a damp-infested hovel in the hope of making money from it looked perplexed. It obviously hadn't worked out the way he'd hoped.

Another channel. Back to the news. Donald Trump filled the screen. He wouldn't be talking about bombs on Tyneside, Ryan concluded. He wouldn't even know where Newcastle was.

Ryan thought of the terrors he'd seen in the city, the face of Teddy McGuffie, and wondered how such horrors could be consigned to fish and chip wrappers already. As if a prompt, he reached for the never-ending stockpile of newspapers his Gran collected. He leafed through a few before his mind returned to the news conference.

Danskin had done well, he thought. Official, sympathetic when appropriate, and reassuring. He also hadn't said much of substance, and Ryan admired that. He imagined how he'd have reacted in Danskin's shoes, and hoped he'd come across as confident.

'One day, I'll find out – touch wood,' he said out loud.

He looked back to the TV. It showed an image of DCI Stephen Danskin addressing a crowd outside Newcastle Civic Centre.

A yellow banner scrolled along the bottom of the screen.

'BREAKING NEWS: Officer in charge of Newcastle bombing misleads public.'

**

Stephen Danskin sat at a desk festooned with papers. He looked up at an electronic whiteboard filled with notes and arrows and circles and asterixis, none of which led anywhere.

He rubbed his brow with a marker pen. Realised he'd used the wrong end and smeared green ink across his forehead.

'For fuck's sake.'

Lyall Parker looked up from his PC.

'Sir?'

'Nothing. Just get on with it, Lyall.'

The room was filled with people talking into phones, animatedly discussing the case, poring over maps and blueprints of the City East campus.

Danskin rocked back in his chair and closed his eyes.

'Sir?'

He opened them to see Hannah Graves standing over him. Despite everything, a smile curved his lips; only for it to disappear when she said, 'Super wants to see you.'

Danskin blew out his lips. 'What, now? Doesn't he know I'm a tad busy?'

Detective Hannah Graves, her cherubic, freckled face pursed in a frown, hesitated. 'No, sir. I mean, yes, sir. But, whatever, he wants to see you. That's WANTS to see you'

Danskin flung the marker pen across the room. 'Yes sir, no sir, three bags full, sir.' He stomped across the room to Connor's office.

When he entered, Superintendent Connor stood at a window, hands clasped behind him, staring out over the railway lines. 'You wanted to see me, sir?'

Connor turned. 'You bloody idiot.'

Danskin's hand went to his forehead. 'It's marker pen, sir.'

Connor looked puzzled. 'What the hell are you talking about? You've got a lot to answer for, Danskin. We've got a major incident going on, we're not forty-eight hours into it, the public are going ape-shit about what we're doing, and you've undermined all public confidence in the force, never mind the investigation.'

It was Danskin's turn to look puzzled. 'I haven't a scooby what you're talking about, sir.'

Connor shook his head. 'This is what I'm talking about.'

He switched on a TV in the corner of the room. Angled it so it faced Danskin. The DCI saw an image of himself stepping into a car. Alongside him stood a woman he recognised. A woman he'd had a heated conversation with.

Danskin had a scooby.

**

The newsroom was party central.

Vorster had uncorked a couple of bottles of champagne and walked from desk to desk, slapping backs and looking like a lottery winner.

In one corner, Bob Mather sat with the entertainment's correspondent. She'd drank most of one bottle herself. Nearby, Leeward Milton had an arm around Emma Steenberg, Megan Wolfe's gofer. Megan was there, too, sipping mineral water.

Raymond Carpenter watched from a safe distance, wondering if he'd get lucky again tonight. David Woods stood alongside him. 'Looks like we're in business again', Woods said.

'I know. And, by the look of Marcus, it's come just in time.'

Vorster popped open another couple of bottles and walked to them, bottles clasped between the fingers of one hand. 'I told you, didn't I? The on-line content would make us. It's how I started, what brought me here. It damn near broke me, too, but it's come good in the end.' He refilled their glasses. 'This time next year, I'll be a millionaire. Again.' He tossed his head back, laughed, and moved on.

'Someone's happy,' Woods said.

'Told you.' Raymond Carpenter chinked Woods glass, his eyes never leaving Megan Wolfe.

'Megan, my angel. My saviour. The love of my life,' Vorster said, flinging an arm around her waist.

She smiled coldly and held a hand over her glass to prevent Marcus topping it with alcohol. 'It's what I get paid for,' she said.

'And you'll be well-paid, too. You hung that dickhead out to dry. Your video's gone global. *'Broke the internet'*, I believe the phrase is.' He looked across the room. 'Hey, Carpenter. What did I tell you about streaming live, you pussy?'

Between lips that formed something resembling a smile, Carpenter spoke like a ventriloquist 'Go fuck yourself,' he whispered.

Megan's voice brought Vorster's gaze back to her. 'Where do we go next with the story?'

'Megan, my dear. Ever the professional. That's for another day. Today, let's rejoice.' He tipped champagne into Megan's glass. She set it down straight away.

'No, seriously. I was just wondering if I could run that piece about the taxi driver in tomorrow's print edition? You know, break up the bombing story a little. Come back to it fresh the day after?'

'Is he dead?'

Megan stared into Marcus's eyes. 'No, but my sources tell me his injuries are horrific. I thought we could run something on the impact it'll have on his life. Run a comparison with acid attack victims, because his scars will be hideous.'

'I like you're thinking, Wolfe, but today is all about the explosion. No exceptions.'

She shrugged. 'Ok. But I would like to delve into the cabbie's story at some point. I think it's got legs. I'd love to get an interview with him. I might, yet. I gather the prognosis is encouraging. They think he's going to live.'

Someone within earshot swiveled their head.

**

Dear Sirs
Not two days ago, you were kind enough to publish my thoughts on the National Health Service.

Since then, we have witnessed the most catastrophic of peacetime events to which our region has borne witness. Many of your readers will argue that the response of our wonderful emergency services dispels my assertation that the NHS should be privatised. Far from it.

In many countries around the world, including those with private medical care, the emergency services respond in similar vein. Indeed, I contend the terrible events serve to prove my argument. A privatised Health Service would see greater funds released to bolster our overstretched police force. We would have more bobbies on the beat. Our security forces would be the best in the world.

The events of December 1ˢᵗ would never have occurred.

Think of that for a moment. Let's put more funds into policing our green and pleasant land, and less on bureaucrats and pen-pushers. Cut the civil servants who waste the taxes they purport to collect.

Our country deserves nothing less.

Yours

F. Roadhouse (Miss)

**

He felt a hand clamp around the nape of his neck. A thumb dug into the base of his skull. Instinctively, he jerked an elbow into his assailant's solar plexus. As the attacker doubled over, he used the man's downward momentum to force him to the ground.

He landed with his knee in the small of his attacker's back and twisted the man's right arm until wrist reached his left collar bone.

'Jesus Christ, man, Ryan. I was only having a laugh.'

Ryan released the pressure on Barry Docherty's arm and stood over him. 'Sorry, mate. Me training kicked in.' He tried not to laugh as his work colleague dusted himself down. 'It's been a helluva week, you know.'

'Tell me about it,' Barry agreed. 'I've had to review a couple of complaint cases and consider an appeal on top of my normal caseload.'

Ryan did laugh this time. 'Yeah, it's a tough life.'

The irony went right over Barry's head. 'Aye, TFI Friday, all right. Any plans for the weekend, mate?'

Ryan fumbled for his security pass beneath the zipped-up coat. 'I'm back on duty. The force needs all the help it can get at the minute.'

'I bet. Do you really do it for nowt?'

Ryan looked surprised. 'Of course. I'm lovin' it, though.' He thought of Teddy McGuffie in his arms. 'Most of it, anyway.'

They stopped to let a stream of vehicles, the privileged few with permission to park on site, turn into the Government office access road. A Metro train disgorged its commuters and the horde joined Ryan and Barry at the gates of one of the region's largest employers.

Barry held up a hand to stop traffic and he and Ryan scampered across. 'So, what do you make of it all? Got anyone for the bombing yet?'

'Howay, man. You know I can't talk about it. Besides, it's got nowt to do with me. I just make up the numbers on the street. It's not like Line of Duty for the likes of me.'

Barry waved to a pretty girl behind them. 'Bet she loves a man in uniform. Get yersel' in there, man.'

Ryan felt heat rise to his face. He'd never been comfortable with girls. 'Haven't got time for any of that.' He looked back. The girl was nice, though.

As they reached the Security Hut, a guy in hooded coat, scarf, and thick gloves gave a derisory glance at the passes of those entering the site and waved them through.

Barry nudged Ryan. 'I reckon anyone could get past security when the Metro arrives. He's not going to step outside his hut for love nor money. Richard Bell reckons he once flashed a sausage roll at the guy, and he nodded him through.'

Ryan laughed. 'Good job Richard Bell's not a bomber then, isn't it?'

They walked in silence through the massive complex. As they approached a revolving door, Barry spoke. 'Listen, I know you can't talk about it but that Danskin bloke made a right prick of himself on telly, didn't he? You sure his name's Danskin, not Foreskin?''

An uncomfortable feeling came over Ryan. He knew his place in the pecking order, but already regarded all members of the City and County force as colleagues.

He shrugged. 'I don't know him personally, but they reckon he's a good bloke. A bit unorthodox sometimes but he gets results. I'm sure he'll get the bastard in the end. Oh, and I gather he does get called Foreskin. So, nought out of ten for originality, Baz.'

They stamped their feet on the rough carpet covering the tiled floor of their building's atria entrance. A yellow 'Heightened Alert' warning greeted them on the LCD Noticeboard.

Ryan looked around the bare walls and empty spaces of the three-story office block. 'You know, I really don't want to be here anymore.'

Barry looked astounded. 'Nobody does. But we've nothing better to do.'

'That's where you're wrong. I'm going to join the force. This is only temporary.'

They stepped into the glass fronted lift. As it rose, Barry Docherty said, 'I bet you'll be here for life, like the rest of us.'

After a beat, he added, 'Unless the bomber gets us all first.'

CHAPTER SEVEN

In the glass-walled Data Room of the City and County police HQ, Stephen Danskin and Lyall Parker sat deep in conference. The DCI had asked Parker to run through what they had in the vague hope a recap would force a connection between his synapses.

'We know it was a bomb hidden in a storage room,' Parker's lilting Aberdonian brogue informed the DCI. 'We know it was on the ninth floor.'

'Why the ninth? Surely it would've been easier to get in and out from the ground floor?'

Parker shrugged. 'Perhaps the ground floor had too many folk passing through. We know there was no CCTV on the ninth, but there are – were - plenty around the entrance and the Ground Floor.'

'It's immaterial because we now know all CCTV footage was destroyed in the blast, so there's no chance to review it anyway.'

Parker nodded. 'Aye. And back-ups stretching back two-weeks with it. We also know there wasn't a warning, or any claim of responsibility, which seems to rule out a terror motive.'

Danskin inclined his head. 'Agreed. They'd be queuing up to get their PR out of it. And the Intelligence Services? Any indication of known cells in the area, just in case?'

'None. In fact, there's relatively few persons of interest to them in the area. We've already run a check against most of them and all seem clear. We've a few to follow up but it doesn't look promising.'

Danskin steepled his fingers. Looked out at the activity in the bullpen, the Americanised name the detectives had given to the office space housing most of the squad.

Officers held impromptu conferences. Some trawled through CCTV footage from the surrounding streets, made a note of vehicle registration details and ran checks on them. Many sat around telephones, taking down information from the public, indexing and cross-referencing it.

Mostly, though, the Incident Room sat eerily silent. The majority were out combing through the wreckage for evidence, or interviewing victims deemed fit to do so.

Parker continued. 'We've checked the list of foreign students, prospective ISIS sympathisers, those with Irish backgrounds. We came up with five possibles. Two were killed in the blast....'

'Suicide bombers, perhaps?'

Parker shook his head. 'Negative. They weren't on the ninth floor where the explosion occurred. Another one's been in Pakistan with relatives for the last three weeks, while the final two were at the Irish Centre in Gallowgate. They've been interviewed and gave no cause for concern. Mobile phone records all kosher.'

Danskin dipped the remnants of a naan into a foil container of congealed masala. 'What about disaffected lecturers? Anyone left their post unexpectedly? Students with a grudge?'

'We're working on it, sir.'

'So, what you're telling me, Lyall, is that we've got diddley-squat.'

'That's about the size of it, sir.'

Danskin rubbed the stubble on his chin so hard it almost sparked 'Bollocks. Looks like we've got a rogue shark out there. The Super will be delighted.'

They sat in silence, trying to make sense of it. Parker chucked the remnants of the take-away into a swing bin. Danskin breathed in the aromatic scent and craved a Kingfisher to finish off the meal.

The DCI stared through the glass window, into the Incident Room bullpen. He saw the door open. Heard the muffle of raised voices. Officers sprang to their feet. Three heads swung towards the Data Room.

'What the...'

Danskin didn't finish the sentence. A breathless Hannah Graves burst in.

'Sir, you're needed. We've got another one.'

**

The rings of Saturn, that's what the ripples reminded the bomber of as they circled towards the edge of the flooded drainage quarry.

Once he was satisfied the burner phone had sunk to the bottom of the algae-infested waters, he clambered from the vehicle and set off through muddy fields and allotments abandoned for the winter.

Beyond the next roundabout, the grey edifice stood tall against its flat surroundings. He checked his watch and figured he'd arrive about the time all hell broke loose. The carrier bag in his right hand swung loosely against his thigh, a comforting reminder that all would be well.

He weaved his way through traffic at Moor Farm roundabout and approached his target. He was already close enough to read the words 'Northumbria Specialist Emergency Care' depicted in large letters on the westward facing wing.

His heart jumped at the sound of sirens. He checked his watch again. Relaxed. 'It's a hospital,' he reminded himself. 'Of course there'll be sirens.'

He made his way towards a building site where diggers lay cutting foundations for a new wing. He clambered into the abandoned cab of one of them. The man oozed off his muddy shoes and pulled a blue outfit from the carrier back. He wore the garb over his clothing, donned a pair of sneakers, and jumped from the cab.

Around the hospital entrance, patients wrapped in blankets puffed on cigarettes. He strode past them, head up, and made his way through the open space of the reception area, beyond the volunteer-run coffee shop, towards a set of glass-fronted lifts.

It was as if he'd triggered it. The moment he pressed the lift button, the alarm sounded. Klaxon-like and strident, it echoed through the open spaces, along the corridors, into the wards and the theatres and the laboratories.

Patients, visitors and staff looked at one another. Security staff scrambled to their stations. Outside, distant sirens approached. Fire, police and ambulance.

The man in his new blue scrubs pictured the logjam at Moor Farm roundabout. He knew he'd timed it right. He stepped inside the elevator safe in the knowledge no-one else would use it; not with the alarm sounding.

On the third floor, the doors slid open. He watched a nurse and porter wheel a bed from the ward into the corridor. Another nurse emerged, a patient on each arm, one trailing a portable drip with him.

'Is it a drill?' he heard a man in pyjamas ask.

'Happens regularly,' a nurse replied, not convincingly.

More raised voices. Two doctors hurried by. 'There's been a bomb warming,' he heard one say, panic in his voice.

He turned right into the next ward. Nurses held an urgent conference around their station. The sister pointed at patient's names on a whiteboard, gauging which were ambulant.

Someone shouted to him. 'Help me get this trolley out here, doctor. We've another three to move yet.'

He mumbled something as he walked on by. He past two individual rooms. Gave the nameplates on the doors a cursory glance. Outside the third, he stopped. Looked left and right. Pushed open the door.

The sign outside read 'Edward McGuffie.'

The door swung shut behind him. There was instant calm in the darkened room; the panic and hubbub outside banished.

McGuffie lay on the bed. A gauze cap covered his skull. Thin films of white tape held his eyelids shut but the purple swelling around his eyes remained.

His face was red, as if the outer layer of flesh had peeled away. Teddy McGuffie's nose was held in place by layers of tape. An oxygen mask covered his toothless mouth. A wire frame prevented his jaw from total collapse.

Wires and tubes and gadgetry emerged from beneath the bed sheet, all connected to an array of monitors, alarms and the assorted paraphernalia required to keep a dead man alive.

The intruder stood over McGuffie. Cocked his head to one side. Followed the line of a drip tube with his eyes. Reached for the connection.

The door flung open. Light and noise and bedlam flooded in. The man thought his heart was going to leap out his chest.

'Sorry doctor. I didn't realise you were in here. I'll watch Mr McGuffie now. We can't move him anywhere.'

The man didn't turn from the bed. He waited for the adrenalin dump to fade before he spoke. Calmly, measuredly. 'I've got this, nurse. You get yourself safe. I'll see to our patient.'

The nurse couldn't wait to get herself safe, and with her went the light and the cries of panic outside.

The man was already unplugging and detaching equipment from McGuffie's body. He stopped. Realised he didn't know what he was doing. He reattached the kit as best he could and settled for switching off the power sockets.

After a second, the monitor, sustained by its emergency battery, flashed red. The numbers on its screen dropped. The spiked line plummeted. An alarm sounded. No-one would hear it over the wailing of the fire and bomb alert outside.

He stayed calm. Regulated his breathing. Delayed until the numbers read zero and the line lay flat.

The man counted to one hundred. It seemed to take forever. He switched the kit back on. Waited to ensure McGuffie didn't rise from the bed like Frankenstein's monster.

Then, the calmest man in the hospital, he left.

**

Ryan was on patrol with Frank Burrows when the call came through.

They were on their third meander between the 15th century Cooperage pub and the uber-modern Law Courts on Newcastle's quayside. They were one of several teams assigned to high-profile sites within the city; their presence to provide visible reassurance to the public.

Ryan regarded everyone with the nervous suspicion of an SAS operative on sniper watch. Frank compiled his shopping list in his mind.

A watery sun, white and cold, filtered through low level cloud of battleship grey. It mirrored the city's mood.

'Copy,' Frank said in response to the Fat Controller somewhere within the Forth Banks police HQ.

Ryan looked at him, expectantly. 'What's the latest?'

'Relax. It was a hoax.'

Ryan expelled air like a horse. 'Thank God.'

'Yeah. Par for the course, I guess. Some idiot seeking his five minutes of fame. Always happens.'

They crossed the foot of Dean Street, Frank wondering how to break the news.

'You ok, Frank? You've gone quiet.'

Burrows nodded. 'Remember that taxi driver? McGuffie?'

'How could I forget?'

'Well, he passed away around the time of the evacuation.'

'Shit no.' Ryan was surprised to feel tears sting his eyes.

'You'll get used to it, son. You've got to.'

'Do you know what happened?'

Frank shrugged. 'All I know is he was hanging on when the alarm went off. His one-to-one nurse left him with a doctor. When she got back, he'd popped it. Truth be told, probably a blessing.'

Ryan shuddered. 'So, at least his case will get priority now. That's some comfort.'

Frank Burrows let out an ironic chuckle. 'I wouldn't count on it.'

'It's murder, Frank. Course it will.'

'Not with the hunt for the bomber going on it won't. All manpower's on that. Sure, the case will be assigned, but it'll be with a junior detective. And he won't get much support. We haven't got the manpower. The cupboard's bare.'

Ryan shook his head. 'That's ridiculous. A man's died here.'

'Son, you've got to see the bigger picture. Think how many died in the bombing. And the figures probably going to go up given the state of some of the injured. We've got to do the greater good for the greatest majority, or whatever.'

'Right. Well, I'll work the case with the detective. At least it'll be one more pair of hands.'

Frank snickered again. 'I admire your motives but, with all respect, you're a Special. You can't help. It's just the way things are. You've just got to let it ride. It's not worth getting angry about.'

'Frank,' Ryan said. 'One thing you'll get to learn. Ryan Jarrod doesn't get angry.'

**

It had seemed a clever idea at the time. He knew enough about procedure to bluff his way through an interview, his presence wouldn't be unexpected, and his uniform was identical. Yet, by wearing it off-duty at the end of his shift, Ryan felt as if he was cheating on a long-cherished partner. But, if Frank was right and no-one of substance was looking at McGuffie's murder, he had to do it.

He took refuge from a wind-driven deluge in the doorway of a micro-brewery built into the railway arches. It gave him time to think, and to observe. The office of Charlie Charlton's Cab's (with stereotypical apostrophe juxtaposition) sat above an Estate Agency, accessible through an unobtrusive doorway. No-one had left or entered during the time Ryan had watched. There was no external CCTV, no alarms. A single window, made opaque by months of exhaust fumes, watched over the street. Most unusual of all, there was no taxi-rank outside.

Ryan ruffled his hair and set off across the road. Inside the building, the stairway was narrow; single-file traffic only. At its head, a small linoleum-lined hallway contained only one door. Ryan pushed it open and entered a time-warp.

The walls of the office were lined with wood cladding. Painted pale-blue and flaking, it had late-60s stamped all over it.

Posters of Hendrix, Pink Floyd and numerous others Ryan Jarrod failed to identify covered patches of damp and mould.

Against one wall, six rigid plastic chairs dared anyone to sit in them. A coffee-ringed table lay in front of the chairs like a sleezy-centrefold, its surface littered with dog-eared copies of Autotrader, Four-Four-Two, and a token Bella magazine.

The office was bereft of taste, tact and customers.

At one end, behind a metal grille, Charlie Charlton tapped a pen on a wooden counter. In front of him, the pages of The Racing Post lay open. Further back, a pallid young woman with lank hair which may or may not have been blonde wore her acne scars better than her uniform. A telephone headset covered her ears.

'I'd like to ask you some questions about one of your employees,' Ryan ventured. 'Edward McGuffie.'

The man didn't look up from his bible. He chewed gum with the voracity of a dog at a bone. 'Not one of my employees.'

'Mr McGuffie drove a cab registered to your company. He was found in Pudding Chare with serious injuries.'

'Like I said. Not one of my employees.'

Charlton's responses threw Ryan. He thought this would've been the easy part. 'I can come back with a photograph of him if I must. It might help jog your memory.'

The man closed his paper. Looked up slowly. 'You don't need show me a photograph. I know Teddy alright. But I don't employ him. He drives my cab. Freelance. Franchised, if you prefer. I don't employ anybody. That way, I needn't pay into a shitty pension scheme for them.'

'Ok. But you do admit he works out of this office.'

'No mate. He works out of a cab. That's what taxi drivers do. When they're big enough to turn up, that is. McGuffie hasn't. But now I know why. He's been hurt. Thank you for letting me know. Good day, officer.'

Ryan was taken aback. He'd believed Frank Burrows when he'd said no-one would treat the case as a priority. It seemed no-one had treated the case as anything. They hadn't even interviewed his employer. Or franchiser, or whatever.

'Who was Mr McGuffie's last fare? It's highly likely he was the last person to see Mr McGuffie alive.'

That grabbed the man's attention like an elastic band around the testicles.

'*Shit*,' Ryan thought. '*I shouldn't have said that.*'

'Dead? I though you said he'd been injured?'

'He was, initially, sir. He's passed away of his injuries since.'

'Fuck. Poor bastard.' Charlton shrugged. 'Still, can't help you much, I'm afraid. Just a minute, though.' He spat out his gum and tossed it at the girl beneath the headset. 'How man, Ilona. Check the rosters for McGuffie's last shift, will you?'

The girl glanced at the man with lifeless eyes. She looked from him to Ryan Jarrod. A nerve in her cheek quivered at the sight of his uniform. She fingered a filthy keyboard at her side and somehow made something out from beneath a grease-smeared computer monitor.

'His last fare was a call-out.' She spoke with an eastern European accent.

'Call out?' Ryan queried.

'A call-out,' Charlton repeated. 'As opposed to a call-in. You know,' he signalled towards the row of threatening chairs, 'Not somebody who called-in.' He shook his head. Mumbled 'Jesus Christ' under his breath.

'Ah, I see,' Ryan said. 'And where was he called out to?'

'Ilona – where was McGuffie called out to?'

The girl checked her monitor again. 'Client asked to be picked up from Manors Metro station.'

Ryan's eyes widened. 'That's, what, half a mile from the University campus? Where'd he get dropped off – do we know?'

Ilona read from the screen. 'Teddy didn't take him far. Says here he wanted dropped off at The Printer's Pie.'

'That's just behind the Mercury offices,' Charlton explained.

CHAPTER EIGHT

In the Mercury offices, Marcus Vorster paced like an expectant father. 'Thank the lord it was a hoax. We'll get column inches out of it, but if it'd been real, and we hadn't been on site to film, it'd have undone all our excellent work. We've got to keep on top of this. If our usual sources aren't coming up trumps, find some new ones.'

David Woods tried to reassure Vorster. 'Relax. Our sources got us to the bombing site first. We got the scoop on the Press Conference. We've got it covered.'

Marcus nodded. 'True. But you're a photojournalist first and foremost, I'd prefer it if our hard news guys gave me the comfort blanket, not a washed-up wildlife photographer.'

Woods opened his mouth to protest but Megan Wolfe got in first. 'Marcus, for heaven's sake, relax. David's right. And remember he was one of the first on the scene at the Uni. Give him some credit.'

Woods mouthed 'thank you' towards Megan and received a smile in return.

'Ag, you're right, Wolfe. Again. Ok, sorry, David. Sometimes the rand signs overtake my mouth.'

They'd been joined by Leeward Milton. 'You ok, Lee?' Megan asked.

'Me? Yeah, sure. Real fine.'

Megan's brow creased. 'Thought it might have brought things back to you, that's all.'

'Uh-huh.'

'You never talk about it much, do you?' Marcus asked.

'Nope.'

'Blood out of a stone. Come on, man. I'm sure you could bring a fresh prospectus on the bombing. Someone who's been through it.'

The Floridian fixed Vorster with a cold stare. 'I don't talk about it. Besides, this doesn't compare to the Gulf.'

'In what way?'

'Are you serious? This was a one-off. In the desert, every single day was a 'one-off'. Only it was you and your comrades in the firing line. When your job's to set off mines, one day your foot will be the one to trigger it.'

Marcus raised one shoulder. 'One foot in the grave', he said, smiling

Milton stood; fists clenched. 'Man, that's not funny.'

'Ok, Lee,' Megan intervened. 'Let it pass. You keep on doing what you're doing. Give me the leads, I'll follow up, you put your stamp on the story and we'll go to print.'

Marcus sneered. 'Hang on a moment. I get a bollocking for the foot in the grave comment and Wolfe gets away with putting a stamp on it.'

Milton stormed out; the door barely left on its hinges.

'Marcus, you're a twat sometimes, do you know that?' Megan said.

'Only sometimes? I must try harder.' Vorster followed ex-Marine Leeward Milton out the door. At a safe distance.

When he was out of earshot, David Woods spoke again. 'Remember you pitched to do an article on the taxi-driver beaten up around the corner from here?'

'Yeah. Didn't get far with it thought, did I?'

'No, but my sources tell me he was at the hospital when it was evacuated. When they got the all-clear, they returned to find him dead. Thought it might give you an extra angle to work on, seeing as Herr Gruppenfuhrer needed convincing on your idea at first.'

Megan put a finger to her chin. 'You know, David, I think it just might.'

'Good. Then, get to work, Meg. You and I, we'll make the Mercury great again. 'Washed-up?' I'll show the Kwa-Zulu who's washed up.'

**

Stephen Danskin knew there'd be a reason. Every head turned towards him as he marched into the Incident Room, and he was quite sure it wasn't because he'd had a shave. Hannah Graves looked towards Lyall Parker who looked at WDS Sue Nairn, the tall woman who'd joined them at the ill-fated press briefing.

Danskin made it easy for them. 'Howay, then. What is it this time?'

Nairn bit the bullet. 'Super wants to see you.'

Danskin groaned. 'Help me out here, guys. Tell me you've got something for me.'

'Not a great deal, Sir' Lyall Parker said in his soothing way. 'We've had reports of a few guys acting suspiciously over the road from the uni on Albert Street. They've been spotted semi-regularly for a month or two.'

'And?' Danskin asked, checking his watch and Superintendent Connor's door.

'We traced a couple of them. Got form for minor drug offences. Nothing major.'

Danskin shook his head. 'Is that it? *Stop Press: Students take drugs shock*'. Shit, man. Anything else for me to go in there with?'

Hannah handed the DCI a sheet of paper. 'Only this, sir. We found a Spanish student. Her cousin's Catalina Mendoza Zabala.'

'Play for Valencia, does he? Give me a clue, Graves.'

'No, sir. It's a she. She's a head honcho with ETA. Or was, until she got herself shot.'

Danskin snapped his fingers. 'That's better. Good work, Graves. Follow it up. I've still got me doubts, like. The lack of a responsibility claim worries me. And, I've no idea why ETA would want to attack a University campus in north-east England. Still, it might be enough to save me nuts when Connor lays into me.'

Filled with no more trepidation than usual, Danskin waited for the stern 'Come' before entering Connor's office. The superintendent wasn't alone. Facing the desk, back to Danskin, stood a tall, board-straight figure, hands clasped behind his back, feet shoulder-width apart, like a guard on sentry duty.

Danskin raised an eyebrow, but the Super didn't bite. 'How's the case progressing, Danskin?' Connor asked.

'We've picked up a couple of new leads, sir. One looks particularly promising.'

'Excellent. Care to share?'

'Yes, sir. We've identified a student with close family links to a Spanish terrorist group.'

'ETA?'

'Indeed, sir.' He waited for Connor's praise. He didn't get it.

'What's your definition of 'close'?'

Danskin swallowed. 'Cousin, sir.'

'You mean second cousin.'

Danskin had no idea. 'Possibly, sir,' he waffled. 'But a relative, nonetheless. She's under surveillance as we speak.'

'Call your team off, Danskin.'

The DCIs jaw dropped. 'Sir?'

'Call them off. You're duplicating effort. Anti-terrorist squad already ruled your student out as a person of interest. There's no involvement.'

Danskin deflated like a punctured football.

'Any other leads?'

Danskin stumbled over his words; grasped at straws. 'We're looking at possible underworld connections. Drug gangs. Unlikely, but we're following up all leads. We've got a full squad looking at the information coming in from the public. We've got a lot to sift through.'

Connor stood from behind his desk, curled his lip Elvis-like. 'The information disclosure line will have attracted nothing more than the usual publicity-seeking cranks and crackpots, I guarantee it. Good old detective work will solve this, and you're telling me you've got nothing. You need to pull your socks up, Stephen.'

'Sir, with respect, I need more men on this. I can't be expected to take on a case of this magnitude with the men at my disposal.'

'I agree, Danskin.'

Stephen Danskin took in air. 'You do? Thank you, sir. You won't regret it. It'll pay back the investment ten-fold.'

'Good. So, allow me to introduce you to your new pair of hands.'

Danskin had completely forgotten there was another man in the room. He turned to greet the officer, then stopped. He wasn't looking at an experienced detective. He was looking at a young, fresh-faced country-bumpkin.

Danskin caught a glimpse of a file on the Super's desk. The name on it, upside down, read 'Nigel Trebilcock'.

Trebilcock spoke. 'Hello, sir. Delighted to meet you. I'm Detective...'

'Treblecock,' Danskin completed.

'It's pronounced Bilko, sir. As in Seargeant Bilko,' Trebilcock said.

'Whatever, Treblecock,' Danskin said. Turning to Connor, he added, 'Sir. Can I have a word? In private?'

Connor shook his head. 'No time. You've got too much on your hands. Trebilcock will provide you with the assistance you need.'

'Sir, one man won't make a difference. I need more than that.'

'It's all you're getting, Danskin. You've got 80% of the station at your disposal already. Now, Trebilcock's come all the way from Cornwall on secondment. Introduce him to your team and get him set to work. He comes with glowing references from,' Connor flipped open the file on the desk. 'Where were you stationed again, Trebilcock?'

When Nigel Trebilcock replied, Danskin looked aghast. 'You're kidding me, right?'

**

'Listen up, folks,' Danskin clapped his hands for attention. 'I'd like to introduce you to Nigel Treblecock.' He waited for the snorts of laughter to subside. 'Treblecock's going to be assisting us for a while.' He glanced sideways at Trebilcock. 'A very short while.'

The squad gathered around them as the DCI continued. 'Right, Treblecock…'

'It's Trebilcock, sir. As in Sergeant Bilko.'

'So you say, Treblecock. Now, Treblecock's with us on secondment. From Cornwall. Would you care to tell the team where you're based?'

'Yes, sir. It's Flushing, sir.'

The laughter returned. A hard-faced bastard with a look of Franck Ribery about him said, 'Christ. Foreskin, and Treblecock from Flushing. We've turned the station into fucking Carry on Constable.'

Ribald laughter followed. Danskin let it die a natural death while his own grin subsided. 'Ok Robson. That's enough. Right, folks; introduction's over. Back to work. There's plenty of time to get to know, err, our new colleague.'

The team dispersed. Danskin looked around the bullpen. Saw a single desk bereft of a paperwork mountain. He inclined his head towards it. 'That's yours, son. Get over there. Keep your head down and your arse up. Oh, and if you think you're getting within a midge's piss of my investigation, forget it.'

Trebilcock made his way to the abandoned workstation. 'Sir, it'll look a bit obvious to the Super if you don't assign me anything, won't it?'

Danskin had to agree. He studied the contents of his own desk. Picked a file from the third tray down. 'Here. Have a look at this.'

He flipped the folder across the station like a frisbee. The contents, a couple of sheets, fluttered to the floor. The file landed on Trebilcock's desk cover up, shaped like a roof's eaves.

He twisted his neck to look at the title of the file.

It read: *Edward McGuffie.*

CHAPTER NINE

Irregular blotches of early-morning frost dusted the roofs like patches of mould. Florence Roadhouse buttoned the top button of her coat and pulled her headscarf tight over her ears. Her early morning walk into the village was part of her routine and a bit of cold wasn't going to stop her.

She made her way to the junction of Broom Lane and prepared to turn left down the steep incline towards the Bay Horse and St Mary's Church. As she did so, her foot gave way on a patch of ice. Not enough to make her fall, but more than enough to make her think.

Ice glimmered and glistened on the footpath like stars in the night sky so, instead of her usual downhill route, she turned right towards Sunniside, where the path was level.

As she walked, Florence allowed her mind to wander. She hoped it would settle on a pearl of wisdom she could share with her fellow Mercury readers. Not five minutes into her walk, raised voices interrupted her thoughts.

At the bus stop outside a gymnasium equipment supplier, a group of teenagers engaged in rough and tumble banter. They were swaddled in puffer jackets. Black and white football scarves covered their faces as if they were protestors against a Communist regime. They spilled into the road, then back to the footpath, like waves lapping ashore.

What Florence saw next chilled her more than the cold.

An old lady stood in the centre of the group clutching a handbag, confused and alone. Worse, she wore only a polyester nightdress.

Florence heard one voice rise above the others. Presumably, the ringleader. She saw the youth lead the woman away from the group. He put his arm around her waist.

Florence gasped. 'Oh, good lord. Pray God, no.'

The ex-nurse forgot her age. Forgot the underfoot conditions. Forgot the boisterous group. All she could think of was the safety of the old woman being led to God-knows-where.

As she closed in, she saw the ringleader also had his face covered. But she knew who it was. The upright flame of hair gave him away.

'James Jarrod, I'm calling the police. Right now. I know who you are. Let her go.'

Jam Jar looked at her, perplexed. 'Eh?'

Florence was within a few paces of him now. The rest of the group had disappeared. 'Let the old dear go, you horrible young thug. Keep that behaviour to the football ground with all the other undesirables.'

Jam Jar still didn't understand. 'Are you nuts, or something?' Then, he got it. 'No, no. You've got it all wrong. This is my Gran. I'm taking her home. She lives in The Drive.'

For a moment, Florence questioned herself but, when she saw the confusion in the old lady's eyes, her doubts disappeared. 'Do you know this boy, dear?' she asked.

The old woman looked at James Jarrod, then at Florence Roadhouse, and back again. She shivered uncontrollably. She said nothing, but she did shake her head.

Florence reached into her own bag. Pulled out her personal alarm. Made out to pull it.

'It's ok, missus. There's no need for that. I'm going, ok?'

'I know you are. And don't think I won't tell the police. You and your brother – if he really is a policeman – are going to be in a load of trouble for this, I promise you.'

She watched until James had retreated a safe distance before delving into the old woman's bag. 'Now let's get you home, nice and warm. You shouldn't be out in this. Not dressed the way you are. You'll end up with pneumonia. Tell me, do you have a Social Worker, dear?'

The old woman didn't move her blue lips. She nodded, but Florence knew she'd agree to anything. Good job she'd got to her before James Jarrod and his football chums got any further.

Florence found a piece of paper in the woman's bag. She unfolded it. It said: *'My name is Doris Jarrod. I live at 122 The Drive, Whickham. Please telephone my son or grandsons on...'*

She read no further. She had her answer and swallowed it, along with a slice of humble pie, as she saw the flame-red hair of James Jarrod dip out of sight over the crest of Broom Lane.

**

Ryan rubbed at his red eyes. Another sleepless night which he'd spent pondering what to do with Charlie Charlton's information.

He'd had no right to question the man. He knew revealing what he'd been up to wouldn't be well-received. Besides, he didn't know who to report it to. According to Frank Burrows, no-one was looking at the case.

Yet, Ryan couldn't stop agonising over it. During his tedious civil service day job, he'd fouled-up so many times thinking of Teddy McGuffie's fate. Finally, he reached a decision. He'd do nothing. For now.

McGuffie had picked up his last-ever client within a few hundred yards of the explosion but there was nothing to link the two incidents. If he could, somehow, find a connection between McGuffie and the atrocity, he'd raise it. At that point, it was sure to be investigated. Until then, he had no choice but to sit on what he'd found.

'Hello. Earth calling Jarrod.'

Ryan came out of his trance. Barry Docherty stood next to Ryan's desk.

'I asked if you fancied a quick pint after work.'

Ryan's eyes brightened. 'You know, I could do with more than one. The Newton Arms?'

'I was thinking maybe The Benton Ale House. It should be quieter. Looks like you could do with a chat.'

'Barry, mate, a talk is the last thing I need. But a pint? It won't touch the sides.' He glanced at the time on his PC screen. 'How about an early finish. 3.30 ok?'

'It's a date,' Docherty said. 'See you in half an hour or so.'

The half-hour turned into twenty minutes, yet they were far from first at the bar.

The Benton Ale house lies half a mile eastward from the HMRC complex. A similar distance in the other direction sits a Department for Work and Pension office. There was friendly banter and rivalry between the two groups, but no animosity. Indeed, they tended to congregate in separate rooms, the way different sides of the same family do at a wake.

The man in the corner booth sat in the HMRC end, quietly sipping a lager. He pretended to read a newspaper but, instead, he watched the bar fill up and sought out prey the way a lioness stalks a herd of gazelle.

As inhibitions decreased and the working day became a thing of the past, the volume ramped up. Cheery voices filled the air, ironic jeers rose when a glass slipped from someone's fingers and shattered on the floor, conversations over football escalated to arguments, and ribald jokes drew exaggerated laughter.

The man in the corner booth set down his newspaper and withdrew his phone from a pocket. He pretended to open his e-mails but took a snapshot of a group of four men jostling for service at the bar. Each wore the tell-tale blue lanyard and security pass of Her Majesty's Revenue and Customs.

One pulled away from the group and said his goodbyes.

And then there were three.

When the three returned from the bar, one held a whisky schooner. Within minutes, he'd downed it. The man heard him say, 'I'd better get off. My Metro's due. More worryingly, so is the missus.' He left amid laughter.

Then there were two.

One, an athletically built young man with strawberry blonde hair, displayed the air of a man with worries. The second, shorter, stouter, drank like a man in a desert. His pint glass was soon empty.

The blonde man tapped an access code into a phone and held it to his ear. He took the call while the shorter man returned to the bar. The blonde twisted his mouth. Tapped the other man on the shoulder.

'Sorry, Barry, I've got to go. That was wor James. Gran's not been well again. Sorry again, mate. I'll see you tomorrow.'

'Ah, howay man. I've just got them in.'

'You'll make short work of them. I've got to go.'

He fought his way out into the frigid winter night.

And then there was one.

The man in the corner booth stood. Made his way to the bar. Stood close to the civil servant clutching two pints of beer. So close that, as he turned, they collided. The beer spilled from both glasses, soaking one man's shirt and another's shoes.

'How man. Watch where your gannin.'

The man from the booth was profuse with his apologies. 'My fault entirely. Really sorry. Here, let me get you another.'

'It's ok. I've salvaged enough for one pint between them.'

'No, honestly. I'll get them in.'

Never one to look a gift horse in the mouth, Barry Docherty let the man 'get them in'. And more. Over the next hour, Barry regaled the man with boring tales of civil service life, how times had changed, how it was no longer gold-plated pensions and jobs for life.

The other man feigned sympathy, all the while gleaning more facts and detail from Barry Docherty.

Finally, when Docherty swayed once too many times and decided enough was enough, the other man played his ace. 'Listen, it's been nice to meet you. I've got a couple of tickets for the Liverpool game in a week's time. I can't make it. I'd rather they went to a good home.'

'Really? I didn't think anybody would sacrifice tickets for that one. Are you sure? I mean, they're like gold-dust.'

'I'm sure. Here.' He pulled two tickets out of his jacket pocket. 'Take them.' He folded the tickets and stuffed them into Barry's shirt pocket. 'It'll pay your cleaning bill.'

Barry chuckled. 'Cheers. Thanks, mate. Nice talking to you.'

They shook hands.

'You too.'

And then there were none.

With a self-satisfied smile, the man slipped the security pass he'd removed from the end of Barry's lanyard into his back pocket.

**

Marcus Vorster's fingers flew over the keypad of his surface pro. He scanned the note he'd typed.

A reminder that the bombing must remain at the forefront of The Mercury's agenda. That heads would roll if anyone's eye slipped from the ball. That all leave was cancelled. And that there'd be an ad hoc editorial meeting to plan a long-term strategy to keep reader figures high and increase on-line hits.

He checked the recipient list.

Raymond Carpenter.

Megan Wolfe.

Mike Cash.

Leeward Milton.

David Woods.

Molly Uzumba.

He hit the 'send' key and shut down his device as someone approached.

'Same again, sir?' the bartender asked.

CHAPTER TEN

In its 1970s heyday, the site on which the Longbenton offices of HMRC stands was a town unto itself. Then occupied by the Department of Health and Social Security, it spanned over eighty-five thousand square metres, and twelve thousand people worked in its antiquated offices.

Three miles east of Newcastle city centre, it boasted the longest straight corridor outside of the Pentagon. It had its own restaurants and bars, retail outlets, and hairdressers. It even had an underground rifle range.

As technology overtook brain power, the old site was demolished. Ownership transferred to Her Majesty's Revenue and Customs, and the old buildings were replaced by soulless blocks of steel and glass.

Six separate but interlinked three-story office blocks arranged in a horseshoe around an armadillo-like central building formed the nucleus of the site. An arrow-straight eastern access road, bordered on each side by two further linear blocks, led to an aircraft hangar-like utilities building which provided storage facilities for tonnes of files and paperwork.

From the air, the whole place looked like a giant tadpole.

Almost 90% of the employees arrived between the hours of seven and eight a.m. Most of them hated the place. The man sitting in a nondescript car on a soaking wet Tyneside morning knew both these facts. He knew because Barry Docherty had told him so.

Parked in a residents-only bay outside the front gates of the office, he knew he didn't have long. While he waited, he studied the security pass in his hands, looked at the photograph he'd captured on his mobile phone the night before, and checked himself in the rear-view mirror.

The photograph on the pass showed a younger Barry Docherty. Different hairstyle. No facial hair. But even a cursory glance revealed them to be one-and-the-same person. The man didn't need to check himself again to know he bore as much resemblance to Docherty as Lady GaGa to Tyson Fury.

He hoped Docherty had been right in what he'd said. That security was lax, and no-one was ever stopped.

A Metro train spat out its commuters at Longbenton station. They trudged over the railway bridge, made their way through the housing estate, and trooped along Benton Park Road. The man watched them approach, hand poised. When about a third of them began their march up the entrance road, he made his move.

Rain fell even harder, whipped into a frenzy by an angry wind. He fell in step with the workers. Lost himself in the crowd. As he watched, the first few office staff flipped their passes towards the guard. Sure enough, he couldn't possibly identify them at that distance and with that amount of exposure.

He was within fifty yards now. He stepped to his right, to the furthest edge of the footpath. Scores of civil servants flashed their passes in the direction of the guard, who waved them through while continuing his conversation with someone hidden in the hut.

The man's pulse raised. He was grateful the beads of sweat on his brow were camouflaged by icy raindrops. Fifteen more paces and he'd be in.

The guard moved to his side of the footpath. Began to inspect the passes more closely. The guard pointed. Indicated for someone to step to one side.

The man looked around. Closed his eyes. The guard was beckoning him, with a pass no-one in their right mind would accept as genuine, to step aside.

He turned. Prepared to bolt back to his car. But the throng behind him made it impossible. And the guard was four paces away.

'Fred', he heard a voice call from inside the security hut. 'Someone's forgotten their pass. Needs a temporary one. Can you do the honours?'

'Aye. Nee bother.'

Fred lost interest in inspecting passes and went to his colleague's aid.

The man thought he was going to be sick, but he had no time to lose. He hurried through the gate with the rest of the employees and headed up towards the offices.

At the rear of Block Five, a service van stood with its back doors open. Inside, ladders, buckets and extendable rods. And a pile of branded coveralls. A hand reached in, grabbed the nearest pair, and dropped them into the plastic bag he carried with him.

The owner of the hand never broke step as he walked to the head of the buildings, took a left, and headed down the eastern road. By the storage facility, the service dock doors stood open. He slipped through them, found a toilet block, and pulled the coveralls over his wet clothing.

He pulled something else out the bag, too.

**

The utilities building was a paradox. Vast outside, the inside was a claustrophobic network of closely ranked lattice-work shelving from floor to ceiling, a hundred foot or more overhead.

Metallic open plan staircases provided access to three floors of archived paperwork and microfilmed records. The interior, with its gridded floors and criss-cross walkways, reminded him of a top-security prison.

The window cleaner's uniform was an ill fit and looked out of place in the dark dusty labyrinth. He wasn't unduly worried. Only a handful of staff worked in the stores and he could easily hide himself in the maze should he encounter someone.

He took a breath of fetid air and began to climb. His feet on the steel staircase rang out like church bells. He paused. Looked around. No-one came. He carried on upwards; ever higher until he reached the upper tier.

A final, dizzying look down to the floor. No-one in sight. Assured his presence had gone unnoticed, he wheeled a mobile stepladder from its position at the top of the stairwell. He brought it to a halt a third of the way along the walkway. He looked up. Counted the shelves. Twelve.

The intruder climbed up the ladder one-handed, the other clinging onto the object he'd removed from the carrier back. On the ninth shelf, he wedged the object between thick manila files. He stripped off the stolen uniform and set it behind the folders.

The man descended the ladder, uncoiling something as he went, and trailed it to the top of the main staircase. One final act, then he took the stairs two at a time and emerged into the cold December air.

**

'This is an emergency. Please leave the building by the nearest available exit.'

The monotone, pre-recorded voice interspersed with a two-tone klaxon drew a communal groan from the office workers. The quarterly fire drills always did. Particularly those outside of summer.

'Bloody hell. It's bollock-freezing out there,' Barry Docherty said as he joined the orderly queue in the narrow confines of the emergency staircase.

'You can't have it all ways,' Ryan responded. 'You moan when you're at your desk and now you moan when you get let off the leash.'

'Aye. I suppose you're right, like.' Barry checked his watch. 'At least we'll miss the ten o'clock meeting with a bit of luck.' They inched downwards. 'We'd be burnt to a crisp by now if this was a real fire.'

'There's a twenty-minute window for us to get out. The escape routes are fire-retardant.'

'Oh aye. As if they built the thing then set fire to it to see how long it'd last. You'll believe owt, Ryan.'

'Don't be daft, man. Never had you down as a conspiracy theorist. You'll be telling me the moon landing didn't happen next.'

'Hadawayandshite. Course it was real. By the way, did I tell you I was chatting to Elvis in the Bay Horse at the weekend?'

Ryan laughed and pushed Barry between the shoulder blades, causing a mini surge down the stairs.

They'd made it outside to discover all seven thousand site occupants had joined them. 'Whoa, a bit busy out here, isn't it?', Barry said.

Instantly, Ryan knew something was wrong. 'I don't like this. They normally do one block at a time.'

Barry craned his neck to see over the masses. 'You don't think it's real, do you?'

He was talking to himself. Ryan had gone.

**

The device worked better than he ever dreamt possible. It ignited with a pop little louder than a champagne cork. The files closest to it caught alight, slowly at first, before spreading to adjacent documents.

The flames reached his discarded overalls. He'd left a tiny capsule of lighter fluid in its pocket. The container went up with a whoosh. The fire grew in intensity. Licked higher.

Exactly as he'd planned it, with nowhere else for the flames to go, crimson tentacles probed the ceiling. They spread along the width of the easternmost wall, seeking escape.

Fragments of charred and burning documents fluttered downwards. The parchment-dry files below provided perfect kindle. Layer upon layer of paperwork caught alight; a hundred-foot wall of fire.

And that was when Lady Luck played her part. The inferno reached the spools of microfilm, its intensity such that that the acetate film decomposed and, finally, began to burn. The smouldering tape released noxious fumes and gases. They drifted upwards, into the air conditioning vents, and re-emerged in the adjacent mail room.

The mail room occupants reacted slowly to the fire alarm; unaware they'd been inhaling carbon monoxide released by the burning acetate. Disoriented, they stumbled out of the room. Became lost in clouds of smoke and, like lemmings over a cliff, followed one another through the first exit they encountered.

An exit that led directly into the fire.

**

Ryan walked quickly down the eastern access road. The idle chatter of the masses became louder the further he travelled. Raised voices floated over the crowds. Urgent tones. Anger and confusion.

He ran towards the voices. Something was very wrong. He pushed groups out of his path, took a shortcut through a deserted block, and emerged to find the voices had become screams.

Dark smoke reached up to darker skies where they clung together in a grim embrace. Young women hugged one another. Men stood, open-mouthed.

The glass western wall exploded in a cascade of razor-sharp fragments. Hell's stomach contents belched through the breach.

Ryan was sprinting full-tilt, breathless and sweating, through a helter-skelter of panic-stricken colleagues. A fire marshal in Hi-Viz jacked barred his way. Ryan barreled straight through him.

The scream became more insistent. Agonizingly so. He looked towards the utilities building and knew why.

Four workers stumbled from the inferno like stunt men, their bodies doused in flame, arms waving in a futile attempt to shake off their agonies. The faster they ran, the more the air fanned the flames.

Ryan was almost to them. Whilst others turned their faces away, he launched himself headlong through the air towards the nearest blazing worker.

As he brought the living Guy Fawkes doll to the ground, he recognised her. It was the pretty girl Barry Docherty guessed had liked men in uniform. Except, she wasn't pretty any longer.

Her blackened flesh pulsed and broiled with blistering buboes beneath her canopy of flame. Her lips were drawn back in a terrified sneer of agony. Ryan thought he saw her mouth the words 'Help me' before he landed on top of her, smothering the flames, depriving them of their oxygen.

Ryan beat at the conflagration with his hands. Rolled over her again and again. He could smell her flesh burning. He felt heat scorch his legs. His clothes began to char, his hands singe, and the stench of bitter charcoal cologne filled his nostrils as his own skin charred with hers.

The flames consumed them.

CHAPTER ELEVEN

Marcus Vorster clutched a Styrofoam mug in one hand and drummed the fingers of the other on the ovoid table. He'd put back the extraordinary editorial meeting by two hours to accommodate the breaking news story but not all his lieutenants were at his side.

Megan Wolfe, looking cool and collected, sat alongside Molly Uzumba. Megan and Molly had worked on rival Fleet Street publications, one The Independent, the other The Times. They remained professional but detached.

Megan was wary of Uzumba's educated accent, aloofness and preference to work alone. She'd have been even more wary if she'd known Uzumba was born plain Molly Brown in a terraced house in Hartlepool and had assumed her grandmother's maiden name to stand out from the crowd.

For Molly's part, she found Megan ruthless, scheming, untrustworthy and way too far up her own backside. Both women were right.

David Woods was also at the table. He bore a worried look, keen to get the meeting over and back on the story. Perspiration beaded his brow despite the chilly air. He kept looking at his watch; his anxiety causing Vorster to increase the tempo of the finger drums.

'Where the hell is everyone?', Woods asked. 'We've got another huge story here and we're sitting around drinking tea and coffee like we're a knitting circle.'

Megan tried to calm him with a look of her crystal-clear eyes. Uzumba shifted in her seat and focused on her i-pad.

The door opened. Raymond Carpenter and Mike Cash offered their apologies on entrance. 'Sorry, folks. Had a few last-minute changes to make to my copy,' a flustered Carpenter offered.

Mike Cash drew his lips together in a smile-cum-smirk. 'We've hit the jackpot the last few days, Marcus. We want to make sure everything's perfect.'

Vorster nodded in assent. 'That's fine, Mike. We've got the nationals all over us wanting insight into the fire. Don't give them anything until we're in print. The team's copyrighted the on-line content. It won't stop the cannibals from cannibalising it, but we're in first. That's what counts.'

Woods looked at his watch again. 'Can we get moving? I haven't had the luxury of dotting and crossing my story yet. I did what I was told. I came here.'

'Okay, okay,' Marcus Vorster held his hands up. 'Let's climb aboard. Milton can join us later…'

'Lee won't be coming,' Megan informed them.

'What? Why the hell not?'

'He's gone home for a few days.'

Vorster threw his hands up in incredulity and tossed back his fringe. 'What do you mean, 'he's gone home?' I distinctly said in my e-mail all leave's cancelled.'

'Seems he'd already left. Some family emergency.'

'Family emergency my sweet arse. The fat lump's taken umbrage with me. What a tart. I warned him not to.'

Megan looked around the table. Raymond had his head down, Mike Cash stared out the window, Molly Uzumba sniffed haughtily. And Megan realised she'd subconsciously scratched her birthmark tattoo.

Megan broke the uncomfortable silence. 'Marcus,' she said, 'You should've known how he'd react. How he is. But let's leave the inquests 'til later. There's lots still to do.'

Vorster clenched his fists, a fountain of coffee spurting from the cup in his left hand. 'I guess you're right, Wolfe. Okay, what we got?'

David Woods spoke first. 'We've got a wraparound spread with images of the blaze taken from the Newton Hotel car park. It's as close as my photographer could get, and it's as if he's right in the middle of it.'

He brought the image up on his device. Showed each of them in turn.

'Class,' Marcus purred. 'What else?'

Carpenter spoke next. 'We've details of the casualties. Three dead, two critical, several requiring inpatient treatment. Every degree of burn you can imagine, smoke inhalation, even carbon monoxide poisoning, would you believe.'

Vorster nodded, a faraway look in his eyes as if visualising the scene. 'Mike? What you got for us?'

'I've looked at the legal consequences. Loss of personal data. The impact on public services and the Treasury purse. Got the team banding it up as a 'how safe are you under this Government' kind of package.'

'I like your bloody thinking, Mike. Nice angle.' He turned to Megan and Molly. 'Ladies, we were supposed to be coming here to discuss how to keep the snowball rolling downhill on the University bombing. We've lost focus on that a bit. Bring us up to speed with your thoughts.'

Megan let Molly speak first. She presented a detailed plan of how to maintain momentum. Drip-feed a couple of new angles a day, continue to build on the public's fears. Marcus was impressed. 'And you, Megan?'

She took a deep breath and spoke off-the-cuff. 'I'm featuring the police enquiry. I'll follow-up on this Danskin bloke. I agree with Molly,' Uzumba raised her eyebrows in surprise, 'We need to keep chipping away at public confidence. The more they worry, the more they'll read.'

Cash interjected. 'Be careful, Megan. Stick to facts.'

Megan spat out a laugh and trotted out the 'don't let the truth get in the way of a good story' line.

Mike admonished her. 'Remember what happened last time you did that, Megan, yeah?'

Megan Wolfe fell silent while Molly Uzumba suppressed a smile.

It was Vorster's turn to check his watch. 'Okay, people. Back to work. Your teams are doing an excellent job. Keep it up. I have a feeling in my bones about this. We're on a winning streak. Keep the dice rolling.'

All bar Marcus rose to leave. 'The On-Line content guys are due in. On your way out, ask them to give me five minutes first, yeah?'

The rivalry between hard copy and digital content irked Carpenter more than most. 'What a shame it's a secure site. They'll have no fancy film to show. Good job you've got us old faithfuls to keep you going, Marcus.'

Marcus opened his mouth to respond, but Woods got in first. 'I wouldn't know about that, Raymond. Look at this.'

They crowded round Woods' surface-pro. He was logged into the Mercury Online portal. A grainy image filled the screen. An image of a building aflame. Vivid reds and crimsons flashed brightly within plumes of black smoke.

'Sound. Is there any sound?', Marcus urged. Woods played with the volume control. An indistinct burble over a roaring noise. 'Nah. Not good enough,' Marcus cursed.

The image shifted with a lurch. It zoomed in on one side of the building. People were running in all directions. As they dispersed, other emerged, human torches, flames covering their entire frames. The wobbly image zoomed in even more, but their faces became an indistinct blur of pixels.

The camera blurred as it zoomed out, just in time to see a figure run through the crowd. It launched itself through the air, rugby-tackled one of the torches, and rolled in a lover's embrace of flame and fire.

Marcus Vorster thought he was going to orgasm.

'These images are off-site? Unbelievable. Looks like we're right amongst it. Fantastic fucking work, David.'

Woods looked affronted. 'That's not us, Marcus. This IS on-site. And our video would be better quality than that.'

'Then, how?'

Woods fiddled with a few settings. 'Someone downloaded it directly onto our server not ten minutes before we started this meeting.'

'You know, I don't give a shit who's film it is. It's ours now. And it'll make me a bloody fortune. Guys, the Mercury's on the rise again!'

He paused for a moment. Asked David Woods to rerun the clip. 'Right, forget what I just said. Molly, you and your team are on the bombing by yourself now.'

Megan Wolfe began to protest. Vorster talked over her. 'Megan, I want you to find who the superhero is. If he's alive, talk to him. If he's dead, talk to the family. Go to the funeral. Offer them your first born. Do anything you like. Just get me Superman's fucking story.'

**

'Time of death, 3.16.'

The quintet around the bed deflated like airbags. The consultant stood back and gave the corpse one last, sad look. The nurses lowered their heads in respect, tears glistening in their eyes.

They should be inured to it all, but it never got any easier. Especially when the deceased were so young. And there'd been far too many of those lately. Too many who should have their lives ahead of them, not behind. Too many who would never marry, have children, forge successful careers. Too many grieving parents and siblings. Just, too many.

They pulled the curtains around the bed and left the blistered and charred body in peace.

**

Dawn broke like the scribbles of a toddler. Irregular streaks of pink and orange overlay a reddish blur before the sun peeked above the horizon's bedsheets.

Jam Jar was in no mood to appreciate it. Without its normal gel, his carrot coloured hair hung long and messily over his eyes. He didn't flip it aside. He didn't want anyone to see the redness or the tears within them.

It was eight-thirty. His paper round should have finished long ago. He didn't care. He wasn't going to school. Not today. Mr Ramesh had offered to deliver the newspapers himself when he heard the news, but Jam Jar declined. He needed to do something.

He was particularly careful to ensure Florence Roadhouse got the Telegraph and Mercury. The last thing he needed was another run-in with the old bat. He needn't have worried. She had long since caught the number 97 into Newcastle to deliver her latest offering to Marcus Vorster and co.

One person he couldn't avoid, though, was his grandmother. He hung outside, composing himself. He hoped she'd be asleep after spending half the night dusting while wondering why it was so dark. She hadn't. Worse, it was a rare lucid day.

'Hello, James. What a nice surprise,' Doris Jarrod said. 'Lovely morning, isn't it?'

Lovely? You haven't a clue, have you? he thought. 'Yes, gran,' he said.

'No Ryan today? Is he at gymnastics again?'

Ryan hadn't done any gymnastics since the age of thirteen but Jam Jar wasn't going to correct her. Instead, he walked to the kitchen, filled a tumbler with tap water, and set it beside his grandmother. He prised open the Nomad box and extracted five pills from the compartment. 'Here's your sweeties.'

'Thank you, Ryan.'

'It's James.'

'Who?'

'Never mind. Listen, gran. I can't stop. Dad needs me.'

The old woman smiled sadly. 'Tell Norman I miss him. That it'd be lovely to see him again.'

'I will. I promise,' knowing full-well that there wasn't any point telling him. His father wouldn't come. He couldn't bring himself to put her into a home yet wouldn't countenance seeing her the way she was. So, it was Jam Jar and Ryan who became her nursemaids.

Jam Jar guessed it was up to him, now.

He kissed the old woman's forehead and stepped out into a bitter sun.

**

The latest in a lengthy line of shitty days was about to get even shittier. DCI Stephen Danskin sat at the wrong side of his desk, his back to the window behind which his team beavered away.

His PC was illuminated, his desk decorated with crime scene photographs and files. He even flipped pages now and again. Yet, it was an illusion. His eyes remained closed.

He inhaled to the count of three, exhaled to a similar beat. Tried to clear his thoughts. Danskin hoped something would germinate within, fertilize his mind, and grow the roots of a theory.

'Don't see what you expect to see.' He repeated his mantra to himself over and over again. It didn't work. It couldn't work, not when there was nothing to see.

He sensed the door to his office open. The lack of a knock signified either Superintendent Connor, or DC Todd Robson. He turned and saw Herman Munster loom over him.

'Didn't hear you knock there, Robson.'

The man looked perplexed. 'Probably because I didn't.'

'It's called irony, Robson. What d'you want?'

'Not me, Sir. Super wants you.'

Danskin let out a groan. Bent forward until his torso covered the desk and grabbed the opposite side of it with the tips of his fingers. Slowly, he inched his fingers back to him and sat upright. 'What the hell does he want now?' the DCI asked wearily.

'Nee idea', Robson shrugged. 'But he's on his way.'

Connor breezed through the door, ignoring Todd Robson. 'Danskin, I need some of your men.'

Robson raised an eyebrow and exited stage left.

'Whoa. You're kidding, Sir, surely?'

'I wish I was. DCI Kinnear's snowed under. He's running every line of enquiry out of this station apart from your University bomber. He needs support in the light of the HMRC fire.'

'Surely that's a fire service issue? There's nothing for us to investigate. Unless...'

Connor held his hands aloft. 'Let's not get ahead of ourselves. There's no indication of arson. Not yet, at least. Their enquiries are in motion.'

'Sir, come on. It doesn't add up. I ask you for more manpower, and you give me Worzel Gummidge on one hand then, with the other, you take away my team to help Kinnear with something that isn't even our business. How am I expected to get results?'

Connor looked genuinely sympathetic. 'I understand, Stephen; I really do. Let's not lose sight of the fact you already have 80% of the station at your call. All I'm asking is you release a dozen constabulary in support of Kinnear. Fifteen at most. He needs help with securing the HMRC site. Stop ghouls getting in, and to provide assurance to the staff there that we're looking after them.'

Danskin thought for a moment. 'You said you were 'asking' me to release them?'

'That's right. But I'll order their release if I have to.'

Danskin smirked. 'Thought as much.' He added 'Sir' as an afterthought.

'Good. Thank you, Stephen. I hoped you'd understand. Oh, and release one detective to help Kinnear out with press releases and enquiries as well, will you? There's a good lad.'

Danskin was left staring at Connor's back. The DCI shook his head. Looked at his people in the bullpen.

Parker and Nairn were too valuable to him.

Sangar and his geek squad were more comfortable talking at IT equipment than to people.

Dealing with press required tact. He'd have to keep Robson.

That left Trebilcock, twiddling his thumbs; a single file in his in-tray. Perfect. But, could he get away with that one? Really? With reluctance, he called through the door, 'WDC Graves? Hannah? Can I have a quick word, love?'

CHAPTER TWELVE

'What 'last fellow'?' Nigel Trebilcock asked.

'The kid. The one who was here a couple of days ago, asking the questions you've just asked.'

Trebilcock looked puzzled. This was his case. Danskin had no right assigning someone else to it without his knowledge. He'd have a word when he got back to the station.

His nostrils flared, caught a whiff of stale alcohol and cheap perfume in the air, and almost gagged. 'Humour me. Tell me again.'

Charlie Charlton gave an exaggerated sigh. Folded away the Racing Post. 'Luca, make iz a coffee, will you?'

Trebilcock noted he wasn't included in the offering as a bearded guy removed a headset and disappeared into a back room.

'McGuffie hadn't been driving out of here for long,' Charlton began. 'Just so we're clear, I don't employ him. I get his takings, he gets the tips and a retainer, but he's self-employed. Pays his own taxes, and such like.' He shot Trebilcock a meaningful look.

'Go on.'

'Well, the night he…the last night he worked, he'd been on a long shift. A quiet day, but a long one. Nothing out of the ordinary. Most the blokes work long hours. Before you ask, that's their shout. No pressure from me.'

'You say it was a quiet day. Can you tell me something about his day?'

'How the hell would I know? I wasn't in the back of the bloody cab with him,' Charlton growled.

Trebilcock tried again. 'What about his fares? Anything unusual there? Did he call in any odd routes? Report any dubious characters?'

Charlton laughed. 'They're all dubious.'

'What about his last fare? Do you have a record of it?'

'You know we do. Ilona told the other guy.'

'Like I say, Mr Charlton, humour me. What exactly did Ilona say?'

Charlton screwed up his face. Rubbed an eye with a forefinger. The guy called Luca plopped a chipped mug in front of Charlie Charlton. He kept the second one for himself.

Charlton blew on his coffee. 'Ilona told your bloke he got picked up not far from Manors and dropped him off,' he thought for a moment, 'I think she said it was the Printer's Pie.'

Trebilcock made a note. Neither of the locations meant anything to him. He'd check them out later. 'Could I speak to Ilona?'

Charlton shook his head. 'Nah. Not possible.'

'Why not?'

'She doesn't work here anymore.'

'Do you have an address where I can reach her? A phone number?'

'I'm not much good at that sort of thing. Admin, like.'

'What about a surname?'

Charlton shook his head. 'Na. I'm not...'

'...I know; you're not much good at that sort of thing.'

Charlton smiled. 'You're catching on, kidda.'

'Is there anything else you can tell me that might help?'

The man with the beard spoke for the first time. 'I could look up our recordings. The drivers have dashcams but the tapes naturally erase after twenty-four hours. Some of them have voice recordings as well and they're automatically transmitted back here. I could check to see if McGuffie's is on here, if you like.'

Trebilcock rolled his eyes. 'Yes, I'd very much like.' He switched his gaze to Charlton. 'Now, why didn't you tell me that earlier?'

'You didn't ask. Neither did the young lad.'

**

Megan Wolfe slammed the receiver into its cradle. 'Thanks for nothing,' she shouted at it.

'I take it that went well, then,' Raymond Carpenter said with understatement.

'Typical bloody hospital receptionist. She said if I really was a relative, I'd have been given a password. They can't tell me anything about his condition without it. Seriously, it's like breaking the enigma code. Good job the security wasn't so tight at the Uni or the Government buildings. We'd have nothing to write about.'

'What's your next move?'

Megan rubbed her tattoo. 'Simple. I turn up at the hospital. Doesn't take a genius to work out he'll either be in trauma or the burns unit. Or the mortuary. I'll just wander in and have a look around.'

Carpenter saw the sullen expression on her face. 'You're not exactly into this assignment, are you?'

She barked a humourless laugh. 'What do you think? My team broke the bomber story…'

'My team, Megan. Not yours.'

She shot him a look. 'Whatever. OUR team broke the story. It was our exclusive. We were the ones who Christened him the Tyneside Tyrant. It's the title that's captured the imagination of the entire country. Marcus has no right taking me off it. Worse, he's left Uzumba to roll with it.'

'You really don't like Molly, do you?'

'That's not the point. The point is, I might as well be doing hatched, matched and despatched as finding out what happened to goody two-shoes at the fire. I'm better than that, and I'm worth a lot more than that. Give me something sexy to get my teeth into, that's all I expect from him.'

Carpenter pushed his chair towards her. Put a hand on her leg. 'Hey, if it's sex you're after..' He cut the sentence short when he saw the look on her face. Held his hands aloft. Backed off.

'Don't even joke about it. It was a joke, wasn't it?'

''Course it was.' His face betrayed the lie. 'Vorster must have his reasons, though. He knows you're the best investigative reporter he's got, never mind news reporter.'

Megan looked at the whiteboard. At the coloured magnetic tiles, each denoting a journalist and the story they were deployed on. Megan's tile sat alone and forlorn in one corner. A thought crossed her mind. Her mouth opened and shut like a goldfish.

'What? What have I said?', Carpenter asked.

Megan had grabbed her jacket and was already on her way out of the office.

**

Less than a mile across the city, another couple sat deep in conference at the base of a different whiteboard. The sound of trains rumbled through the open windows, making Lyall Parker's words difficult to hear.

Parker shivered frequently. He was deathly white, but he'd worked with Danskin long enough to know closing the window wasn't an option. Danskin believed heat dulled the thinking process. Minds function better in the cold, he'd told the Scotsman.

'The final forensic report on the explosive device is in. It's a basic timer. Not overly complex for someone who knows what they're doing.'

'So, we were right to assume the perpetrator has some experience with explosives.'

'We were,' Parker confirmed. 'The problem is, that's about all we know about the device. It was obliterated in the blast.'

Danskin thought for a moment. 'How long would someone set the timer for? An hour? Two? If we knew that, we might get something on CCTV. The Uni's images might be up in smoke, but the street cams around the city will be ok. I know we've got folk trawling them, but we need to make the haystack smaller if they're to find the needle.'

'I'm ahead of you, Stephen. Our intelligence tells us the usual time scales are one hour, twelve hours, or twenty-four hours.'

Danskin rested his unshaven chin against his fingers. 'An hour's too risky. Wouldn't give him time to get far enough away.'

'Or her,' Lyall Parker reminded.

'I bet it's a male but I take your point, Lyall. Rule one hour out. Twenty-four hours would mean it'd be planted in the early hours. I get there'd be few people around to spot him – or her – at that time, but any activity would be suspicious at that time in the morning. Even in a University.'

The silver-haired DI tended to agree. 'Mid-afternoon, then?'

Danskin nodded. 'That's my guess. Lyall, get a list of all service vehicles who were signed-in around that time. Check for any students who missed their lectures, lecturers who missed their classes. And tell the surveillance squad to focus their efforts on reviewing footage between one pm and five pm the day before.'

Parker nodded. 'And remember the student who was given the all-clear because he was with family in Pakistan?'

Danskin wrinkled his brow then nodded.

'Well, seems he wasn't in Pakistan. He missed the flight. There was a Sarfraz Iqbal on board, but not our Sarfraz Iqbal. Turns out he was shacked up with a lassie in Elswick. Parvin Uday's her name. And guess what? Her father IS on the intelligence services list.'

'Get the bugger in here for a word'

'He's already on his way, sir.'

A third voice interrupted the conversation. 'Could I have a word, sir?'

Danskin rolled his eyes. Nigel Trebilcock.

'Not really, Treblecock. I've got a few things going on, don't you know.'

Trebilcock remained unmoved. 'I won't keep you long. I just wanted to say, sir, that no matter how little you think of me, I'm perfectly capable of running my own investigation.'

Danskin remained silent for a long while. He and Parker exchanged looks. 'Treblecock, I haven't a scooby what you're on about.'

'You sent someone to interview the owner of the cab firm McGuffie worked for. Without my say so or knowledge.'

'Listen, lad. I can do what I want unless the Super tells me otherwise. But, for your information, I didn't send anyone. It may have escaped your attention but I've no bugger to send.'

Trebilcock considered the DCI's riposte. 'He said somebody had talked to him.'

'Name? Description?'

Nigel Trebilcock hesitated. 'I don't know. I didn't ask.'

Danskin sniggered. 'You didn't ask? Are you sure you're capable of running your own investigation?'

'Yes, sir. I am, sir.'

'Ok. You find out who it was, and I'll pay some attention to it. Pound to a penny, it turns out to be press. But, if not, I promise you, you'll have my ear. Is that good enough for you?'

Trebilcock smiled. 'Yes, sir. Thank you, sir.' He left thinking he'd won some respect.

'Stupid boy,' Danskin whispered to Parker in a passable impression of Captain Mainwaring. 'Right, Lyall. You get the surveillance squad looking at the tapes. When this Iqbal guy gets here, put him in the interview room. I want to observe him before going down.'

'DCI Danskin,' a breathless female voice interrupted.

'Jesus Christ, I'm as popular as a Greggs in Pennywell today.' He turned to see Hannah Graves' cheeks flush beneath the freckles. 'Hannah. I thought you were supposed to be with DCI Kinnear.'

'I am, sir. Or at least, I was. I'm not sure, now.'

'Howay man, lass. What do you mean?'

'I mean, sir, I think you might need me back.'

He took a deep breath. 'Go on.'

Hannah Graves next words ran through him like an electric charge.

'The fire service has come up with something. The HMRC fire? It wasn't accidental. They found evidence of an incendiary device and an accelerant.'

CHAPTER THIRTEEN

'Ladies and gentlemen, I shall read a short statement relating to the fire at Her Majesty's Revenue and Customs Office in Longbenton. I shan't be taking questions at this stage, but you will be kept informed of developments via official press releases as more information emerges.'

At least they'd had the decency to let him inside the Civic Centre this time, with a handy exit immediately behind him to ensure he could disappear without being ambushed. Danskin looked to his left where Sue Nairn stood in support. He'd left Parker at the station to interview Iqbal.

'The Fire Services have shared with me their preliminary report on the fire. Although I emphasise the findings are preliminary, I am releasing the key fact today to ensure we are being totally transparent with members of the public.' Danskin looked around the room. No sign of the damn woman from the Mercury. Relieved, he resumed his prepared speech.

'I can tell you the fire was not accidental. It was a deliberate act intended, at best, to disrupt Government services, at worse to kill, maim, or endanger life.'

He was well-accustomed to the volley of flashbulbs by now, so he remained still, allowing the press photographers to capture his image.

'I am unable to share more details at this point in time as I'm sure you'll appreciate we are not prepared to disclose anything which may jeopardise our lines of enquiry. Thank you.'

Danskin collected his papers and shot through the exit door leaving the inevitable barrage of questions rhetorical ones.

Once Nairn closed the door behind her and they were alone in the council antechamber, Danskin's body sagged with relief. He slunk into a chair, head back, eyes closed. 'Ok, Sue. Give it to me. What's Connor going to annihilate me about this time?'

Sue Nairn smiled. 'You didn't say owt so he's got nothing to complain about.'

Danskin blew out air. 'I needed to hear that. Thanks. Do we have anything from Lyall on Iqbal yet?'

'Yeah, he was in touch while you were making preps for the release. He's finished with him. Waiting for you to get back before deciding next steps.'

Danskin curled his lips. 'Doesn't sound promising. If he'd found, or even suspected, anything, he'd take the next steps himself.'

'Aye. He even left Iqbal alone with Todd Robson for ten minutes.'

Danskin snickered. 'The poor bastard. But if Robson didn't get anything out of him, it looks like he's in the clear.'

'Lyall's also traced the girlfriend. His exacts words were, 'pretty as heather in bloom, bright as a Hebridean midnight.'

The DCI chuckled. 'Sounds like Lyall. What about the father?'

'Nah. He's disowned her since she came to the west. Sangar's geeks have run their software over her social media profiles and phone records. Results came back straight away. She's had no contact with him for years.'

'Shit. Another blind alley.'

'Looks that way, sir.'

'Anything else to cheer me up with?'

Sue Nairn pursed her lips. 'Just a thought. What about checking the finances of those at the University?

Danskin shook his head. 'What? All of them? We'd never get permission. Why suggest that?'

'It just seems we've got nowhere with any theory we've proposed, so I was wondering about gambling debts. There's the Stowell Street Chinese community, and you know how much they're into their gambling.'

Danskin shook his head more vigorously. 'Fucking hell, Sue. That's ISIS, ETA, the IRA and now the Triad. You'll be suggesting the Cosa Nostra or Hitler Youth next. We're in fucking Newcastle, man; not a Hollywood set.' He saw Nairn bristle. 'Never mind. I wondered about the Khmer Rouge, myself.'

Sue threw her head back and laughed, no longer affronted.

Danskin relaxed back into his chair. Closed his eyes again. 'Anyway; you reckon the briefing went ok?'

'Well, the only thing is..'

Danskin opened one eye. 'Yes?'

'The press vultures are bound to put two and two together at some point. Probably soon. They'll come up with eight. Link the bomb to the fire and make a meal of it. Wind everyone up into a frenzy.'

Danskin nodded. 'I know that. Thing is, they might be linked. I need to get back to the station.' He rose to leave. As Danskin and Nairn stepped out into the brisk air, a question came to him.

'I wonder why that Wolfe woman wasn't here?'

**

'How were things at home?', Megan Wolfe asked.

'Cool,' came the rumbling reply.

Raymond Carpenter raised a quizzical eyebrow at the exchange. He felt there was a shared joke in there, somewhere.

'Lee, you need to know Vorster's not too happy with you,' Megan warned. 'Slinking off like that when he's getting horny over the Tyneside Tyrant story didn't go down well.'

'I couldn't give a damn. He knew he was pushing my buttons. I'd end up squatting him like a fly if I hadn't gotten some air.'

'You're up to speed with the story?' Carpenter asked. 'And the fire? You know about that, too?'

'They do have the internet back in FLA, you know. I might have been away physically but, head-wise, I've been right here.'

Again, Carpenter felt he'd missed something. He felt uncomfortable. He smiled at Megan as he rose to leave, made an ok sign with his fingers as if seeking confirmation things were alright between the two of them. She smiled back. It was barely perceptible, but sufficiently for Raymond Carpenter to feel his tension ease as he let himself out.

'Thank Christ he's gone. Lee, I want to run something past you. It needs to be completely between you and me, understand?'

Leeward Milton furrowed his brow.

'I need you to say it.'

'Sure. We went off the record two minutes ago.'

'Thanks. I appreciate it. Call me insane if you want, but hear me out.'

Megan smoothed down the hem of her skirt as she stood. Scratched at the birthmark on her arm. She wandered to the window overlooking the cobbles of the Groat Market. At the folk plying their trade from market stalls, others hustling by from one appointment to another, a few more seeking warmth and a cold beer inside the Old George. She took a deep breath and began.

'Marcus invested a fortune in developing e-news. He built up platforms and offices across the world. But it was too soon. People weren't into the internet. There weren't enough subscribers for a service, and businesses hadn't cottoned on to the benefits of advertising via websites. By the time there was a market for it, other new e-publishers arrived. They had money to invest. Marcus had already spent his. The Mercury empire was swallowed up by the competition.'

Milton shuffled in his seat. 'Can we get to the point, honey? I've got work to get back to.'

Megan gave him a dismissive wave and continued unabated. 'Marcus once told me that the terms of his inheritance demand he establish and own a business. His parents refused to sanction their wealth if Vorster sat on his arse and frivolled it away. That's the only reason Marcus keeps this crummy place going.'

'Megan, I'm real sorry but I've a story to write...'

Wolfe snapped her fingers. 'That's just it. What if THIS is the story?' *What if* his parent's money is running out? *What if* he needs a business – a SUCCESSFUL – business, to keep his lifestyle? *What if* he needs the Mercury to skyrocket?'

She looked directly into Leeward Milton's eyes. He saw a fire rage deep within hers.

'*What if,*' she concluded, 'Vorster is creating his own stories?'

**

The ice-cream parlour opposite The Coble was closed and shuttered for the winter, the streets and car parks deserted. Litter flew by like sprinters out the blocks. Gulls, battered and buffered by North Sea winds, surrendered themselves to the whims of the tempest. Yet, this was David Woods kind of weather. He loved it.

While a few old-timers sought shelter inside The Coble's snug interior, Woods nursed the dregs of his stout at a wooden table and bench in a small square outside the hostelry. No-one else braved the elements. He'd photographed polar bears at the top of the world and observed penguin colonies at its base. In contrast, Newbiggin-By-The-Sea's bracing climate was a piece of cake.

Woods coveted the relative isolation of his adopted town. He worked the city out of necessity. He lived in his windswept cottage overlooking the Point's historic church out of love. He spent hours at his bedroom window watching kittiwakes and other seabirds ride the North Sea storm currents, or circle the air over St Bartholemew's.

Built to resemble a mediaeval castle, the church stood headstrong against the gales and storms. The only nod to the inhospitable climate was its flagpole, which jutted horizontally from below its rampart-like tower rather than stand proud and vertical to the windswept heavens as it once had, before a nineteenth-century tempest tossed both flagpole and part of the tower into a furious North Sea.

David pushed the last of his beer aside and set off along the deserted promenade towards his remote home. The wind ruffled his hair, the saline spray from the curled fingers of breakers stung his eyes, as he paused to look out over The Couple; an off-shore art installation set atop a semi-submerged plinth.

The artwork depicted a young couple searching the horizon for the return of loved ones lost to the waves. David found it the perfect place for contemplation. And he had plenty to contemplate.

He'd traced her through the Woodhorn Northumberland Archives. He'd done that easily enough. After all, it wasn't a common name. What puzzled him was the fact the records indicated someone had beaten him to it.

Now, why would someone else want the back story of Florence Roadhouse?

**

Twenty-two miles south-west, someone was feeling the cold. Florence Roadhouse sat in her parlour with her arthritic hand deep within a pre-heated, lavender-scented mitten. Her typewriter remained in its cover on the mahogany table by the window. A day's respite wouldn't go amiss. Mr Vorster had plenty of her unpublished letters to consider for the time being.

But, Florence wasn't used to inactivity. She forced herself to her feet, straightened gingerly, and furniture-walked her way to the window where she watched tits and robins cling precariously to fat balls strung from her washing line. A pair of starlings looked on enviously at the acrobatic smaller birds, occasionally swooping to gobble up discarded titbits from the sodden lawn.

An armada of grey-hulled clouds weighed anchor overhead, ready to release their next deluge. She turned the heating up another notch and let her mind take her far away from the Tyneside winter.

Florence closed her eyes and imagined dappled sunlight etch her face through the fronds of a tropical rainforest. She let her scrawny muscles absorb the heat, felt herself relax as she imagined the call of birds - more exotic than those in her garden – rent the air.

She heard the incessant buzz of insects. Could almost feel the flies around her. She shooed them off with a reflexive flick of her arm and allowed herself a faint smile of embarrassment.

Her fantasy resumed with the howl and chatter of distant monkeys. She felt her linen uniform cling to skin slick with sweat and humidity. Florence's nostrils flared as her imagination took in the heady scent of pine, her ears picked out the sound of thick plops of rainfall as they splattered against dense foliage.

A twig snapped underfoot. Was it a twig? Time seemed to stand-still. She heard blood pound her temples, felt her heart knock against her chest wall.

Raised voices, loud and insistent, echoed around her. Shouts, high-pitched. Feverish. It wasn't a twig, it was...

Another safety clicked in the trees above.

The rat-a-tat of rapid gunfire.

The screech of jungle creatures deafened her.

As they faded, human voices replaced them. Falsetto screams of the dying.

The ground beneath her feet quaked as bodies in their dozens fell around her.

Florence Roadhouse opened her eyes and welcomed the sight of bland, familiar birds in her garden and the sound of rain against her parlour window.

Most of all, she cherished the comforting feel of a bitter cold day in north-east England.

CHAPTER FOURTEEN

DCI Stephen Danskin stood in front of the briefing room's open windows and let the frigid air wash over him while his team sat huddled around the boards. He began the briefing with his usual mantra.

'Remember, guys, we don't see what we expect to see.'

He moved in front of the board, above which hung a map of Tyneside. Two red circles highlighted the crime scenes. Danskin used the tip of a marker pen to tap on one of the circles.

'Northumbria University, City East campus.' A 'before and after photograph' of the building provided a stark reminder of the devastation.

'Fact. A timer was used to detonate an explosive device on the ninth floor. This was likely – but not indisputably – placed in location between the hours of 1pm and 5pm the day before the incident.'

Three clock faces drawn on the board served as a reminder of the detonation time and the probable hours of placement. Danskin walked as he spoke, most eyes followed him; some remained fixed on the board.

'Fact two: the perpetrator had some knowledge of explosives.' The board showed a blue circle with the letters IQ inside.

Danskin moved to a rogue's gallery of photographs. 'Don't close your minds to any avenue, nor to any motive. But, persons of interest include Maria Gonzales and,' he indicated the photographs of a tanned and attractive girl, 'her connection to the late Catalina Mendoza Zabala.'

Todd Robson let out a wolf-whistle while Ravi Sangar opened his mouth to remind Danskin that there wasn't any digital footprint to link Gonzales to the crime. Danskin had already moved on.

The DCI tapped three other photographs. 'This is Sarfraz Iqbal and, these two, father and daughter, Adnan and Parvin Uday. We can rule out the lass, Lyall is monitoring Iqbal, and we've asked Interpol and the security services for further help on the older man. At this point, I have to say their involvement is unlikely, but it's all we've got.'

He listened as others mooted their own theories, scrawled the more relevant topics on the board, and poo-pooed the more outrageous.

After a gulp from a bottle of water, Danskin drew a line down the centre of the board. He went through the same process with the HMRC fire. It didn't take long.

Finally, he circled the common denominators. There weren't many. While he summed up, he continued walking amongst the rank and file of his team.

'Keep on open mind on this,' Danskin urged, 'but let's think of the probability ratios. One: the crimes were either committed by one person with knowledge of a range of explosive devices. Two: we have a copycat out there. Bloody buggery if we have.'

The profanity lightened the mood.

'Three. We're looking for two separate individuals, each with a motive against separate organisations but at the same time. Four: it's a sheer bloody coincidence.'

He let his words sink in. 'We need to prioritise. For the time being, let's rule out three and four. I'm not buying the coincidence. We'll work on the theory it's either the same loony-tune, or a copycat. That's where our focus lies until we exhaust our options.'

He paused long enough to catch the eye of every officer in the room. 'We're going to get him. Or her. I swear, we'll get the bastard.'

He returned to the crime board and gave it a last look. He was surprised to notice someone had managed to add a third column while he walked the floor. Within its parameters, Danskin noted a quickly scrawled blue H, an object that looked like a brick, and a child-like drawing of a car.

Danskin raised an eyebrow. 'Explain.' An order, not a question.

After a long moment, a voice spoke. 'What if we have three incidents?' Nigel Trebilcock.

Danskin stared back. A muscle twitched in his cheek. 'Explain,' he repeated.

'Well, we had a hoax, didn't we? The warning SMS messages to the hospital.'

The H and the brick scrawled on the board began to make sense. Hospital and cell-phone, not a brick. Much as he hated to admit it, Danskin thought Trebilcock might be onto something.

He scratched the bristles of his jawline. 'So, you're suggesting it mightn't have been a hoax? That something went wrong and, for whatever reason, the device failed? Different MO each time, but it's possible.'

Trebilcock shrugged. 'Possibly. But that's not what I'm thinking.' Trebilcock found the courage to step forward. He rapped the knuckle of his thumb against the drawing of the car. 'Sir, you charged me with investigating the murder of the taxi driver, Teddy McGuffie. When the alarm sounded at the hospital, he was alive. By the time the all clear was given, he was dead.'

Dots began to join in Danskin's head. 'You believe the taxi driver knew something that could incriminate or identify our guy? That the culprit had the hospital evacuated to give him the opportunity to finish the job he started?'

Trebilcock waited for the put-down.

When Danskin spoke, it was almost as if he was talking to himself. 'Weeyabugger. I think we can rule out number two, now. It's not a copycat. We know we're looking for one person.'

Louder, he said, 'It's the same bloody person. Brilliant. Great work, Nigel. Great bloody work.'

Astonishment crossed Nigel Trebilcock's face. Danskin hadn't called him Treblecock, or even Trebilcock. He'd got a Nigel. A big, fat Nigel.

Trebilcock though he'd burst with pride.

**

The vehicle stalled as he pulled into the kerb, but he abandoned it where it lay. He clambered out and took in his surroundings.

He stood in a run-down housing estate on the outskirts of the city centre. Broken glass and discarded takeaway cartons littered the footpath. Sheets acted the role of curtains in the windows of those houses that weren't boarded up. Graffiti-strewn walls and smashed fences told him the social status lay midway between traditional working class and precariat.

Concrete bollards separated the different sections of the estate. Intended to prevent boy racers, they offered natural boundaries within the community which served to encourage a gang mentality. He'd been in worse places, but not many.

His target lay half-a-mile downhill, though he set off in the opposite direction. Careful not to attract attention, the man looped around the estate, doubled back on himself, and emerged within sight of his goal.

It was hard to miss.

The man buttoned up his coat, wrapped a scarf around his face, and pulled on a pair of ski gloves. Barely an inch of flesh remained exposed. Slowly, he circumnavigated the target three-times, scrutinising it every step of the way.

There were numerous access and egress points. All were locked, bolted and shuttered. Nowhere offered unchallenged entry. CCTV cameras sat proud against surrounding walls. People busied themselves nearby. All wore photographic ID. This wasn't good. Not good, at all. He sighed and resigned himself. He'd have to give this one a miss. He set off into the wind.

As he did so, something caught his eye. A sign:

'Tours: This Way.'

Tours. They did tours.

Perhaps all was not lost after all.

**

It wasn't the fact the heating was turned up to melting point. It wasn't the interminable wait in the pharmacy, nor the awkward, stilted conversations of those around him. It wasn't even the pain and discomfort, or the forlorn expression on the faces of his father and brother either side of him.

What did it, was the thought of the poor girl who's life he'd failed to save. That's what brought Ryan Jarrod as close to anger as he ever got.

He'd asked about her as soon as he came around. They wouldn't tell him. It was only an hour before his discharge a kindly young nurse had held his arm and told him she hadn't made it. She'd passed away in the early hours a couple of days ago.

Ryan cried. Unashamedly. The nurse told him it was a natural reaction to shock. Told him to let the tears flow. He'd been lucky, she said. The rainwater puddles on the ground, the dampness in the atmosphere, all had helped him survive with mainly superficial burns.

Ryan didn't feel lucky. He thought of the girl. How her parents had been there for her when she entered the world, but she left it in the arms of a stranger who she'd never even spoken to. He didn't know her name nor she, his.

He wiped moisture from his eyes with hands swaddled in layers of bandages so thick he appeared to be wearing Micky Mouse's gloves. The consultant had told him his hands took the brunt of the flames, but they'd heal. The burns were second-degree but some had been categorised as deep partial thickness in nature. These would need cosmetic surgery at some point, skin grafts and the like, but she assured him he'd make a full recovery.

His lower abdomen, where he'd pressed the girl to the ground in his futile attempt to save her, also needed attention. His 'pelvic area,' she'd called it. 'There'll be no long-lasting effects,' she'd said, 'But you'll be out of action for some time.'

Ryan hadn't known whether she was referring to his hands or his crown jewels. He didn't really care. All he knew was that he wanted to get well not for himself, but for the girl. And for Teddy McGuffie. So that he could ensure somebody, in some way, paid for it.

He tapped his feet restlessly. The hospital pharmacy waiting area was inadequate. One row of seats around the edges of the hexagonal shaped dispensing kiosk, two lines of five seats facing it. Ryan sat in the centre of the front row, either side of him Norman and James Jarrod sat as still and silent as mannequins.

'Ryan Jarrod,' a voice called.

Ryan stepped forward. The young Asian girl behind the kiosk pushed a shopping-bag sized carrier stuffed with lotions and potions and sufficient dressings to bind Tutankhamen, towards him. 'Sorry for your wait. I just need you to sign for these, then you can be on your way.'

Ryan held up his hands. 'Can you just stick your pen between my teeth for me, please?'

The girl, Sunni, her nametag said, looked up. 'Sorry. Perhaps your grandfather could sign for you?'

Despite the circumstances, Ryan laughed for the first time in days. 'I'll tell him you said that. It's my dad. A bit of a late starter, you could say.'

The girl apologised for the third time in a minute as Ryan motioned with his head for Norman Jarrod to step forward.

While his dad completed the paperwork, Ryan felt a strange sensation touch the base of his skull. The feeling, a warm tingling numbness, crept up his head. It was the feeling of being watched. The sensation disappeared at the same time as Norman Jarrod swept up the carrier bag.

When the Jarrod clan made for the exit, Sunni called the next patient.

'Ilona Popescu.'

Ryan swiveled his head in recognition of an unusual forename. He saw a waif-thin girl with dirty blonde hair and a bruised, closed eye cast a glance in his direction.

Norman and Jam Jar were already outside. Ryan had no choice but to follow them.

CHAPTER FIFTEEN

Megan Wolfe eschewed the Printer's Pie, the favourite haunt of Mercury journalists, in favour of the newly-opened and hedonistic Eden in the entertainment complex known as The Gate. Although breathless from the uphill walk, she relaxed in the knowledge she'd go unrecognised amidst the thrall of office workers enjoying their festive lunches.

Megan's companion took in the surroundings. 'Wow. First time I've been here. Sure is a transformation from its Tiger Tiger days.'

'Yeah. Upped its game, hasn't it?'

Leeward Milton speared a fork through a wood-fire grilled gammon and took most of it out with one enormous bite. 'We're here for a reason, I guess,' he mumbled through a mouthful of salty meat.

Megan locked ice-blue eyes with his. 'I wondered what you thought of my theory.'

Milton chewed on his gammon for a while. Wiped his mouth with a napkin. 'I think you're playing a dangerous game. I think you should forget it and concentrate on the kid from the fire, like the good girl Vorster asked you to be.'

She waved an olive in his direction. 'Come on, Lee. Don't you think it's worth looking into? Something Raymond Carpenter said set me thinking. I mean, I'm Vorster's best investigative reporter by a country mile. Why side-line me from the biggest story he's ever had? Unless, Marcus has something to do with it, and he doesn't want me to uncover it? What a story it would make, Lee. It'd set me up for life.'

'Or ruin you forever. If you're wrong, and he finds out, he'll stake you out for the bugs.'

Megan slapped the table in frustration. 'I thought you of all people would think he could be capable of such a thing.'

Milton sipped on a bottle of Coors. Smacked his lips. 'Oh, he's a self-promoting bastard of the first order, for sure. He's ruthless. Mind, he says that about you, too.' Megan made a face. 'And,' Milton continued, 'He's got no empathy. Just look at the way he crashes all over me. No thought to what I've been through. How I react to the things he says.'

Megan noticed the gammon on the end of Leeward's fork tremble as his hand shook. She rested hers on his wrist. 'Hey. I'm sorry. Let's forget it. I'll go back to making some shit up about the Wunderkind. Keep him happy. It's just, you know, I thought he had a lot to gain from this and nothing to lose.'

Leeward beamed at her, his moon face creased in a smile.

'What?' she asked.

'I've been doing some research of my own. You do know he's writing his life story, don't you? He's signed a million-dollar publishing deal. Our Marcus Vorster is selling his soul to the devil. I figure he could do with a few headlines of his own.'

Lee Milton waited for Megan's eyes to sparkle with excitement. Waited for her thrilled response. Her barrage of questions. It wasn't the reaction he got.

'For fuck's sake,' she said.

'Huh?'

'Over there. Coming this way. He's stalking me, I'm sure.'

Leeward Milton glanced over his shoulder.

Raymond Carpenter strode towards them.

**

Frank Burrows said his goodbyes as Barry Docherty arrived.

'Who's that?', Barry asked Ryan.

'That's Frank. I'm shadowing him with the Specials. Quite touched he came, actually. Brought me a pile of magazines.

Barry leafed through them. Men's Health. The Mag. WhatCar. Beneath them, Town and Country, and People's Friend. Barry raised an eyebrow.

'I know,' Ryan laughed, 'Think he's just wiped out the hairdresser's stock library.'

'Daft question, but how you doing?'

'I'm not sure, really. Very sore. A bit down. Could be worse, though, all thing's considered.'

Barry nodded. He was sat next to Jam Jar who wore earplugs while his thumbs blurred at lightning speed over the hand-held games consul. Opposite, Norman Jarrod stared blankly at a TV soap opera. Only Spud, consigned to his pen save he leap on Ryan's injuries, yelped in exuberance at Barry's presence.

'How long you out of action for?', Barry asked at length.

'Worst should be over in three weeks, they reckon.'

'So, back at work in the New Year?'

Ryan grimaced. 'Not sure, really. Don't think I'll ever go back, if I'm honest.'

'Howay, man. I know it'll have terrible memories but get back on the bike as soon as you fall off it is what they say.'

'Nah. I'm not cut out for it, Barry. My heart's set on joining the force.'

Barry looked at Ryan's swaddled hands. 'Will they still take you?'

The words hit Ryan like a low blow. It was something he'd never considered. 'Sure,' he said, not really sure at all.

The silence was interrupted by a rap on the door. No-one moved.

'I'll get that, then, should I?' Ryan asked.

He rose to his feet, trousers held away from his burnt groin. When the door swung open, his face froze.

For her part, her eyes roamed over him. Neat hair, slim but honed frame, honest eyes. He was younger than she'd expected, but she'd had younger. Megan Wolfe announced herself with a simple, 'Hi.'

'Yes?'

The bluntness of his tone took her aback. 'I wondered if I could have a quick word with you? About the incident at work.'

'No, I don't think you can.' Ryan's words were as crisp and clear as her Arctic-ice eyes.

Megan tried a charm offensive. Looped her hair around an ear. Gave him a dazzling smile. Even fluttered her eyelashes. 'Ah, I understand. You're a civil servant. Official secrets, and all that. Don't worry. It's you I'd like to talk about.'

Ryan snorted. 'No thank you. Besides, the fire's part of an ongoing investigation. I can't talk about it. I'm a Special Constable, you see.'

Megan arched her eyebrows in genuine surprise. 'Really? How interesting. Oh, sorry. I haven't introduced myself. I'm Megan Wolfe, and I'm…'

'I know who and what you are.' The 'what' came out with obvious distaste. 'I saw how you stitched DCI Danskin up. He's a decent man, you know. You were way, way out of order.'

Wolfe and Ryan locked eyes for a long moment, a gunslinger's standoff.

'Everything ok here?' Barry Docherty arrived at Ryan's shoulder.

'Yeah. Miss Wolfe is leaving us just now.'

Megan blinked a couple of times. 'Yes. I am. For now.' She turned her back. Began walking down the driveway. She stopped. Spoke over her shoulder. 'You intrigue me, Ryan Jarrod. In a good way.'

Ryan and Barry watched her disappear.

'Still ok?' Docherty asked.

'Aye. Howay, let's go down The Horse. There's some Europa League shite on. We'll watch that.'

Within minutes, they were at the bar. Not in The Bay Horse, but the Wetherspoon's next door. The Horse was having one if it's regular mop-ups after a rainstorm. Barry got them in before Ryan realised the mistake.

He made jazz hands, indicating his inability to hold a glass. 'We didn't think this through, did we?'

'Not really,' Barry laughed. He set Ryan's glass on the bar-top and tossed a long pink straw into it. 'There we go. Nowt's the matter.'

'Hadawayandshite. I'm not using that. I'll be like one of those ducking swans me gran had when I was a kid.'

Barry ruffled his friend's hair. 'That's more like the Ryan Jarrod I know. And, to cheer you up some more, ta-dah.' He produced two sheets of hall-marked paper from his pocket.

'What're they?'

'They, my friend, are tickets for the match. Liverpool. This weekend.'

'No way. Where'd you get them?'

'It's a long story. You up for it?'

'You bet I am.' He shifted uncomfortably in his chair. 'I think.'

'Good,' Barry said. 'It's a date.' He looked at the beers in front of them. 'Tell you what, I'm not thirsty. Why don't we nip back to mine to watch tonight's game? It'll have kicked off but we can catch it on one of those Plus One channels.'

Ryan watched a pink straw bob in his tankard. 'Sounds good to me.'

'Great. We'll pop to Lance's for a bag of chips. You can fantasise I'm a dusky handmaiden as I feed you them.'

'Cheeky bastard,' Ryan said, feeling good about himself for the first time since he found Teddy McGuffie in the alleyway,

**

Stephen Danskin got home at eleven-thirty, pizza box in arms. He, too, felt good about himself. He snapped an Americano pod in the Tassimo and whistled a snazzy tune.

'Alexa, play country music artists,' he instructed. Willie Nelson's On the Road Again struck up. Danskin made an ok sign with his left hand. 'Good choice, Alexa.'

He swept up crime information he'd scattered around his living room floor. No need for it now. The investigation had taken off. Connor had bought into his one-man-three-crimes theory. The Super had magicked up support from the Prince Bishop force. What's better, he'd told Danskin he was in overall charge but had ordered Rick Kinnear to manage the day-to-day operations of the Mackem newcomers.

The DCI knew, with three crime scenes to trawl but only one man to find, the chances of finding a lead had tripled. Somewhere, the perpetrator will have made a mistake.

Willie Nelson morphed into Carrie Underwood into Rascal Flatts while Danskin scoffed on his pizza. He sensed his mood lower. He felt bad about Trebilcock. He hadn't given him the lickings of a dog, yet the lead was down to the Cornishmen. Danskin had pre-judged him; 'seen what he expected to see.'

R Dean Taylor started singing about Ghosts in his House. Danskin sighed. Plenty of them here. His eyes settled on a photograph of three people. Danskin, an attractive brunette a few years younger than he, and a young girl of eleven with a mass of curls and freckles, and the gap-tooth grin of youth. They'd all look much different now.

Alexa's choice went downhill. Every song seemed to be about whisky or lost love. Danskin lost his appetite, let alone his love. And, he realised, he was no further forward in the investigation. All he knew was that they were looking for one culprit. Somewhere, there had to be a logic behind the acts. Some connection.

A slice of pizza hung lazily between his fingers. A triangular slice cut from a round object stored in a square box. A geometric puzzle that defied logic. What if there wasn't a logic to the crimes? What if a madman was committing random acts for no rhyme or reason? Logic would never find him.

Now thoroughly depressed, the improbably named Sherman Tank wailing about both whisky and women in the same song proved too much.

'Alexa, shut the fuck up.'

CHAPTER SIXTEEN

Norman Jarrod did his best, but his bedside manner left a lot to be desired. He was no nurse

Ryan bit his lip as his father peeled the lowermost layer of dressing from his raw and weeping left hand, applied ointment to the wound with the delicacy of a nightclub bouncer, and draped fresh bandages around it as if he were Anthony Joshua's cornerman.

Norman saw the colour drain from his son's face. 'Do you really think you're up for this, son? It's only been a few days, you know.'

'Dad, sitting around the house is doing my head in. Besides, me right hand's improving already.'

'Aye, that's as maybe but look at the state of this one. What happens if someone bumps into you? Not to mention,' he nodded towards Ryan's nether regions, 'you know.'

'Yes. I do know. How could I forget?' He saw his father's downcast face. 'Sorry, dad. I shouldn't take it out on you. I know you're doing your best.'

'Aye. I am. My best's never been good enough, though. Not for your mother, God rest her soul, or your Gran. I don't want to go down the same road with you and James.'

Ryan wished he were well enough to hug his father. Instead, he settled for a 'Hadawayandshite, man.'

Norman managed a smile, and pulled open Ryan's bedroom curtains. Snow fell; the first of winter. Large, down-like flakes fluttered to earth in the still air like feathers from the ruptured pillow of grey sky.

Ryan looked out over roofs coated in a thick white blanket. An igloo-shaped lump was the only evidence his Fiat still sat on the driveway. Ryan Jarrod pushed at the window with his forearm. A dusting of snow fell inwards, coating the carpet at his bare feet.

A silent hush invaded his space, the dense blanket of snow absorbing sound like a silencer. He used his elbow to switch on a socket. Metro Radio sprang to life.

'...and, if you plan on going to the match today, stay tuned. A pitch inspection is scheduled for eleven o'clock. We'll bring you the latest from our reporter live at St James' Park. And, right now, here's Liam with the weather.'

'Thanks very much indeed, Warren. Snow will continue for much of the early part of the morning, slowly turning to rain. This afternoon, temperatures will rise before plummeting below zero later this evening.'

Ryan elbowed off the radio. 'Looks like you've nowt to worry about, dad. I reckon the match will be off. Typical of my luck. Just bloody typical.'

**

Stephen Danskin woke knotted in a bedsheet and with a non-alcoholic hangover from Hell.

He raised his head from his pillow and groaned. His clock told him his meeting with DCI Rick Kinnear was due in twenty minutes. He pulled his phone from beneath the pillow and dialled.

'Rick, I'm tied up with something at the mo,' he said, unknotting himself from his bedding. 'Can we do this over the phone?'

Kinnear replied in the affirmative. Danskin had asked him to mobilise the Prince Bishop force as security cover. While Danskin led the investigation, Kinnear's role was to ensure the culprit had little opportunity to strike again.

'The lads are covering all likely targets in the city centre,' Kinnear assured. 'We've a visible presence in Eldon Square, and uniforms travelling on all metro trains. There's an armed squad patrolling the airport, and a smaller deployment at North Shields ferry terminal.'

Danskin considered for a moment. 'Railway station? You got that covered?'

'It's covered, but I'm not using our people. Transport Police are on top of it. I've even got a firearms squad on Northumberland Street. Fenwick's Christmas window display always draws a horde of kids. Can't risk the publicity of kiddies getting drawn into this man's plans.'

'Good idea,' Danskin replied, though the thought of hairy-arsed armed men looking over a display of animatronic reindeer and elves presented an uncomfortable paradox. 'What about the match?'

'Don't worry, Stephen. Apart from the airport, that's our main focus today. Tripled the presence in and around the ground. Sniffer dogs and search checkpoints all lined up.'

Danskin had a vision of the Sunderland-supporting Prince Bishop squad policing Newcastle United's stadium. 'Bet they were fighting over themselves for that assignment.'

Kinnear snickered. 'I don't think they'll be taking any prisoners, put it that way.'

'I just wish we had a healthy view of where he might strike next so we can better-utilise our resources.'

'That's your job, Stephen. And good luck with it. '

Danskin almost heard the bitter gloat in Kinnear's voice, but he may have imagined it. 'I will, Rick. Just give me time.'

'That's the one thing you mightn't have, pal.'

Danskin chewed his lower lip. Didn't he just know it?

**

The man who'd locked himself in the toilet for half an hour after the final tour of the day yesterday couldn't resist an early morning visit. He'd done all he could. Now, everything depended on the vagaries of the weather.

The oddly-asymmetrical cathedral stood on a hill not four-hundred yards from the city centre. Visible from all approaches, north, south, east and west, it dominated the skyline. This was a cathedral with a congregation second-to-none. This was St. James' Park; the physical home of Newcastle United and a spiritual home to much of Tyneside.

The stadium loomed menacingly in front of him, the upper tiers barely visible in the blizzard's swirl. Council staff worked diligently, sweeping snow from the surrounding roads. No sooner had they cleared a path, fresh snow covered their tracks once more.

He pictured groundsmen frenziedly working on the playing surface inside the stadium, keeping it snow-free for play. Undersoil heating would help, but the turf would need treatment to prevent waterlogging.

In a section of the stadium car park fronting onto Barrack Road sat a fleet of television vans, thick cables coiling around them like tentacles. Producers and directors and cameramen stood by. Some looked skywards at the elements. Others looked at their watches.

He checked the time, too.

10.50.

In ten minutes, he'd know whether his work the day before was in vain.

**

Ryan's phone rang.

'Game on,' Barry Docherty told him. 'Refs given it the all-clear.'

'Brilliant. Doubt it would have got the go-ahead if it wasn't on Sky.'

'Me, and all. So, what time do you want to set off?'

Ryan thought for a moment. 'Do you mind if we go early? I don't want me hand jostled too much if I can help it so I'd prefer if we got there before the masses.'

'Aye, nee bother. I suppose we'd better give the pre-match pint a miss, as well.'

'Too bloody true. I don't think sipping a pint of Almasty's through a straw would sit well with the Mean Eyed Cat's regulars.'

Barry laughed. 'You've got a point there. Ok, Ryan. I'll be around in an hour or so. Get your gear on ready.'

'It's already on, mate. Replica shirt, even my lucky underpants.'

'I think it'll take more than your lucky underpants today. We're in for a drubbing, I tell you.'

'No change there, then.'

'Aye. Y'know, I divvent know why we bother. See you soon, Ry.'

'See you.'

Ryan hung up and shook his head. He even needed help to wrap the black and white scarf around his neck. He went to find his dad.

**

Five minutes to kick off. Weatherman Liam had been right. Rain fell as the temperature rose, turning the approach to the ground into a slithering mass of icy sludge.

The stadium wasn't full. The extra security checks meant thousands were still outside when the final refrains of Local Hero faded and the referee called the captains to the centre-circle.

On the TV gantry, the commentator led into an advertisement break as his co-presenter, an ex-pro, finally made his way from hospitality. The director in a studio van outside ran his final checks during the break. The commentator's microphone level. The special effects mic for background crowd noises. He checked the functionality of each of the five cameras on the main gantry, the remotely-operated cameras behind both goals. Finally, he checked the reverse-angle camera, situated on a platform strung beneath the roof of the smaller East Stand.

'Geoff, clean your lens, will you? Rain's blowing your way. We want a shot of the managers in the dug outs when we come back. You're in the driving seat with that.'

Geoff pulled a rag from a knapsack at his feet and wiped the cloth over the front of his camera. 'Ready to go, boss.'

The director counted down. 'Three, two, one... go, Martin, go,' he cued the commentator.

The referee blew his whistle, the crowd roared. A Newcastle forward passed back to his skipper, who hoofed the ball forward. It hit the sodden turf and skidded straight out for a goal-kick.

'Bloody great start,' Ryan said.

It set the tone for a dispiritingly poor half of football. One man didn't care. In fact, he didn't even notice. He wasn't watching the action. From his seat in the Milburn Stand Press Box, his eyes never left the cameraman covering the reverse angle.

**

'Jesus Christ, this is piss-poor,' Ryan complained.

'Look on the bright side, mate. At least there's been nowt to make you clap your hands. Still, we're not behind yet. That's something.'

'How long left?'

Barry checked his watch. Twenty-five to go.'

Behind them, a man in the press-box checked his watch, too. As far as he was concerned, there were only ten minutes left. Then, the action would begin.

The rain fell in torrents. Pools of water formed on the pitch. Players mistimed tackles, the ball stopped dead in its tracks, and generally behaved like a huffy child.

The crowd became increasingly restless. None more so than the man in the press box. Despite the cold, sweat oozed from his brow.

He trained his phone on a spot opposite and prepared to press 'record.'

Three minutes to go.

**

Ten minutes later, nothing had happened. On the pitch, or off it. The man in the Press Box looked around. Something had gone wrong, and there was nothing he could do about it. If he could, he would have left, but Press didn't leave early. He was trapped.

With the clock showing eighty-four minutes played, a muffled roar from the highest tier grabbed the man's attention. When he finally dragged his eyes towards the action on the field, he saw the ball nestled in the back of the Newcastle net.

'Oh for fuck's sake,' Barry complained. 'Fucking typical.'

'He should never have let that bounce. He should've known it'd skid away from him.'

'Absolute shower of shit, the lot of them. Roll on the transfer window.'

'What's the point? The stingy git will never put his hand in his pocket.'

Barry flicked the Vs at the triumphant Liverpool fans celebrating above the Leazes End. 'Do you want to get away early, mate? Avoid the crush?'

Ryan saw droves of people leaving their seats. 'Think we've missed the boat there, like, but aye; let's gan.'

The man in the press box wished he could go, too.

**

Forty-five minutes after the final whistle, the rain stopped. The TV crew began to pack away their kit as cold hit like a middleweight. It jabbed at the senses, weakened the spirit, and addled the mind.

'Reverse-angle' Geoff dismantled his camera, coiled its leads into a hoop, and bagged his headset. Finally, all his equipment stored in two rucksacks slung over his shoulder, he took a tentative first step onto the ladder.

As his head disappeared from view, he caught sight of a third bag. Without thinking, he grabbed it and made his way to the motorcade where he dumped all three bags in the nearest van before jumping into his car for the trip home.

The cavalcade of Sky TV wagons hadn't reached Chester-Le-Street when the middle one disintegrated in a seething ball of blazing shrapnel which took out a dozen vehicles and closed both carriageways for the remainder of the weekend.

CHAPTER SEVENTEEN

Stephen Danskin trudged into Superintendent Connor's office with the air of a man sentenced to several years in a Siberian gulag. Rick Kinnear was already there. The fact he bore an even worse hang-dog expression was no consolation.

'I've sat on this for twenty-four hours, gentlemen,' Connor began. 'I've considered it every which way but loose. I've tried to see it from where you sit. But, for the life of me, I can't begin to understand how you fucked up so royally.'

Like kids called to the headmaster's study, Danskin and Kinnear stared at a spot somewhere between their feet. Neither spoke. Connor tried again.

'Stephen, you've been on this case for weeks now. The only thing you've given me is that you think the same person's responsible. Three weeks of investigation, and you've no proper leads, no forensic evidence, no suspects. You've questioned a couple of Jonny Foreigners and where has that got you?'

'Nowhere, sir,' Danskin mumbled.

'Exactly. You've got nothing. Zilch. Sod all. Four major incidents, and not a bloody inch closer to resolving them. Meanwhile, I've got press, TV crews, MPs, and Uncle Tom Cobbly on my back wanting answers.'

'Sir, with respect...'

'Respect, my arse, Danskin. And don't you dare trot out the line about manpower again. You've got every spare man across two counties working for you. Speaking of which,' Connor turned his attention to Kinnear, 'You were supposed to make sure this never happened again. You've had the role a couple of days and already your incompetence has reduced the A1M to a Fast and Furious set.'

Connor let a silence settle. Waited until both men lifted their head. 'Ok. What's done's done. Stephen, I presume you've concluded the same man's responsible?'

DCI Danskin reigned in his emotions. Brought his thought processes under control. 'We are working on that theory, sir; yes. We believe the bomb was meant to go off inside the stadium, or in the van outside, during the game. We see no reason for someone to target a convoy of TV wagons.'

Connor took a seat opposite the two men. 'Something went wrong?'

'We think so, sir. It's possible the weather played a part, perhaps the cold or damp affected the device. It's the first time the perp's attempted an outside detonation.'

Connor nodded. 'Any other implications in its failure to explode on time?'

Danskin remembered something Sue Nairn had flagged up. 'It's possible whoever's doing this may not be such an expert on explosives as we first thought. He's got some knowledge, certainly; but its perhaps not his chosen territory.'

The Super rapped the desk with his knuckles. 'And that helps us how?'

The question took the wind out of Danskin's sails. 'Unfortunately, sir, it widens the field even more.'

'Bollocks. So, we're further back than we were previously?'

'That's about the size of it,' Danskin was forced to concede.

'Double bollocks. Rick – what happened?'

'Sir?'

Connor breathed in noisily. 'You were leading on security. I charged you with protecting the city. Begged, stole and borrowed half of my neighbour's force to help you do your job. I'm paying God-knows-how-much over budget. I think I'm entitled to ask, 'What happened', don't you?'

'Yes, sir. Sorry, sir.'

Under normal circumstances, Danskin would probably have enjoyed Kinnear's obvious discomfort, but not today.

'I ask again. What happened?'

'Clearly, I had several potential targets to protect. I prioritised those I thought most vulnerable. Including St James Park. I trebled the normal match day deployment. At short notice, I set up body scanners and bag searches. They were all conducted thoroughly. By doing so, many were late gaining access to the ground but I facilitated a smooth operation.'

'But not so smooth the bomber didn't get in or around the stadium.'

'Superintendent Connor, I even brought in sniffer dogs…'

'Did they all have sinusitis or something, because they clearly didn't sniff anything, did they?'

Kinnear shifted uneasily. His face reddened. 'The dogs were deployed on the queues of fans entering the stadium. If the bomb either came with, or was hidden in, the TV vans, the dogs wouldn't identify them.'

All three men considered their next words carefully. Danskin broke the silence first. 'Sir, can I suggest something?'

'For God's sake, Danskin. That's what you're here for. You don't need permission to speak. It's not Dad's fucking Army.'

Stephen ignored the gibe. 'I suggest a couple of things. Firstly, as far as the press is concerned, we act as if it's a separate incident. It happened in Durham. We let Rick handle the press enquiries and stick to the argument it's an isolated incident. I'm sure they won't buy it, but that's what we tell 'em.'

'You wouldn't be avoiding the press in case you make another cock-up, would you?' Stephen was relieved to see Connor give a dismissive wave to his own theory before he could respond. 'And the second?'

'Well, I'm just thinking. From what Rick says, there's no way the device could have got into the stadium on match day. I'm happy that his procedures were spot-on.'

Kinnear smiled at the support, and Connor gave a slight tip of his head. 'So,' the Superintendent concluded, 'The device was either planted in the van, or the crew brought it with them to blow themselves up? I don't see how that's the case if you're convinced the crimes are the work of the man who's also responsible for the other incidents.'

'Me neither, Sir. So, what if the bomb was brought into the stadium in the days leading up to the match and, somehow, made its way into the van afterwards?'

Connor chewed on a knuckle. 'It's a long shot, Stephen, but a shot all the same. See what you can find from CCTV and the club staff.'

He spoke again, more to himself this time. 'It's all we've bloody-well got.'

**

Marcus Vorster was jumpy. Wired. His hands moved continuously; his eyes darted from face-to-face. 'Great copy, guys. Really great copy. But one thing's missing: why'd we not get video footage? That's where the Rands lie: not in hard-copy, but in hits and on-line content.'

The news staff waited for someone to react first. When no-one did, Vorster picked one of his crew out.

'Woods, you're our photographic expert. Why weren't you there?'

'Firstly, I wasn't on duty. Secondly, even if I was, how was I – how was anyone – expected to know a van was going to go up in the middle of a motorway?'

'Because I pay you top-dollar, that's why. I knew you were all washed up. Ag, I don't know why I ever took you on in the first place.'

Megan came to his defence. 'Remember who was one of the first on the scene at the Uni? Remember who got the stills of the HMRC fire? Yes, David Woods, that's who. You're becoming a tyrannical dictator, Marcus. That's not what I came here for.' The audience looked at her, mouths gaping. 'There,' she concluded. 'I've said it.'

Vorster tossed back his fringe. Stared at her. Fidgeted. 'All right, Miss Wolfe. David, let's see how you fare with the on-line guys. Pound to a penny they'll have you burnt out within a week. Consider yourself transferred. Now, get out of my sight.'

Woods' chair screeched as he rose. 'You're so wrong about me, Marcus. So, so wrong. You need to get to know your people. As you'll discover.'

'Out!'

The others sat in an uncomfortable silence. As for Vorster, he continued as if nothing had happened. 'We all know the TV thing is linked to the other incidents. That's our line of attack for the next few days.'

Mike Cash interjected. 'Police are holding the line that there's no connection. From a legal viewpoint, we need to be sure of the facts first.'

Marcus snorted back a laugh. 'Facts? What have facts got to do with it? I believe Miss Wolfe said something similar not three weeks ago. Ok, then, we'll prove it. Raymond, Molly; that's your remit.'

'Don't you think Megan's best suited for that role?' asked Raymond Carpenter. 'She's a history of investigative reporting second-to-none in this outfit.'

'No!'

The rebuke was instantaneous. Out the corner of her eye, Megan saw Leeward Milton shoot her a look that said 'you know, you could be right about him'.

Vorster lowered his tone. 'No, Megan. I want you to stick to the superhero story. You've started, so you'll finish.'

Megan looked disappointed. She was surprised to note Carpenter looked even more disappointed.

Vorster smiled. 'Ok, guys. Let's get the show on the road. And I guess I should apologise. Things got a bit heated there. But, you know, this is destiny we hold in our hands.'

He caught everyone's eye in turn.

'My destiny.'

**

Ryan Jarrod sat in a moribund silence broken only by his grandmother's gasps and snores. Still, at least she had an excuse for not speaking. His father and Jam Jar; they just didn't know what to say.

He had a newspaper spread in front of him but found it nigh on impossible to turn the pages. He was about to give up and leave Doris Jarrod in peace when he heard a light tapping on the door.

When he opened it, he was face-to-face with a woman as old as his grandmother. Both eyed each other suspiciously.

'And you are?', the old woman asked.

'Excuse me, don't you think I should be the one asking the questions?'

The woman tilted her head. ' No, I don't. And, I know you don't live here.'

'Perhaps not. But me Gran does.'

A light went on behind the woman's eyes. 'Ah, yes. Of course. The policeman.' She brushed past an astonished Ryan into the house.

When he joined her in the lounge, the woman had claimed his seat. 'Don't worry. I'm her friend. I thought I'd make sure she was ok, after the run-in with your brother and his hooligan friends.'

This got more surreal by the minute. 'What?'

'Never mind.' She gave him a dismissive wave. 'Burnt your hands, have we?'

Ryan's training sprung into action. 'How do you know they're burnt?'

The old lady laughed. 'By the dressings, silly. Here, let me have a look.'

Despite himself, he let the woman unwrap his hands. Listened as she tutted and tisked. Asked him if he had any fresh dressings. When he indicated the bag next to Doris's chair, she dexterously applied fresh dressing to the wounds.

'There. Your right hands coming along nicely. Another day and you can get away with some gauze padding. But the other; my, quite a state isn't it? You need to be careful with that for a while longer yet.'

He inspected his hands as if he'd never seen them before.

'Right,' the woman said. 'I can see young Doris here is in good hands. Pardon the pun. I'll be off and leave you to it. Nice meeting you, Mr Policeman.'

She was out the door and heading from whence she came before Ryan could ask, 'Wait, I don't know your name.'

With her back still to him, she replied, 'I don't know yours either. Makes us equal.'

CHAPTER EIGHTEEN

Christmas Day.

Stephen Danskin picked at a plate of turkey roll, instant mash and frozen veg. The TV screen was blank, no music playing, even Alexa wasn't speaking to him. He was alone with his thoughts. Worse, he was alone with his memories.

He shoved his plate aside, spooned out a hunk of Mint Choc Viennetta, and imagined his mineral water had the bite of vodka. His tenth Christmas alone and it didn't get any easier, even with the picture of the attractive brunette and curly-haired child strategically turned to face the wall.

'Fuck it.'

He grabbed his coat and headed downtown to the office.

**

Ryan and James sat either side of the battered sofa, their grandmother in her straight-backed orthopaedic chair. They'd wrapped a plate of Christmas dinner in tin foil, brought it to her, and sat while Doris Jarrod refused to eat her brussels sprouts.

'Get yourself home, kidda. I'll stick this one out,' Ryan told his brother.

James smiled his appreciation and was out the door before Ryan had time to change his mind.

Ryan flicked through the channels with his bandage-free right hand. Doris's old friend had been right. A sterile pad covered by a couple of thin layers of gauze across his palm allowed him a degree of dexterity for the first time in a week. He came across a re-run of It's a Wonderful Life, allowed himself an ironic smile, and told his grandmother she'd enjoy it while she waited for the Queen's Speech.

Ryan cleared the half-full plate from Doris's lap-tray and took an age to make a cup of tea one-handed. When he returned, Toy Story iii blared at full volume. Five minutes before the Queen was due to address the nation, Doris Jarrod fell asleep.

The palm of his hand itched like crazy as the burns healed. To take his mind off it, Ryan reached for the pile of newspapers next to Doris and began leafing through them to kill time until his gran woke up and he could say his goodbyes.

**

Lyall Parker was in the office when Stephen arrived at the station. They exchanged Happy Christmases and shook hands.

'Anyone else in?' Stephen asked.

'Hannah's been in.'

Danskin rubbed an index finger into the corner of an eye. 'Where's she now?'

'I sent her down to get the tapes of the cab driver, McGuffie. Ravi's not done with them yet but hasn't come up with anything so far. Says there's nothing but static. Thought I'd have a wee listen myself.'

Stephen bobbed his head. 'What about the others?'

'Working from home, most of them. Thought we'd get more out of them if they were with their families. I've got them trawling the internet for anything of interest, some doing research into the Pakistan connection or the Spanish lassies. Todd agreed to lead a couple of the lads revisiting tip-offs coming through on the hotline in case they weren't all bollocks, after all. Treblecock's on that, too'

'They won't find owt, but good idea to give them all some time with their families. They've had precious little of it lately.'

Lyall Parker studied the DCI. 'How are you doing, Stephen?'

Danskin shook his head. 'It's not easy, Lyall. Not easy at all.'

There was nothing Parker could say, except 'I'll get you a coffee.'

He returned just as Hannah Graves walked in holding a memory stick and a signed-for chitty. Stephen and her embraced, pecked each other on the cheek, and shared season's greetings.

Parker loaded up the recording as Stephen slurped his coffee. While they waited, Hannah updated them. 'The manifest says this is the recording of the final moments of McGuffie's last shift. We join it at the point where he picks up McGuffie.

'Where to, sir?'

Silence.

'Short trip. No problem. Weather's awful again, isn't it? What you been up to today?'

Silence.

Danskin stared at the computer. 'Why aren't we hearing what he's saying?'

Hannah read Ravi Sangar's notes. 'The privacy screen's shut. Baffles the noise.'

'What the fuck's the point of recording anything, then?'

Hannah spoke again. 'If you're going to be robbed or attacked, it's not going to happen if the robber's behind a screen. But, if the screen or door's opened, it'll be picked up.'

'Suppose,' Danskin conceded.

'What's Sangar done to enhance it?'

'He's turned up volume to the max, tried to fade out background noise. Listen.'

Danskin and Parker recoiled as McGuffie's voice yelled at them with all the force of a Space Shuttle launch.

'Fucking hell,' Stephen said.

After McGuffie's voice faded and their ears stopped ringing, a buzz of discordant static hummed through the machine.

'What's that?'

'That,' said Hannah, 'Is our man.'

Stephen played the recording again, and a third time. 'That all we got?'

'At the moment, yes, sir. It is. But Sangar's still working on it. Trying to pick out speech patterns in the static's cadence.'

Danskin sniffed. 'Huh. Good luck with that.'

Lyall spoke. 'At least it's something, sir. Something to work on. And, more importantly, to keep the Super off your back.'

'That's only going to happen if I coat my spine with Teflon.'

The three sat in a silence broken by Danskin. 'Ok, Hannah. Get yourself home to your mother. She'll be missing you.'

'Thanks, sir.' She shook hand with Lyall Parker. 'Merry Christmas, Lyall.'

'Same to you, Hannah. Take care of yourself.'

'Merry Christmas, sir.'

'Happy Christmas, Hannah,' Stephen replied.

She stood on tiptoes and kissed his cheek once more.

**

Ryan wriggled the fingers of his pink and scarred right hand to increase blood flow after its period of inactivity. He checked his watch. Cleared his grandmother's stone-cold tea. A spot of drool emerged at the corner of the sleeping lady's mouth. Ryan reached for a tissue and tenderly dabbed away the sputum.

Seeing the once vibrant woman he'd known throughout his childhood locked inside a shell broke his heart. No matter how much he disagreed with his father about her treatment, he knew how he felt. This was a different person. Not the mother Norman Jarrod had known, nor the grandmother to whom Ryan had been so close.

He'd read the Mercury's coverage of the outrages from front to back. He'd read the sports pages. He'd even done the daily word quiz. All he had left were horoscopes or letters to the editor.

There was the usual mix of comments on TV programmes, celebrities, the odd social comment. One grabbed his attention. It spoke about football hooligans, and how people weren't safe in their own village.

Ryan thought back to how patient the queues outside St James Park were when they were being searched and scanned; how there'd been no trouble whatsoever. Then, he remembered sitting in the same chair he was now, listening to an old woman's cryptic comments about his brother and football hooligans. He must ask him about that.

Doris Jarrod slept on, not knowing if it was Christmas or Easter. Ryan wiggled his fingers again and picked up another newspaper.

The word puzzle proved too much for him this time. His horoscope told him he would meet a stranger who would play a big part in his life, a career opportunity was about to open, and family matters would take precedence. He looked at his grandmother. He gave the astrologer one out of three.

He scanned the pages. A letter mentioning civil servants and their gold-plated pensions caused him to shake his head and move on. Doris stirred slightly in her chair. The cushion slipped out from behind her back. Ryan gently replaced it. One more paper, then he'd rouse her and get himself off home.

Something caught his attention.

Dear Sirs

I would like to bring to your attention the state of our city centre. Constant rebuilding work causing untold difficulties for pedestrians and transport alike. And, I ask you, for what?

The building work is a blight on our landscape and won't even bring jobs or money to the city. The construction of endless tower blocks of student accommodation from all points east and west, all for the benefit of a transient population of here-today-gone-tomorrow students.

City planners: stop it now, I say. Return our city to the proud people who live their life and spend their hard-earned wages and pensions is in this city of ours.

Yours

F Roadhouse (Miss).

Ryan wrinkled his nose. What was it that concerned him? He checked the date of the newspaper. Four days before the explosion at the University building which changed his life forever.

He held his breath. Something, but what? He picked up a newspaper he'd discarded. A letter about civil servants. A letter, penned by the same person, four days before the fire.

Heart racing, he retrieved another. Football hooligans.

He visualised an explosion in a TV van; a van returning from St James' Park.

He leapt to his feet. He had to tell someone. He had to tell DCI Stephen Danskin.

Ryan had to tell him who the bomber was.

**

Ryan took his frustrations out on the living room carpet. He paced back and forth in his boots and coat as he waited for his cab. Yesterday had been an absolute farce. He'd tell Danskin that, too.

When he uncovered the bomber's identity, his first thought was to rush straight to the station. Except, with only half a functioning hand, he couldn't drive. Except, his dad was too pissed to take him. Except, he'd never get a cab, not on Christmas Day.

Instead, he dialled the Police Information line. Was on hold for forty minutes. In the end, he gave up and dialled 999. The operator had been less than helpful.

'This is for emergencies only, There's a dedicated hotline number if you have anything to disclose about the major incidents. I can give you it, if you like.'

'I've already got it. Nobody's answering. That's why I've called 999.'

'It's Christmas Day, you know. There won't be many staff in. You could try again.'

'No chance. I need to speak to DCI Stephen Danskin. Now. It's important. I know who's doing it.'

Ryan expected an urgent response. That the operator would see sense and divert the call. Not a chance.

'You and over a hundred others. Why should your information be any more reliable than the rest of them?'

Ryan took a frustrated gulp of air. 'Because I know what I'm talking about. I'm a Special Constable.'

'Listen, I don't care if you're a Special Fried Rice; your information will take its place in the queue. I'll pass your details on. Someone will call you back, in the next three to four days.'

'What?! She could strike again by then.'

'I'm sorry, sir. That's the way it works. Good day.'

Ryan was left staring at a disconnected handset. It's a good job he never got angry.

He'd spent what remained of Christmas Day planning what he'd say to the DCI and imagining how Danskin would react when he had the killer's name in front of him.

So, at a little after 8am on Boxing Day morning, Ryan Jarrod ploughed another furrow in the carpet as he waited for the cab to arrive.

CHAPTER NINETEEN

Megan Wolfe rolled out of bed and shook her hair free of knots; the consequence of a dire night's sleep. A day of rest for Megan was a chore rather than a joy, and a lack of spent energy resulted in a restless night.

She'd tried to burn off energy. Boy, did she try.

She slapped the bare buttocks alongside her. 'Come on, soldier. Time for you to get a move on.'

Her partner sat up. 'Is it morning already? Time flies when you're having fun.'

Megan looked towards the clock which read eight a.m. She showed him eight fingers.

'Eight out of ten? Is that all the fun you had?'

She stuck out her tongue as she unfurled both thumbs from the palm of her hands.

The man chuckled. 'That's more like it.' He climbed out of bed, naked and unashamedly proud.

Megan arched her eyebrows. 'Well, if you put it like that, I dare say we've another hour or so.'

The man grabbed her shoulders and spun her back onto the bed.

**

At the same time as Megan Wolfe tumbled back into bed, Florence Roadhouse was straightening hers. It didn't take long. As ever, there was only one side to straighten.

She waved a duster around her ornaments while a pot of Earl Grey brewed. She pulled open her curtains and watched birds peck hungrily at her feeder. An icicle hung from her porch like a stalactite, running with water as the temperature rose.

Florence buttered herself a slice of toast. She switched on the TV. The news. The sales began today, and shoppers had been queuing since the early hours. The reporter interviewed them as they waited for the doors to open.

'As if they've nothing better to do on a Boxing Day morning', she said to herself with nothing better to do on a Boxing Day morning. Not without her precious newspapers.

Her eyes fell on her typewriter. Sales. Shopping. Shopworkers having to work on a public holiday; a religious one at that.

Florence shuffled to the typewriter, pulled off its plastic hood, spooled in a sheet of A4 and moved her swollen fingers over the keyboard.

**

Beneath the railway bridge not half a mile from the Forth Banks police station, a freezing-cold woman in green puffer jacket and red yellow and blue bobble hat disengaged herself from a damp and smelly sleeping bag.

She checked the contents of a rusty biscuit tin alongside her. The young woman counted out the few coins inside it. It didn't take her long. Two pounds seventy-five pence. Barely enough for a coffee. She shivered. Coughed.

A taxi turned under the bridge. Its lights glinted off the greying mounds of street-side snow. She shielded her bruised eyes from the glare as the cab carrying Ryan Jarrod drove past her.

Ilona Popescu was alone once more with an empty stomach and a head full of memories of home.

**

On the fourth story of the City and County Police HQ, Stephen Danskin looked over the railway tracks leading into the Central Station. He saw a single car, a taxi, veer right from beneath the arches and splash through the slush-covered streets.

Lyall Parker was there, too, but Danskin addressed Ravi Sangar. 'Tell me more about the voice recording you got from the taxi. How it helps.'

Sangar scratched his beard. 'It's not so much what was said; more the pattern of speech. We can't decipher the words, unfortunately.'

Stephen snickered. 'I know. It nearly blew my lugs off.'

'That's because you listened to it. You should have watched it.'

Danskin and Parker shared a puzzled glance. 'Come again?'

'Look.' Sangar attached a lead between a PC and a hand-held portable device. He also inserted the memory stick Hannah Graves borrowed yesterday. Within a few moments, with no hint of static or any other sound, a jagged line similar to an ECG scan, appeared on the monitor screen.

Danskin furrowed his brow. 'What's this? It looks like we're Third Umpires viewing Ultraedge.'

Sangar motioned with arms crossed below waist height. 'You've just lost a review. What this is, is the patterns of speech. The cadence. As unique as a fingerprint, once you interpret it. We can often determine an age range, an accent, even the mood of the speaker.'

Danskin sat down opposite the monitor. 'Explain it to me.'

Sangar clinked a pen against his teeth. 'Ok. Remember a song you learnt at school. Row, Row, Row Your Boat?'

Intrigued, both Danskin and Parker replied, 'Yes.'

'Well, watch this.' Sangar removed the memory stick and recited into the device. 'Row, row, row your boat, gently down the stream.'

The screen showed a uniform pattern of spikes, equal height, equally spaced.

'What this tells us is the first three words are replicated exactly. No change in tone, or expression. Equally spaced. In regular speech, that might indicate we're listening to someone with a speech impediment. A stutter.'

Danskin pursed his lips. Dipped his head.

'Now, the next sequence also duplicates a word. Merrily, this time repeated four times. You might think you'd get a similar result. But watch what happens.'

Danskin and Parker stared at the screen as Sangar sang, 'Merrily, merrily, merrily, merrily life is but a dream.'

The graph peaked and troughed, distinct levels of intensity coinciding with raised and lowered notes, and gaps in timing.

'See how this differs from the first? It's still repeated words, but the patterns – the cadence – is quite different. This isn't a stutter. This is someone singing. Or, perhaps, speaking with a sing-song accent.'

'Fascinating. And, you can pick up patterns from static? It doesn't need to be words?'

'Hole in one, sir. It's considerably more difficult. And, of course, we'll never know what was said. But we can learn a lot about the speaker. It just takes more time.'

Parker asked the next question. 'But, there's so little to go off. Such a wee conversation with the driver. You cannae learn much from that, surely?'

Sangar smiled. 'You're right, sir. But the guy in the cab said much more than that. We have one minute thirty-five seconds of static waves. Our man had a brief telephone conversation with someone from the back of Teddy McGuffie's car.'

Danskin's ruminations were interrupted by the sound of sudden activity in the bullpen. He tisked and prepared to berate the culprits.

The activity outside was urgent. People gathered around PCs. Typed in data. Scrolled down search results. Sue Nairn dashed to the crime boards and studied them. Nigel Trebilcock's face was wreathed in smiles. Others punched numbers into telephones.

Todd Robson, in front of a PC, tipped his head back and roared with laughter. Others looked at him. He pointed at his screen. Folk gathered around. They joined in the laughter. Looked towards someone standing at the back of the room.

Superintendent Connor's door rattled open.

Danskin, Parker and Sangar heard his voice above the others.

'What the hell's going on?' Connor roared. He pointed towards the rear of the group.

'And who let a civilian in here?'

**

Todd Robson slapped the desk in front of him. He could barely answer Superintendent Connor for his laughter. 'Sir, the civilian let himself in. He knows the passcodes. And, get this, he reckons he's cracked the case.'

Danskin was out his office faster than a buttered bullet. 'What's funny about that? Come here, lad. Tell me what you know.'

'DCI Danskin, my name's Ryan Jarrod. I'm a Special Constable. I was on duty the night of the University bombing, and I was the one who found the taxi driver, McGuffie.'

Danskin spoke to Trebilcock. 'You know about this, Treblecock?'

'No, sir.'

'Well, you should do.' He turned his attention back to Ryan. 'Okay, Ryan. I think it's worth hearing you out.'

Robson guffawed. 'You'll regret it.'

'Shut it, Robson. Young man – you've five minutes. Tell me who it is, how you found out, and why you think he's doing it.'

Ryan gazed around the room. Saw a number of faces he recognised; Parker and Nairn from the press conference, Danskin, of course, and Superintendent Connor. The roof of his mouth turned to sandpaper. He licked his lips.

'First off, sir, it's not a 'he'. I believe the perpetrator to be female.'

Stephen Danskin twisted his face. 'That's not a promising start. We're pretty sure it's a man. Never mind, carry on. You've still got more than four minutes.'

'I think you may be wrong.'

Danskin raised an eyebrow. The young man with the bandaged left hand and a Michael Jackson glove on the right was sure of himself. The DCI admired him for that. 'Tell me why you think I'm wrong.'

Ryan withdrew a pile of newspaper clippings from beneath his coat. He passed one to a pretty detective standing next to him, another to the man Danskin had called Treblecock, and a third to Danskin himself.

'Four days before the University bombing, the letter held by the Detective on my right appeared in The Mercury newspaper. I've highlighted part of it in red. Read it out, please.'

Hannah Graves was about to protest at the young man's insolence, but she relented when she saw a smile on Stephen Danskin's face.

'...*The building work is a blight on our landscape and won't even bring jobs or money to the city. The construction of endless tower blocks of student accommodation from all points east and west, all for the benefit of a transient population of here-today-gone-tomorrow students,*' Hannah read.

'Thank you.' Ryan turned to the next detective. 'Detective Treblecock,' the room filled with laughter. Superintendent Connor hushed it with a look while Danskin again smiled. He was beginning to like this lad.

Ryan continued unabated. 'Treblecock, please read out the letter I've given you.'

Nigel Trebilcock obliged. '*Today, I encountered a mob of young men, football supporters all, harassing an old woman in my once peaceful and quiet village. When will our police force act against such thuggery, or must we rely on vigilantes.*'

'Thank you, Detective Treblecock.' More stifled laughter. 'This letter appeared four days before the Newcastle Liverpool match, after which a TV van covering the game exploded.'

Danskin widened his eyes towards Lyall Parker, who raised an eyebrow in return.

'Now, DCI Danskin, please read out your letter.'

Danskin waited a moment before lowering his eyes to the page. 'My letter says: *Let's put more funds into policing our green and pleasant land, and less on bureaucrats and pen-pushers. Cut the civil servants who waste the taxes they purport to collect.'* Let's guess, Ryan. This letter appeared four days before the HMRC fire.'

Ryan beamed. 'It did, sir. The fire in which I received my injuries.' He held up his hands, though stopped short of dropping his pants.

The detectives looked at him anew. The female detective who'd read out the first letter, Hannah Graves, put her hand against Ryan's back and gently rubbed. Connor nodded to himself. Lyall Parker's mouth curved in a smile of appreciation.

Stephen Danskin winked at the young Special Constable; an act that brought a blush to his face and extracted an 'Aah' from Hannah Graves as if a colleague had brought a new-born baby into the office.

DCI Danskin brought the group back to the matter in hand. 'One minute left, Ryan. Tell me who's doing it.'

'I will, sir. The letters were all written by the same person. It must be the perpetrator of the crimes. The writer of the letters is a Miss F. Roadhouse. She is your bomber.'

Todd Robson fought hard not to laugh. 'Sorry to rain on your parade, kidda, but that's where your theories go arse over tit.'

'Why's that, Todd?', Danskin asked.

'Because I've done a quick internet search of this Miss F. Roadhouse.' He swiveled his monitor so Danskin could see. Placed the cursor over a link. Clicked, and an image appeared. 'Her name's Florence. And she's a hundred and thirty-six if she's day.'

Danskin leaned in for a closer look. As usual, Todd had exaggerated, but possibly only by fifty years. Whoever she may be, she wasn't the culprit.

The others laughed at Ryan no more, but they knew his allegations were balderdash. They began to drift away to their duties. Connor turned towards his office, and Ryan Jarrod blushed more furiously than ever.

Until Danskin dragged a ruler down the whiteboard. The screech stopped everyone in their tracks.

'Robson, what's the one thing I tell you lot more than anything.'

It didn't take Todd Robson long to answer. 'Don't see what you expect to see,' he said in a childish mimicry of Danskin's favourite motto.

'Aye. And that's exactly what you've just done.' Danskin clapped his hands. 'Listen up, you lot. Mr Jarrod might be mistaken about who's doing it, but he's given us our first real lead. The perpetrator's either someone this Roadhouse knows, or someone who's using her name as a front.'

Lyall Parker joined in the refrain. 'Or, it could be someone from the newspaper which prints the letters. Someone from The Mercury with something to gain by these acts.'

'Of course. Brilliant thinking, Lyall. Graves, I want you to delve into every nook and cranny of this woman's life. Sue, you follow-up on her family, friends and acquaintances. Robson and Trebilcock – you work with Lyall on digging out everything you can on this newspaper. Lyall, how long will it take you to pull together an initial dossier on the rag and its staff?'

'I can get something worthwhile to you in three hours, sir.'

Danskin clapped his hands. 'Ok, guys. What are you waiting for? You know your tasks. Get on with them. Tell you what, we'll reconvene in the amphitheater first thing in the morning. It's still Christmas, after all, and we need all the guys to hear this. Let them enjoy the rest of the day. We'll reconvene eight-thirty a.m. Not a minute later.'

The group dispersed to their various desks and cubicles to draw up what they knew. Phone calls were made, PCs burnt with frenzied activity, and the room was alive with electricity. Ryan Jarrod watched it all from the rear of the group. He gave a smile of satisfaction. All this was his doing. He'd proved to himself he could do this job. That's all he ever wanted to know. Slowly, he made his way to the exit. Opened the door. Put one foot outside.

'Hey, Ryan. Would you care to join us for the briefing?'

Ryan pointed to his own chest. 'Me?'

'Who else?', Stephen Danskin asked. 'After all, there'd be no briefing if it hadn't been for your detective work.' He turned to Detective Superintendent Connor. 'Assuming you have no objections, sir?'

Connor pretended to think it over for a moment. 'It's improper to allow anyone not directly involved in the case access to such a briefing, Danskin; as well you know.'

Ryan tried not to show his disappointment in any way other than a slight droop of his shoulders.

'And,' Connor continued, 'As Mr. Jarrod is very much directly involved, of course I have no objections.'

Ryan let out a 'Yesss!' before correcting himself. 'I mean, thank you, sir. I'd appreciate the opportunity.'

'Just one more thing, Jarrod.'

'Yes, sir?'

'Stick to the 'Yesss' next time, will you? It suits you.'

CHAPTER TWENTY

Marcus Vorster sat in a wing-back leather chair in his office at The Mercury building. Dressed in expensively tailored jeans, Ralph Lauren polo shirt with a speckled Arran sweater tied around his neck, he looked every-inch a male model wannabe.

Opposite him, his chief news team rested on two plush burgundy sofas.

Vorster rolled a whisky tumbler in his hand. 'I just want to thank you for your work over the last couple of weeks. I don't say it often enough, but I appreciate you guys.' He raised his glass in toast. 'Chin chin.'

The single malt hadn't been shared with his team, but they murmured thanks whilst shifting uncomfortably in their seats. A relaxed Marcus Vorster was an unpredictable beast.

'I know I've brought you in on Boxing Day because we're on a goldmine story here, but I wanted to spend five minutes with you before letting you off the leash.' He took a sip of whisky and smacked his lips in appreciation. 'I want to apologize. I've been hard on you of late.' He offered a shark's smile. 'Well, more hard than usual.'

Megan Wolfe, Raymond Carpenter, and Molly Uzumba shared glances. Leeward Milton stared straight back at Vorster.

'I'm a lucky man. I have the best team anyone could wish for. Especially now I'm rid of the deadWoods,' Marcus Vorster paused, waiting for them to acknowledge his pun. When they didn't, he carried on.

'I want you to know, I'm going to change my ways. New Year, new approach. I'm determined to show you guys what you mean to me. Together, you and I will make history with this story. But, I sense we've built up an air of tension. Perhaps because of me, who knows? So, first, let's get everything out in the open. Clear the air, you know?'

Leeward was the one to break the silence. 'Talk's cheap, Marcus. No-one objects to being driven hard. They do object when it gets personal.'

The smile which never reached the eyes returned. 'Ag, that's fair comment, Leeward. I've been unfair on you, especially. I want you to know, because of my background, it's nothing to do with..., you know.'

'My colour. You can start by saying the word.'

It was Marcus' turn to squirm in his seat. The leather made a noise like a fart. 'Ok, Leeward. It's nothing to do with your colour.'

Milton considered the words. Seemed to accept them. 'Then, what is it?'

'You're unpredictable, Leeward. That's what it is.'

'Example?' Milton responded.

'Like, the other day. When you stormed out. Went home like a pussy because I commented on your time in the Gulf.'

Milton's eyes darkened like coal. 'You didn't comment. You joked. No-one jokes about war and the things it does to you.' He drifted to a different place. A different time. 'War changes you. Hurts like hell. Seeing guys you live with maimed. Questioning yourself why you're the one that survived.' His voice hardened. 'No-one jokes about such things.'

Vorster held his up his hands. 'I was out of order. I'm sorry. I'll change.' He leant forward. Extended his hand. 'I promise.'

Milton hesitated for a moment before accepting. 'Ok, Marcus. No problem.' He squeezed until he saw a muscle twitch in Vorster's cheek. 'And I'm no pussy, man.'

Marcus lifted a crystal decanter from a side-table and refilled his glass. 'This feels like a therapy session. Who's next?'

Raymond Carpenter spoke. 'Marcus, I don't have a problem with your methods. They've proved successful. But I do have a request.'

'Request away.'

Raymond looked at Megan, squeezed alongside him on the two-seater. 'I want Megan back on the main story. She's the best. She and I: we gel. We bring the best out of each other.'

Carpenter paused. Waited for Vorster's sarcastic response. When none came, he continued. 'You took your best investigative reporter and put her on a people story. Megan's hard news. That's where she belongs.'

Vorster looked at Wolfe. 'How do you feel, Megan?'

'Actually, I'd quite like to follow up the boy-in-the-fire story.' Carpenter looked at her, open-mouthed. 'He's a Special Constable and I sense there's something else in there. Something I can tease out. But, of course, I still want a slice of the main pie as well. But only if I can go rogue on it, Marcus.'

Carpenter appeared both perplexed and crestfallen. 'What? You mean you don't want us to work together anymore?'

'Not really, no.'

Vorster made a T-shape with his hands. 'Time out, guys. Time-out. We're a team here, Megan. But I'm happy to give you your head for a few days. See what you can come up with.'

Carpenter folded his arms across his chest.

Marcus turned his attention to Uzumba. 'Molly? Anything I can do for you?'

'Yes. You can bring David back onto the team. You were too harsh on him. He's a good man. Not a conventional newsman, but he brings something to the team. A fresh perspective. And, he's brilliant at capturing the mood of a scene on camera. You've plenty videographers on the digital side. We haven't many as good as David with a lens.'

Megan agreed.

'Lee? You feel the same as the ladies?'

'We could manage without him, if I'm real honest. I don't think he contributes much to the deal. But, I can't be a hypocrite. You were harder on Woods than you were me, and that aint right. So, bring him back, I say.'

Marcus finished his whisky. 'Folks; you've got yourselves a deal. Merry Christmas, what's left of it. Now, get out of here. We've got ourselves a shitload of money to make. I haven't changed that much,' he smirked.

They were the first genuine words he'd spoken all meeting.

**

Florence Roadhouse continued with her tales, oblivious to the fact her audience sat with head resting on chest, mouth open, snoring peacefully. Doris Jarrod had just about stayed awake while Florence recounted her early life story, but she'd slipped over to her peaceful place long before the story had really begun.

Florence sipped tea and stared into space as she spoke about the medics she'd encountered, the places she'd seen, and the travails of wars she'd witnessed. Her face betrayed her emotions. A smile here, a frown there; a twinkle in her eye quickly replaced by a tear, and laughter substituted by a sadness in her voice which Doris would have empathised with in her prime, but now wouldn't recognise even if awake.

When Florence told of the jungle and the heat and the sniper attack, her hand tremored. She brought her arthritic hand up to support her better one, then had to set down the cup. She stopped talking. She'd exorcised sufficient ghosts for now.

Florence limped to the window to assure herself she was back in Britain. All was as it should be: the sky grey, trees bare, remnants of snow where her garden borders lay. With Doris Jarrod slumbering in Florence's favourite chair, the long-retired nurse prepared to make lunch for them both.

Outside, the car stood out of sight, but in a position where the driver could see in. He watched as Florence's outline drifted by, the net curtains at the window making her appear as a veiled spirit.

He clenched the wheel, knuckles white. The man lay his head against the steering wheel and flexed his fingers to circulate the blood. His breath came in snorts. Condensed against the windscreen. His heart pounded like a jackhammer and he heard blood ping as it pulsed at his temples. He'd planned for this moment for so long yet, now it was here, he didn't know what to do.

With an anguished wail, David Woods put the car into gear and drove away.

**

Danskin had asked Ryan to report to Hannah Graves first thing. For Ryan, first thing meant seven. Fortunately, Hannah was already at her desk. She chaperoned him for the first half-hour. It mainly consisted of Hannah telling him where he could and couldn't go. Which was almost everywhere. Nevertheless, he'd warmed to her. Found her engaging company, gentle and kind, yet with a hint of steel beneath the surface.

Sadly, she'd had to dash off to attend to her duties. While Ryan waited for the conference to begin, he spent the time milling around the canteen. He felt out of place, as if he were attracting odd looks from a force familiar with each other and wary of interlopers. Ryan left his sandwich uneaten and retreated to the reception area.

He hung about, reading posters about crime prevention, all the while avoiding the stares of a curmudgeonly desk sergeant. With relief, he spotted Frank Burrows carrying a mound of paperwork into an adjacent room.

Frank greeted him warmly, asked why Ryan was there and, when he'd told him he was waiting for Danskin's briefing, Burrows congratulated him with a slap on the back like a parent dislodging a mint imperial from a child's windpipe.

Finally, twenty minutes early, Ryan took the stairs to the basement and loitered outside the major incident conference room. Ten minutes before the briefing was due, someone arrived with a set of keys and let him inside.

The room was as cold as the streets outside, and as dark as night. He found a light switch but the glow was minimal. Ryan shivered, partly because of the chill, but mainly with a mix of excitement of nerves. He felt the way he did before his childhood gymnastics competitions, an urgent need to pee despite an empty bladder.

Instead, Ryan studied his surroundings. At the front, a lectern populated a small stage similar to the one in his old school hall. A laptop sat atop the lectern, pointing towards a pull-down canvas screen. In front of the stage, plastic seats had been set up facing front. Ryan estimated about eight rows, ten to twelve seats to a row. Ryan judged where he should sit. The front appeared too eager; the back proclaimed disinterest. He decided he'd sit around six rows back, three seats in.

To the rear of the room, a coffee machine hid behind a screen of baffle boards. Not sure whether he should help himself, he dithered before slotting a plastic cup beneath the spout and pressing a button marked 'mocha.' No sooner had the cup filled than he heard voices outside.

Hurriedly, he went to take a seat. He caught a foot on a chair leg, felt himself fall. The hot drink spilled onto his healing groin. He stifled a scream, tried to stand up, only for him to bring down two more chairs.

As he clambered to his feet, trouser-front stained, the door opened and Danskin and the entire crew flowed through. Embarrassed as fuck, Ryan tried to slink into his chair. No such luck.

'Ryan. Glad you could join us. Good to see you, good to see you.' Danskin meant to put Ryan at ease but only succeeded in drawing him to the attention of the others. Ryan flushed furiously and cursed the family habit.

As the others took their seats around him, Ryan heard a few mutterings. Not least from behind him. 'What the hell's Foreskin playing at now? I didn't realise it was bring your little fuckers to work day.'

Ryan stole a glance behind him and saw the Franck Ribery lookalike glowering at him. Ryan began to blush once more, not helped when Hannah Graves put her hand on the nape of his neck and said, 'Don't, Todd. He's all right, you know?'

From the front of the room, Danskin spoke. 'I suggest you listen to Graves, Robson, because there's one thing you need to remember. In ten years, young Ryan will be up here in my place and you'll still be down there, listening to him. I wouldn't wind him up, if I were you.'

The room filled with sniggers while Ryan afforded himself a shy smile despite Robson's eyes burning into the back of his neck like lasers.

On the stage, Lyall Parker connected a light probe to the laptop and fiddled with the connections. An off-centre blue radiance caught the edge of the screen and most of the wall behind it. Parker twisted the lens and the image veered more wildly, crashing against the wall like a speedway rider into the safety fence. He scratched his head. Tried again. Eventually, Ravi Sangar came to the Scotsman's assistance and aligned image to screen with microscopic precision.

Sangar retook his seat as Danskin stood and clapped his hands for attention. 'Listen up.' The hubbub dwindled and died. 'This is our first real lead on this case, thanks to young Jarrod, there.' Heads turned in Ryan's direction as he battled with the flush rising to his cheeks.

'As you know, we have a link between the atrocities and letters written to The Mercury newspaper. Lyall's pulled together a quick overview of some persons of interest employed by the rag. Thanks to those who have contributed. A few things to remember. At this point, they are not suspects. This is background information only. Next, we haven't ruled out that this is all just a coincidence. Unlikely, but keep an open mind.'

Ryan scanned the room. Some of the detectives made notes, others leant forward, listening intently. A few slumped in their chairs, arms behind their heads as if they heard this every day. He returned his attention to Danskin.

'Before Lyall begins, I'm going to ask DS Nairn to make a few points about the letter-writer, Florence Roadhouse.' He paused. Looked around the room, seemingly catching the eye of everyone. 'Finally, what is the most important thing to remember?'

Like a chorus of schoolchildren greeting their teacher, they recited 'Don't see what you expect to see.' Satisfied, Danskin took the end seat on the front row.

Sue Nairn, tall and erect, stood. 'Today, we're focussing on those who received the letters, not the one who wrote them. Why?' she asked rhetorically, 'Because Miss Florence Roadhouse is elderly, partly-infirm, and incapable of constructing, placing, and detonating a device.'

Sue maintained a silence to ensure her words had registered. 'Secondly, she's a nurse who spent her working life saving, not taking, lives. She served in the NHS and, before that, as a field nurse to the armed forces in conflicts across the globe.'

A detective a few rows from the front raised his hand. Sue stopped for the question. 'If she was in the forces, she could have knowledge of explosives, could she not? I mean, I'm just thinking *don't see what you expect to see,*' and all that.'

Ryan noticed Danskin give an approving nod.

'Correct, Geoff. But someone of her age, and in her health – she's severely arthritic – isn't physically capable of it,' Nairn answered.

'What about someone she knows? A relative of hers?'

'She has no living relatives. She's a spinster with no siblings or cousins. Her parents, obviously, are long gone. That's why, for now, today's focus is on those who have handled her letters. Primarily, those working in The Mercury newsroom.'

Sue Nairn waited to see if her answers prompted more questions. When none came, she voiced a doubt of her own. 'A word of caution before handing across to Lyall. Roadhouse is an inveterate letter writer. We've discovered she writes to The Mercury as many as four times a week. She's done this for years. Not all are published. Usually, one in four is selected for print if she's lucky. We need to consider what it is that triggers a response from our bomber.'

Her audience murmured their agreement. Danskin tapped a pen against his teeth.

Finally, Nairn concluded her segment. 'Is it coincidence? Are we barking up the wrong tree? Let's bloody hope not. Hopefully, Lyall will be able to convince us.'

Lyall Parker strode to the lectern.

CHAPTER TWENTY-ONE

As the City and County police discussed the merits of the lead, across the city in The Mercury offices Molly Uzumba and Megan Wolfe sat at their desks, Molly engrossed in a telephone conversation while Megan stared at a split-screen image on her desktop PC. One displayed her research material, the other the contents of a rival publication. Along the bottom, a further tab remained minimised. It read 'Marcus Vorster'.

Nearby, the Tyneside Tyrant scanned a draft copy of the morning's second edition. When he realised features editor Luke Padwell had excluded Roadhouse's latest claptrap from publication, he lost interest. He switched his attention to the women.

The man lumbered over, laid a hand on Uzumba's shoulder and took a seat next to Megan. 'Things ok, girls?'

Molly signalled for him to hush and continued her conversation. Megan replied without shifting her attention from the screen. 'Good, thanks.'

'A bit formal, aren't we?'

Megan smiled apologetically. 'Sorry. I'm in the middle of this,' she explained by way of explanation.

The man leant in close. 'What you working on?'

Megan closed down her monitor screen. Tapped the side of her nose with a forefinger. 'That's for me to know. I'm working alone, remember.' She flashed him a smile. 'Nothing important, really. Just checking a few things out.'

He returned her grin. 'Ok, I'll leave you to it. I have to be somewhere, anyway.' The man grabbed his coat. 'See you later, girls.'

'Yeah, see you,' Megan said, while Molly waved a hand in his direction.

The man's smile turned to a scowl the moment his back was turned.

**

Lyall Parker spoke so softly, Ryan had to lean forward to hear. So, too, did everyone else in the room.

'Clever,' Ryan thought. Parker's gentle Scottish accent, reminiscent of a commentator describing a golfer hunched over the decisive put of The Open Championship, meant everyone had to concentrate hard on his words.

'…very early days,' Parker was saying. 'The guys doing the background research have found a mine of information on this set-up already. Give us time, and we'll get to the bottom of this.'

'Thing is, Lyall,' Danskin interjected, 'Time is the one thing we mightn't have. Who knows when we'll see the next letter, and whether that'll be a one to trigger the Tyneside Tyrant into action.'

Lyall agreed. 'Ok, Stephen, I get it. I'll get the squad digging up more on the key players once we're finished. What I will say right now, we've got a lot to do. From what I can tell, The Mercury's a tawdry set-up from top to bottom.'

'Howay, Lyall, man. Just get on with it.'

Parker clicked the mouse. A composite picture appeared on screen. Top left, Leeward Milton. Centre, Raymond Carpenter. Right, David Woods. Beneath them, from left to right, Molly Uzumba, Mike Cash, and Megan Wolfe.

Right in the centre, between the two rows, the grinning face of Marcus Vorster.

Believe me,' Lyall Parker said, 'It could be any one of the buggers.'

The detectives in the auditorium studied the lean, angular face in the centre of the screen while Parker spoke.

'Marcus Aaron Vorster. Born Natal Province, South Africa. Also born with a silver spoon in his mouth. Or, more accurately, a golden one. His father, Aaron Vorster, owned a string of gold mines. Like most in Natal, no single mine was particularly productive, but the cumulative wealth they generated was significant. Put simply, the man was minted rich. Minted, that is, until this happened.'

With a click of the mouse, Vorster's face disappeared to be replaced with an image of a burnt-out wreck of a car.

'The general belief, supported by Wiki, is that Aaron Vorster and his wife perished in a car crash. That's not strictly true. They died in their car, certainly, but it was as a result of ambush by a pair of disaffected black employees. This,' he pointed to the screen, 'Was the result. The sad irony is, Vorster Senior bequeathed half his wealth to charities aimed at improving conditions within black townships. The other half he left to his only heir; his son, Marcus Vorster.'

A voice interrupted Parker's presentation. 'So, this seems to rule out Vorster if we're thinking he's after publicity to boost his income. You're saying money wouldn't be a motive for Vorster, so this isn't our guy, right?'

'Och, no. Not at all. Because there was a wee problem with the inheritance. Aaron Vorster wanted his son to earn his money. The old man set up a string of lawyers and accountants to check Marcus did just that. You see, the will stipulated at least 50% of the inheritance be committed to the development of business ventures.'

Danskin rubbed the bristle on his jawline. 'What about the rest of it? Did Marcus trouser it?'

'Not exactly. The rest was – is – paid out as an annual stipend. And it's paid in arrears, on the proviso Vorster still owns and runs a business. The amount he's awarded has a direct correlation to the profits of his business.'

Lyall Parker's words piqued Danskin's interest. 'Which means he needs The Mercury to be a success.'

'Precisely, sir. At first, it wasn't an issue. Vorster invested a huge swathe of the initial inheritance setting up his concept of On-Line journalism in Durban and Johannesburg. His advertising strapline became 'Don't read the news, don't watch the news, be the news'. Click on a quote, and you heard the speaker say the words. Click on an image, and a video played. It presented an immersive experience for the subscriber. Trouble is, there wasn't enough of them.'

Another click and the image of two uber-modern tower blocks filled the screen. Both bore The Mercury logo above the entrance. 'Vorster expanded his empire. Proclaimed he'd take on and beat Murdoch and Maxwell...'

'We might as well call it a day now, then,' Todd Robson shouted. 'Anyone with aspirations like that has to be twattish enough to be our man.'

When the laughter subsided, the Scotsman continued. Parker enlarged one of the images. 'This is Houston. Vorster had this purpose-built for his expansion to the States. It never opened. Before its launch, he shifted his attention to New York.' The other block appeared on-screen. 'Vorster decided the Big Apple was the place to be. At ridiculous expense, he bought this building, two blocks away from The New York Times HQ.'

Vorster's face reappeared on screen. 'That's when it really went tits-up. He tried to take on the NYT, which itself was experimenting with digital roll-out at the time. Vorster's ego meant he wouldn't back down. He slogged it out with NYT for several years, but there was only ever going to be one winner. Vorster was left with little choice. He shut down his American enterprise and returned to South Africa with his tail between his legs and his inheritance dwindling.'

The door opened and Superintendent Connor filled the frame, arms folded, observing intently.

'Of course, Vorster still needed a business in order to access his father's inheritance,' Parker continued. 'He scaled back some of the excesses of his lifestyle and made one final attempt at breaking the market. He moved his operation to Paris. Like many of his decisions, it proved a costly mistake. The relocation, across continents, cost millions. He couldn't possibly hope to recoup the outlay. It prospered, briefly, but in the face of increasing competition, it was doomed to fail. You see, by now almost all traditional print newspapers had jumped aboard the tech bandwagon. Put simply, there were too many snouts in the trough.'

Sue Nairn asked the next question. 'I get that, Lyall. But, come on - we've had Durban, Jo'burg, Houston, New York and Paris. Sounds like a cosmetics or fashion advert, so I've got to ask: why the hell pick Newcastle, of all places?'

'Pure chance, Sue. Chance, opportunity and not a little desperation. Towards the end of his time in Paris, Vorster attended a conference. Alongside him sat the proprietor of The Journal. The Newcastle Journal. He was looking to sell up. It was going for a song. Cheap as chips. Vorster needed an outlet – any outlet – to keep his old man's money flowing. He bought it; lock, stock and barrel. He introduced some of The Mercury's tech content but switched more emphasis to print. It kept costs down. As we know, he's still here.'

'But,' Stephen Danskin interjected, 'In desperate need of a ratings boost. There's some real food for thought there, guys. Lyall, Todd, Treblecock: you've done an excellent job getting this together so quickly.'

'Thank you, sir,' Parker said. Nigel Trebilcock beamed. Todd Robson remained impassive.

Danskin addressed the rest of the room. 'Let's not jump to conclusions. It's still early, and we've got nothing to link Vorster directly to the crimes. Besides, we need Lyall to brief us on our other persons of interest. Lyall, you said it could be any of them?'

'Aye, I did.' Parker returned to his I.T. Called up another image. The huge, grinning face of Leeward Milton smirked down on his audience.

**

When confronted by an angry bear, the last thing you should do is poke it with a stick. Unfortunately, that's precisely what the girl behind the counter of Beaverbrook's Jewellers did to Leeward Milton.

Shopping wasn't for Milton at the best of times. Throw into the mix the crowds inside one of Europe's largest shopping malls, Gateshead's MetroCentre, on the day the sales began in earnest; it all added up to his worst nightmare. Well, second worst.

Milton had driven around the car parks for the best part of half an hour without finding a vacant spot. In the end, he decided the only way he'd get parked was to take his already spotless car to the valet station on the Yellow Mall ground floor.

Leeward was well-used to crowds. He'd worked in New York. He'd spent two years working from an office adjacent to the Champs-Elysees. He was a frequent traveller to frenetic London, and he took his kids to Busch Gardens at least three times a year back home. Yet, today, being around people bugged him.

Milton entered the mall with a dark heart and darker thoughts. He strode through the masses with intent, shoulders back, muscles tensed. People avoided the big man as best they could. Inevitably, the malls were so jam-packed he barged into several shoppers. They didn't complain. One glance warned them off. The ex-linebacker marched on, unchallenged.

Milton himself wasn't thinking straight. He'd missed the shortcut to the Red Quadrant which meant he was obliged to weave his way through the impatient kids queuing for the MetroGnomes performance in Town Square One.

His mind was elsewhere. On Marcus Vorster, Megan Wolfe's theory about him and, finally, the cold-blooded hatred he felt for the South African bully. So, when he stepped into the relative calm of Beaverbrook's, the last thing he needed was a prod with a stick.

'Good morning, sir. Lovely day for shopping, isn't it?' The girl wore oversize, Coke-bottle glasses which magnified her eyes. Sat on her narrow face, she looked all the world like an alien escapee from Area Fifty-One.

'Hmmm.'

'Are we after a gift for a loved one?'

'Well, I am. Sure as hell don't know about you.'

Unperturbed, the girl ploughed on. 'We have some classic silver on special offer today. Can I interest you?'

'No. Gimme a twelve-carat ring. Any. You choose.'

The girl with the alien eyes simpered. 'Only twelve carat, sir? I'm sure the lady's worth more than that. We've higher grade gold available for the same price twelve was pre-sale, if I may be so bold.'

'Look, are you gonna give me what I want or do I just the break the goddamn case and take some myself?'

The girl's eyes grew even larger. Her mouth formed a perfect O. She began to protest. thought better of it, and completed the transaction. Satisfied, Leeward Milton stormed out.

He caught sight of a carriage clock as he exited the outlet. Couldn't believe the time. He checked his own watch. 'Christ.'

Milton broke into a run. He swerved through the crowds, knocked women and children over as he fled. Folk watched, bemused.

He'd almost reached the exit when the explosion came.

He sensed, rather than heard, it. Instinctively, he threw himself to the floor. Curled into a ball and rolled for cover. The shrieks hit him hardest. Piercing, falsetto, almost child-like screams.

He refused to open his eyes. Couldn't open them. He was back in the Gulf, on a patch of parched earth. He knew carnage lay beyond his closed lids. Detached limbs, the maimed, the dead, and the dying.

Other sounds filtered into his brain. More howls. Yet, there was something different about them. Cautiously, he unfolded an arm from around his head. Dared to open one eye.

He was curled up behind a rack of shopping baskets in the entrance to Primark. People stood around. On two legs, and with two arms. What he'd heard were howls of laughter, not agony.

At the front of the crowd, closest to him, a three-year old child with tear-stained cheeks stared down at him. The boy held a stick in his hand. Attached to it, a red balloon emblazoned with the Frankie and Benny's logo. At the child's feet lay another rod, with the ragged remnants of a green balloon hanging from it.

A burst balloon.

Sheepishly, Leeward Milton clambered to his feet and brushed himself down. He was late for his therapy appointment. Boy, did he need it.

CHAPTER TWENTY-TWO

Superintendent Connor pulled up a chair alongside Danskin as Lyall Parker continued.

'Now, here's an interesting one. Leeward Milton. Unofficially, Vorster's second-in-command. He's been with Vorster since the beginning.' He paused to ensure he had the full attention of the room. 'Yet, they cannae stand the sight of each other. Be it jealousy, prejudice, competitiveness or something else, they respect one another, tolerate each other, but they don't get on.'

Connor whispered something to Danskin, who nodded. 'Lyall, stick with discussing Milton for now. We'll make our own mind up about the state of their relationship.'

'I'll try, sir, but there are links which I need to make. Okay, Leeward Milton is married. Wife and kids live on the west coast of Florida. Milton visits them half a dozen times a year. His wife, Lois, has never travelled with him wherever he's worked. And, he's worked in plenty of places.'

The screen showed an image of a newspaper cutting. 'Milton is not a journalist by trade. Far from it. The son of a US serviceman, he followed his father into the services. Until, in the Gulf, this happened.'

He zoomed in on the cutting. 'Milton was the only survivor when the jeep he was driving hit a landmine. Two of his colleagues died instantly. A third lost both legs. The other squaddie lost his eyesight and his mobility. A paraplegic, he drove his motorised wheelchair into the Hudson two years later. Leeward Milton walked away without a scratch.'

One of Ravi Sangar's men asked a question. 'So, what's the connection with Vorster? How'd he end up working for him?'

Parker raised his eyebrows in surprise. 'I thought you of all people would know, John, being a techy and all. You see, Milton was arguably the world's first vlogger before the term had even been invented. The internet was in its infancy. The world wide web didn't exist; only a string of separate pages or individual sites with no links between them. Milton, though: he had his own page. And, to it, he posted surreptitious footage and pinned it to his site.'

Parker called up an archived video Milton had taken of his comrades, talking about day-to-day life in the Gulf. They spoke matter-of-factly about killing and the risk of being killed. It wasn't particularly well shot but it remained powerful stuff even now, let alone then.

'Vorster stumbled across Milton's footage when he began planning his empire. In fact, it was Milton's vlogs that gave him the idea for an interactive newsreel rather than the traditional print medium. It seemed logical to recruit Leeward Milton. In that era, who better?'

The detectives were so engrossed in Parker's brief, the silence deafened. A detective in front of Ryan broke the spell. 'Out of interest, what was Milton's role in the Gulf?'

A hint of a smile played on Lyall Parker's lips. 'He was a combat engineer. A deminer. Put another way, bomb disposal.'

Todd Robson let out a low whistle. 'Pound to a penny, he's our man.'

Another voice agreed. 'I'm with you, Todd. If he could disarm mines, it's not the greatest leap of re-engineering to construct them.'

One of DCI Kinnear's men spoke next. 'Can't doubt he's got the means, but what's his motive? If our theory that greed's behind all this, why'd Milton risk everything for the benefit of a bloke he openly despises?'

Theory and contra-theory spun through the air like vocal spiderwebs. 'If he's such an expert, why didn't the St James's bomb detonate on time?'

'Howay, man. Keep up. He's used to pressure mines, not timing devices. It's him, I tell you.'

'I'm not convinced. If we think back to the first incident, what's he doing trailing up to the ninth floor of twelve to plant an explosive? With his knowledge, he could've placed it somewhere more convenient, surely? He'd have the skill to plant a device anywhere, inside or out the building. Why risk discovery?'

Danskin had heard enough. 'Whoa, whoa. Let's hold these thoughts, yeah? I'm loving the debate. It's all valuable stuff. But, what did I say at the start? 'Don't see what you expect to see.' Save all this for the bullpen because Lyall's got the lowdown on a few more yet. Lyall, back to you.'

The voice that spoke wasn't that of Lyall Parker.

'9/11.'

Heads spun to look at Ryan Jarrod.

'The bomb was on the ninth floor because of 9/11.'

Ryan took silence as permission to proceed. 'The South Tower was hit second but collapsed first. Why? Because the plane hit at its weakest point. Towards the corner, at or around floor eighty of a hundred and ten: which is three quarters of the way up. I've read the reports of the University bombing. It went off in a storeroom. On the corner of the ninth floor. The ninth floor was three quarters of the way up the building.'

Superintendent Connor looked at DCI Danskin who looked at Lyall Parker who stared, open-mouthed, at Ryan Jarrod.

'Fucking hell,' Todd Robson whispered.

Hannah Graves ruffled Ryan's hair. Or, he imagined, ran her fingers through it.

Ryan blushed once more.

**

Stephen Danskin called for a quick recess. While the officers stood around slurping coffee and dunking ginger snaps, Hannah Graves sidled up to Ryan. 'How'd you know all that?'

He shrugged. 'Dunno. I read it once. Must have stored it up in my brain somewhere. It just sort of came to me.' When she smiled at him, Ryan noticed a cute dimple appear in her cheek. So cute, he missed what she said. 'Sorry, what did you say?' he asked.

'I said you made them think. I haven't seen the DCI react like that for a long time. Even Todd seemed impressed.'

'So, 'fucking hell' is Todd-speak for well done, is it?'

Hannah laughed. 'No, fucking hell is Todd-speak for just about everything. But he didn't rubbish you. That's praise indeed.'

Ryan thought for a moment. 'You don't think I spoke out of turn, do you? I mean, I am a guest here.'

'No, son. You didn't.' Danskin spoke from behind him. Hannah Graves slunk away and became lost in a fug of steaming coffee and condensing breath. 'Not many would have the guts to speak up like you did. Especially after I'd told them to shut up.'

Ryan ran his padded hand up and down his hip to relieve the itch in the healing flesh. 'Sorry, sir.'

Danskin shook his head. 'Don't apologise. I'm pleased you felt able to contribute.' He smiled at the teenager. 'You'll go places, son. You realise that, don't you?'

'Nice of you to say so, sir. I'd like nothing more than to work with you. Properly, like.'

'Whoa. Had your horses, young man. You've a good while to go yet and, much as I admire you, it's down to you how far you go. A good place to start is knowing when to keep your gob shut.'

His eyes locked with those of Ryan. He waited until he was sure the youngster understood. 'So, here's your first mission, should you decide to accept it, and all that shite. Comprendez?'

Ryan nodded enthusiastically.

'Good,' Danskin said. 'As for me, I'd appreciate your help. On the outside, of course. Just with research, like. Or any theories you have. Keep your head down and your arse up. If Connor catches wind of what you're up to, I'll deny it and you'll be out the specials before your feet touch the ground.'

Ryan's eyes sparkled with excitement, even as the DCI continued. 'You don't interfere, Ryan. Don't do anything – and, I mean ANYTHING – that jeopardises the official investigation. You don't talk to anyone, you don't question anyone, you don't put yourself anywhere you shouldn't be.' The DCI cocked his head to one side. 'That's assuming you want to help, that is.'

'Yes, sir. I'd love to, sir.' Ryan rattled out the words before the DCI had a chance to reconsider.

'Good. That's settled, then. I'll speak to you later. Meanwhile, Lyall's got a few other buggers he wants to talk about.' He raised his voice so he could be heard above the buzz of conversation. 'Back to business, guys. Parker, get us on the road again.'

Once everyone had retaken their seats and Danskin had urged them to keep theories and questions for the bullpen unless they wanted to be there until New Year, Parker resumed his update.

'Next in The Mercury pecking order, after Vorster and Milton, comes Raymond Carpenter. Unlike Milton, Carpenter is a newsman through-and-through. He's a widower. Lost his wife at an early age.'

Parker saw one or two straighten in their chairs at that little nugget. They quickly relaxed when he added, 'Cancer. No suspicious circumstances. He never re-married. Threw himself into his work.'

Lyall called Carpenter's image up onto screen. Two pictures appeared. Carpenter, and an elfin-faced woman immediately recognisable to Danskin and Ryan. Megan Wolfe.

'Carpenter's known in the business as a steady pair of hands. Truth is, he's never broke a major story, never appeared as a talking head on TV, never rattled any cages. In fact, our intelligence indicates he's built his reputation purely because, wherever he goes, so too does Megan Wolfe. They've followed each other around from the regionals, to Fleet Street, and back again.'

Parker enlarged the image of Megan Wolfe. 'She's the real power behind the partnership. Although, technically, he's her superior, Carpenter's Andrew Ridgeley to her George Michael.'

'Are they shagging?'

Lyall chuckled. 'They're not in a relationship, Todd, no. But I wouldn't be surprised if they'd shagged, as you put it. She has a reputation for it.'

'Lucky bastard.' Then, as an afterthought, 'If you need someone undercover on her, I'm your man.'

'Thank you, Todd. I'm sure the DCI will note your offer.'

'Aye. And I'll ignore it, and all,' Danskin said amidst laughter. 'Now, if Robson can shut his erection up for a minute, get on with it, Lyall.'

'Thanks, sir. That's about all we've got on Carpenter. Variously described as 'deep', 'a bit creepy,' 'loyal', and 'not one for the trenches,' little else is known about him. As for his sidekick, Wolfe; well, she's renowned for flirting with the boundaries of press freedom…'

'Bet that's not all she flirts with.'

'Robson!'

'Sorry, sir. Gan on, Lyall. I'll shut up.'

'As I was saying, her name's appeared above several controversial stories. Not least when she managed to wheedle a hooker into a role as a Parliamentary researcher just so she could set up the then-Home Secretary, photos and all, for the sake of a story she'd planned, manipulated, and published.' Another picture appeared on screen. That of a well-known and much-loved singer, a family-man who'd received the MBE for his charitable work.

'Rumour has it, she deployed almost the exact same techniques with our friend here. Except, this time, she used two girls. Another call-girl. And herself.'

Parker heard the intake of breath. Waited for Robson's comment. 'Go on, Todd. You know you want to.'

Todd faked pulling a zipper across his mouth.

'When his version of events came out,' Lyall Parker continued, 'He alleged Wolfe slept with him willingly and, when she swapped places with the second girl, Wolfe took photographs of the liaison. Wolfe denied any involvement, of course, but the photographs of our man and the second girl 'broke the internet', as they say, when they mysteriously appeared on-line. Less than three months later, he topped himself.'

'Seems like a nice girl,' Nigel Trebilcock deduced. 'Any more tricks up her sleeve?'

DI Parker couldn't prevent his eyes sliding towards Danskin. 'Several, but none as underhand as these.'

Stephen Danskin chewed on his lip.

**

As the day progressed, the clouds lifted over both the Tyne valley and Raymond Carpenter's mood.

Megan had been impulsive for as long as he'd known her. Given time, she'd come around. In his mind, he'd already sown the seeds. He'd sat with her over coffee. Made small talk. Nothing consequential, nothing controversial.

But, when he offered her a lift and she'd accepted after a moment's hesitation, he was sure they'd work together soon. 'Who knows', he thought, 'with the right story, we might just…'

As he watched Megan Wolfe knock on the door of a house in Whickham, the sun appeared in the sky and in Carpenter's thoughts.

'Hi,' Megan said as the boy with the strange hair opened the door. 'Can I have a word with Ryan?'

'Not in.'

'Ah. When will he be back, do you know?'

Jam Jar shrugged. Megan reached into her shoulder bag. Passed over one of the ubiquitous business cards. 'Please. Tell him to call me.' She flashed a smile at the teenager.

'If I remember. Not sure he'll do owt about it even if I do.'

'Well, he won't do if he doesn't get it. I'm sure you won't forget. Please, tell him I'm not bad, really.'

Jam Jar shrugged again. Looked her up and down, eyes lingering where a teenage boy's eyes always did. 'Not half bad,' he thought. Except, he didn't think it. He said it.

Megan reached for James Jarrod's arm. Stroked it gently. 'And I think you're a cutie, too,' she smiled, eyes sparkling.

With the capriciousness of his years, Jam Jar's face changed. Eyes wide, mouth open, face flushed the colour of his hair, he took a step back into the hallway and slammed the door shut. Megan put her mouth to the letterbox. In her huskiest voice, she said, 'Don't forget to tell him, big boy.'

In his car, Carpenter watched her toss back her head and laugh. Under his breath, he spoke out loud. 'Yes, with the right story, we really might.'

**

Less than half a mile away, the blue skies had little effect on Florence Roadhouse. She hated this time of year in this part of the world, where winter nights linger like an unpalatable truth and memories come tinged with a sour bitterness.

Her gaze flitted to the photograph of the man in uniform, but that was a road best left untraveled. There were many worse off than her, she told herself. She thought of Doris Jarrod, alone and abandoned by inadequate social care. And of those with families required to work throughout the festive season in the face of commercialism.

Florence stopped herself in her tracks. 'Good heavens. Don't tell me I'm going all socialist in my old age. Can't be having that, can we?' So, she turned her thoughts to those forced to live on the streets or in inadequate housing whilst migrant workers and immigrant skivers prospered in council-donated homes.

Florence Roadhouse had found something to take her mind off her loneliness. She reached for a sheet of A4 paper. Realised one was nowhere near enough. She picked out half a dozen more from the pack and fed the first beneath her typewriter roller.

So began her latest self-conducted therapy session.

CHAPTER TWENTY-THREE

In the depths of City and County police HQ, Stephen Danskin had established a league table in his head. Despite his posturing, his 'don't see what you expect to see' mantra, he always did it. He wanted his best men focused on those most likely and this required a running order.

While Lyall Parker ran through the backgrounds of Molly Uzumba and Mike Cash, Danskin already had those two rooted in the relegation zone. Mid-table saw Carpenter and Wolfe, as inseparable as Brighton and Hove. At the top of the ladder sat Milton, edging out Vorster on goal difference.

All that remained, with a game in hand, was David Woods. Right on cue, Woods face appeared on screen.

'David Woods,' Parker was saying. 'An enigma. In the time we've had, we've unearthed almost nothing about his early life. We do know he's an accomplished photojournalist, first rising to prominence with National Geographic where he was twice nominated for Wildlife Photographer of the Year.'

Todd Robson let out an exaggerated yawn and stretch. Danskin took the hint. 'There's more subtle ways of doing it, but Todd's right,' the DCI interrupted. 'Cut to the chase, Lyall.'

'Not much to cut to, Sir. He got a couple of credits as a researcher on one of Attenborough's 'Life' series, Went back to National Geographic. End of.'

'Do we know what brought him to The Mercury?' Trebilcock asked.

Parker rubbed his top lip. 'Not really. He came to the North East as part of a team reporting on the local phenomena that was Freddy the Dolphin. For those of you too young to remember, Freddy was a bottle-nose dolphin who lived in and around Amble harbour in the late eighties. He, the dolphin that is, stayed for about five years. Woods stayed for much longer. He fell in love with the area, took early and semi-retirement, and settled in Newbiggin where he went off-map.'

'Fell in love with Newbiggin? Fuck me. That's not a phrase you here often. Doesn't explain how he ended up with Vorster's crew, though.'

'That's something we still don't know. Presume it's because of his photographic knowledge but, equally, it could be for his research background. Give us more time, we'll find out.'

Danskin screwed his eyes tight. Pinched the bridge of his nose. 'Freddy the Dolphin didn't end up being bombed out the water, by any chance?'

'No, sir.'

That placed Woods firmly in the lower reaches of the imaginary table. Wearily, Danskin took the stage. 'Thanks, Lyall. A good start given the timescales. Now's the time to put the meat on the bones. Ok. Here's what we do. I want all of these guys researched within an inch of their life. Put a tail on them. Ravi, get your boys on their Social Media profiles, re-run the CCTV footage of the crime scenes looking for these in particular.'

Superintendent Connor interrupted the flow. 'I don't want to lose sight of the other leads. Kinnear, I want you to work with the Bishops and follow up on the Pakistan, ETA, and any other leads that come to light, no matter how unlikely they seem.'

'Sir.'

'And,' Connor continued, 'while you guys do your stuff, I'm passing the details of the case to Imogen Markham. She's a profiler I've worked with before. I want her to determine what it is in Roadhouse's letters that triggers an attack. Look at how the perp translates her letters into target sites. We might second-guess when and where he's headed next.'

Danskin grimaced. 'A female Cracker. That's all I bloody need,' he thought. He pulled at his cuffs, outwardly ignoring the Superintendent's intentions. 'Lyall, you take a team and look into Milton. Sue, you're on Vorster.'

He searched the room for those eager to lead a strand. His eye fell on a Junior Detective. 'Alan, you got Uzumba.' He picked out Gavin O'Hara next. 'Gav, you got Carpenter and, by default, Wolfe.'

Todd Robson raised an arm in protest. Before he could speak, Danskin allocated Woods to him. Robson slumped in his seat, arms folded.

That left Cash. Conscious of Connor sat alongside him and Trebilcock in the audience, Danskin allowed the Cornishman to lead on Mike Cash.

'Thank you, sir. What about the taxi driver? Do you want me to continue investigating his death?'

The DCI had completely forgotten about McGuffie. 'For all it's worth, why not? Which reminds me: Ravi, you get anywhere with your voice machine-thingy yet?'

Sangar shook his head. 'Not yet, sir.'

'Well, add that to your list as well. I want something ASAP so we can rule it out, if nowt else.'

Hannah Graves raised an arm. 'Sir, I think I'm ready to lead a strand.'

'Hannah, you can be on standby. Next in line, so to speak. In fact, why don't you follow up on this Florence Roadhouse? Don't think there's anything in it but let's not lose sight of the possibility she has more than an indirect part in all this.'

The audience began to shuffle in anticipation of the conference end. 'Before we go, I want this to be done on the QT. No direct questioning at this stage. I don't want any of them knowing we're onto 'em. Especially,' he sought out Trebilcock, 'Cash. With his legal background, we have to be squeaky-clean. He'll be onto us like a flash if he suspects we're overstepping the mark.'

'Is it safe to put a tail on them, sir?'

Danskin rubbed a hand over the crown of his head while he thought. 'On reflection, no. Not at this point. Like I said, we do nothing to jeopardise this line of enquiry. If we get any direct threats, if there are further letters, we'll think again. Until then, good old-fashioned detective work.'

He shooed the assembled group towards the door. 'Go on, then. What you waiting for? Get yersel up to the bullpen and start work. I want results, and I want them soon.'

Over the screech of chairs and excited chatter, Danskin spoke again as the room emptied. 'Hannah. A word. In my office.'

The young detective sucked in air through closed lips, a sound like a wave retreating over a pebbled beach. She'd overstepped the mark. Hannah prepared herself for a bollocking until she saw Danskin use his eyes to motion someone to join them. Graves didn't exactly smile, but the dimple in her cheek returned.

Ryan Jarrod moved towards them.

**

The door closed behind him. He waited until the fluorescent lighting flickered to life and his pulse rate settled.

The room he stood in was a cluttered, windowless affair in the basement of The Mercury offices; a room he knew well. Two ancient metal filing cabinets stood on sentry duty either side of a desk so littered its surface appeared made from crumpled paper, post-it notes, and polystyrene Coke cups.

Features Editor Luke Padwell's workstation made the local waste recovery plant look pristine.

The man known as The Tyneside Tyrant looked around and wondered where the hell to start. He ignored Padwell's desk and began rifling through the cabinets. He tossed unmarked loose-leaf folders onto the floor. The contents spilled at his feet. The papers were in no order, without structure or logic.

'At least,' he thought, 'No-one will know I've been here.'

He knew from the On-Line calendar he had fifteen minutes until the meeting finished. Perhaps five more before Padwell made it back. He checked his watch. Twenty minutes to find a needle in a haystack, if there was a needle in the first place.

He resumed his search. Expense Invoices mingled with half-written articles. Word puzzles lay alongside pre-prepared obituaries of the living. Restaurant reviews were filed with travelogues. He'd seen better systems operating at the bottom of rock pools.

On the desk, he peeled off a chain of post-it stickers. Looked beneath the telephone. Swept away a Burger King carton. Finally, he pulled at the desk drawer. It was locked.

'Yes? Can I help you?'

He jumped at the voice behind him. 'Oh. Err, hi, Luke. You ok?'

Luke Padwell's permanently raised eyebrows bore a higher arc than normal. 'I'm fine.'

'Didn't mean to intrude. Just wanted something and I saw you were in a meeting so, um, guessed I'd better find it myself.'

'I'm sure it could have waited.'

The man clenched and unclenched his fists. 'I suppose. Sorry if I startled you.'

Padwell chuckled. 'I think you're the one that's been startled. Anyway, meeting finished early. I'm here now. What can I get you?'

There was a moments hesitation. 'I'd like to see your pending stock of Letters to the Editor.'

**

At the junction of Orchard and Forth Streets, river-side of the Central Station, The Telegraph Inn stands as a monument to pubs of yesteryear. Nineteenth century, small and intimate, only the pine flooring and pastel red and cream décor stands it apart from the spit-and-sawdust of its heyday.

The Telegraph Inn was far from the most prepossessing of locations for a first date, if that's what this was.

Hannah Graves sat in a cosy booth at the rear of the pub. She'd changed into fresh clothes taken from her locker; black high-necked top, short red and black tartan skirt over black leggings, Doc Marten boots. She'd teased a single curl over her forehead where it hung like a coiled spring.

Alongside Hannah, Ryan Jarrod wore the same jeans, T-shirt and baggy sweater he'd worn all day. He was surprised it bothered him. Less than an hour ago, he'd sat bolt upright and tense. Now he'd man-spread and sunk into the seat. While his arm wasn't around Hannah, it did lay across the wooden surround of the booth behind her. Ryan convinced himself it was the beer, but feared it was something else.

Hannah's voice brought him to reality. 'So, how do you feel about us working together?'

'Cool. A bit surprised, mind. The DCI swore me to secrecy and said only me and him should know he wanted my help. Next thing, he's handed me over to you. Anyone else know?'

'Good god, no. I guess Stephen realised he had enough on his plate leading the case. Wanted someone he could trust to work with you on his behalf?'

'You mean he doesn't trust all the team?'

Hannah chuckled. 'Not to keep their mouths shut.'

She refilled her glass from the prosecco bottle on the table. He sipped his beer. They both spoke together. They laughed. 'You first,' Ryan insisted.

'I was just wondering what you made of the team.'

'I don't make judgements. Not sure Todd Robson likes me very much, though.'

'That's Todd. He's like that with everybody.'

Ryan thought for a moment. 'Nigel doesn't seem to fit in.'

'He's the new boy in town. And, if you do happen to work with the lads again, never call him Nigel. He's Treblecock. It's all a bit clannish. You'd be thought a bit quirky if you stepped out of line. The others wouldn't like it.'

'It was me who found him, you know. The taxi driver. The one Nig... the case Treblecock's working on.'

Something in his voice drew her attention. She turned to face him. 'I know you did. It's a bit of a cliché but the first one's always the worst.'

Ryan nodded. 'Me and Frank. Found him in Pudding Chare.'

'I know.'

He pulled his mind back to the present. 'Anyway, where do you live, Hannah?'

'Got a one-bed flat in West Jesmond.'

'Nice.'

'Not if you knew how much it cost me. Still, on the bright side, I can have a wee and make a coffee without moving. What about you?'

'I'm with my dad and brother. And my dog. A pug who thinks he's a rottweiler.'

Hannah laughed. 'I had a dog when I was little. A schnauzer. Loved the bones of her, bless her. When my mam and step-dad split up, they sent her to the rescue centre. It broke my heart.'

Ryan's arm slid off the back of the booth onto her shoulder. 'They get you like that, don't they?'

'They sure do.' She reached behind her and gave his left hand an empathetic squeeze.

Reflexively, he hit her with the force of a rabbit-punch.

'Ouch.'

'Sorry, Hannah.' He waggled his padded hand in front of her. 'It's still bloody sore, you know?'

'Of course it will be. Sorry. I wasn't thinking.' After a beat, 'You've got a helluva punch on you, Ryan Jarrod. Do you work out?'

He laughed. 'No. I used to go to the gym, but not that sort of gym. I was a gymnast as a kid.'

Hannah twisted the curl at her forehead. 'Like, in a leotard and all that?'

Ryan blushed. 'Yes. In a leotard. And all that,' he said.

'How long ago?'

'I stopped about four or five years back. I'd been going since I was a kid.'

She raised her glass to her lips. Looked into his eyes. 'Why'd you give up?'

A long pause. 'Mum used to take me. She got ill. Couldn't take me any more. Then, when she passed away, dad was either too busy or couldn't be arsed to keep it up.'

Ryan felt her hand take his, ever-so-gently, over the wad of padding. 'I'm so sorry, Ry.'

His eyes misted over. 'Ry. That's what she used to call me. Sorry. It gets me, this time of year, you know?' Ryan excused himself and made for the gents.

He returned more composed but the moment – if there had been a moment – was gone. After a silence which lingered uncomfortably long, their talk reached the safe ground of the case.

'So, not only are you lumbered with me, you've got that Roadhouse woman to contend with, an aal.'

Hannah nodded. 'Nothing in that, though. You have my full attention, don't worry.'

'Aye, but you'll need to keep in touch with her all the same, just in case.'

'True. I might pop over there to see her tomorrow, actually.'

'Where's there?'

Hannah tipped the last few dregs into her glass. 'Whickham.'

'Really? Bugger me. That's where I live.'

'And you didn't know?'

Ryan flushed slightly. 'No.' A pause. 'Guess I'm not much of a detective after all.'

'Don't knock yourself, Ryan. Stephen thinks you are good detective-in-making. That's high praise, trust me. But you know what he said. Keep out the way. You're not to get involved.'

'I know, but howay man. It's my village. Never mind what Foreskin said.'

Hannah stared at him. Made her intention stone-cold. 'No. You won't. Promise me, you won't go near her. And, another thing, Ryan: please don't call the DCI 'Foreskin'. It's not nice.'

Ryan rested his head against the booth. 'Hang on a minute. I've got to call Nigel 'Treblecock', but can't call the DCI 'Foreskin'? What the hell?'

Hannah bristled. 'Just don't, ok? Stephen deserves better.'

'Stephen, is it? Not sir? Or the DCI?'

'Look, I've known him for a long time. I think the world of him, and he me. Just, Ryan – don't call him that, ok?'

Realisation dawned. Ryan pulled away from her, face contorted in disgust. He reached for his jacket. 'You and him? Ah man, Hannah, come on. He's old enough to be your dad, for fuck's sake.'

She tossed back her head and laughed, the dimple in her cheek quivering. 'Oh, Ryan; really. Of course, Stephen and I haven't. But you're right about one thing. He is old enough to be my father.'

Hannah fixed Ryan with a cold, clear stare. 'Or even my step-father. Ryan, Stephen Danskin used to be married to my mother.'

**

Alexa selected some calming, classical music for him tonight. He was no Morse, but a place existed for the classics in his collection.

Danskin sat in the high-backed leather chair, eyes closed, and rolled a glacier mint around his mouth. There was a time he'd have cradled a vodka. Often, when he found a breakthrough in a case, it'd be a bottle, not a glass, in his hand. This would have been one of those occasions. Time to release the invasiveness of the case. Time to let it all out. Time to unwind with his vodka and his family.

Danskin opened an eye. Stared at the ceiling. Lowered his gaze until it sought out the undecorated Christmas tree. Found the four cards on his windowsill. And finally settled on the photograph of Louise and Hannah Graves. Eleven-year-old Hannah sporting curly hair, a gap-toothed grin, and dimple in her cheek.

Stephen Danskin spat out the mint and went in search of his Corsodyl.

CHAPTER TWENTY-FOUR

New Year's Eve dawned crisp and bright. A cold, white sun hid behind wispy clouds like a child behind a curtain. As the city eased lazily into life, Marcus Vorster raised the day's pace.

He bid a buoyant good morning to his reception staff, hummed a discordant tune to himself in the elevator, and breezed into the meeting room unusually early with a fresh, if temporary, plan to attract new, and retain existing, readers.

Leeward Milton and David Woods were the only ones in attendance when Vorster arrived. They acknowledged Vorster's mood with the wariness of a blind dog. Sports Editor Stewart Walker took the seat alongside Woods. Suzi Mawhinney, her Christmas excesses betrayed by the fact he complexion mirrored that of an angry Alex Ferguson, arrived next. Luke Padwell, Carpenter and Wolfe waltzed in together.

Cash was rostered for duty tomorrow so that left only Molly Uzumba. The heads of department exchanged small talk while they waited for her arrival. As soon as she took her seat, Vorster rapped knuckles on the orbital table.

'Morning all. Firstly, some good news. Most of you have tomorrow off. Providing, of course, you have your copy ready for the following day.' His grin invited the others to smile, too. They didn't. Vorster cleared his throat.

'Leeward, Raymond, you other news guys: you know your focus. Stick with the Tyrant. We'll continue to run with it, but I want you to know: we're going to lighten the mood. Shift emphasis onto some good news stories. Re-energise our readership.'

'That's a change of tune,' Megan said. 'I thought you wanted to squeeze the story until it squeaked?'

'And so we will, Megan. That's why you and your friends can leave now and continue your digging. But, New Year, new beginnings. For a few days, we're giving our readers a reprieve from doom and gloom. They can have two or three days off to fill their heads with mindless trivia. Then, we come back at it like impala in season. They'll be begging for more by then, I promise.'

Milton wore a quizzical expression. Megan mouthed something to him, and the Floridian nodded in return. They all rose to leave, Woods muttering about a waste of time while Uzumba reminded Vorster he always granted them New Year's Day off anyway.

Marcus Vorster said nothing until the news team left the room. 'Ag, ignore them,' he said. 'The floor's yours today. Hit me with your plans for an uplifting New Year edition on January second. Suzi, you first.'

Mention of her name brought her out of an approaching slumber. She moistened her lips. Gave some half-baked proposition about a 'where are they now' feature on local actors and music stars with better days behind them. Rather like herself, Vorster thought, accepting the idea all the same.

'Luke. What do you suggest?'

Padwell pulled out his notepad. 'A couple of these stray into Suzi and Stewart's territories so I hope you don't object. What I had in mind was turning chunks of the content over to our readers and subscribers.'

Vorster nodded. 'Tell us more.'

'Well,' Padwell continued, 'We always have a review of the Christmas TV around this time of year. I thought we could make this a bit offbeat. Ask our readership to write the reviews. If we're not infringing any copyright, for the on-line content we could run it along the lines of Gogglebox.'

Vorster nodded again. Encouraged, Luke continued. 'And, with all the festive sport, select a few readers who've contributed to Stewart's output and see if they'd report on the January fixtures and FA Cup ties.'

'Don't have a problem with that, Luke, the Sports Editor consented. 'Happy to give you a couple of names, or I could approach them myself.'

'This is all great stuff, Luke.' He fixed Padwell with a stare. 'Anything else for us?'

'Yeah. If you're looking at a bright new beginning, how about we go overboard with the New Year's fireworks? We always cover it but get our best videographers on it, a few of the photo guys as well for the print version. Perhaps get a few of the kids who are there to do the voiceover'

'Ok, Luke. Nothing new in the fireworks but I'll buy the kiddie angle.'

'And moving forward, starting with our first edition of the year, I suggest we invite a few of our readers to write a commentary. A Carole Malone, Katie Hopkins type of column. It mightn't attract any new subscribers, but it would almost certainly ensure we retained those we've already got.'

Vorster rubbed his palms together. 'I like it. How would you kick-start it?'

'Funny you should mention that,' Padwell said, almost as if reciting a script. 'We've a regular contributor already; an inveterate letter-writer who inundates us with contributions.'

Luke Padwell opened his portfolio case and withdrew sheathes of paper. He scattered them across the table. 'As it happens, she's been particularly prolific over the last week or so. I suggest we weave all these,' he flapped his hand over the documents, 'Into a single article.'

He looked at Mawhinney, Walker and Vorster in turn.

'Lady and gentlemen, I give you our first guest columnist: one Florence Roadhouse.'

**

DCI Danskin slammed down the telephone handset as if he were hammering a nail into a fence.

'Bad news?' Lyall Parker asked.

'Aye. Nowt more than I expected.'

'Pray tell,' the Scotsman coaxed in the gentle tones of a concerned priest.

Danskin sighed. 'That was the Super. The Local Authority's refused to cancel the New Year's Eve fireworks. Connor wasn't happy but he relented. Said it gave the public a sense of normality. That we had things under control.' He let out an ironic laugh. 'If only.'

'Aye but as you say, it was expected. And they've already agreed to move it to Exhibition Park from the Quayside. It's not a built-up area. There'll be nowhere to plant anything.'

'I know that, Lyall. I'm not stupid.'

'And there's been nothing in The Mercury. We've no reason to suspect our man will change his MO. Relax. It'll be ok. Kinnear's men will polis it. We can get on with our day job.'

Danskin reluctantly agreed. 'It's still something else for us to worry about, Lyall.' He wheeled his chair to the door of his office. 'Ravi. Get your arse in here a minute, will you? I need an update.'

Ravi Sangar stifled a yawn as he entered. 'Sorry, sir. Been up most the night working on the voice recordings.'

'And?'

Sangar shook his head.

'Ah man. Not exactly Professor Higgins, are you? What's taking so long? You were confident your machine could crack it.'

'It can, sir. And it will. One theory we're exploring is that the accent isn't local. Or, even British.'

Danskin became alert. 'American? That leads us straight to Milton.'

Only Parker dared correct Danskin in the manner he did. 'Sir, don't see what you expect to see, remember. What if it's Asian? Takes us back to the Pakistani connection or, more likely, South African. Leads us back to Vorster.'

Chastened, Danskin sank down in his chair. 'Shit. You're right. Or, it could be a restaurant worker from Chinatown. Or a foreign student. Or Mork from the Planet Ork. Bollocks. Ok, Ravi. Get back on it, mate.'

'Sir.'

'Oh, Ravi. We haven't missed anything, have we? I mean, there's nothing hidden away in the On-Line Mercury content about tonight's fireworks. No e-mails from Florence Roadhouse?'

'I've already checked. Nothing from Roadhouse.' He hesitated. 'But they do intend to live-stream the display tonight. They often do, but Vorster's giving it the big build up today.'

'Still as confident, Lyall?' Danskin pinched his lower lip between thumb and index finger. 'Who's Vorster sending to cover it, do we know? Tell me it's not the news guys, for God's sake.'

Sangar wavered. 'Carpenter and Woods seem to be allocated, sir.'

'Shit-a-brick'

He dashed into the bullpen. 'O'Hara. Robson. Where've you got with your two?'

Gavin O'Hara spoke first. 'We've had Carpenter checked out. His Social media presence is restricted to professional content. He's got no personal accounts on Instagram, twitter or Facebook. Ravi's boys had no CCTV sightings of his car at any of the locations. Of course, he might have parked out of camera range.'

'Hire car?' Danskin interrupted.

'None, sir. Not in his own name, at least. That's as far as I've got. Nothing to link him to owt.'

Danskin's attention shifted to Robson. 'I know you started with a blank sheet of paper on Woods. What you got on him?'

'To be honest, nothing significant, sir. He's still a man of mystery but there's nothing suspicious to date. I found a brief bio about him in National Geographic from way back, and that's all we've got.'

'What did it say, man. I need to know.'

'He's an orphan. Left on the doorstep of a pub as a baby.'

'Where?'

Robson breathed in. 'I thought you'd ask me that.' His face underwent a series of contortions as he rehearsed the words. 'Wirey Drug,' he mumbled.

'Where?'

'Wirey drug. That's what it says here.' He waved a sheet of paper beneath Danskin's face.

'Yr Wyddgrug, you knacker-heed' Danskin thrust the page back into Robson's hands.

Robson looked affronted. 'That's what I said. Wirey drug.'

'Yr Wyddgrug is the Welsh name for the town of Mold.'

'So why didn't he say Mold?'

Danskin rolled his eyes. 'Because they're Welsh, that's why.'

'Well, they shouldn't be.'

Danskin fought to restrain himself. 'Any other pearls of wisdom, Todd?'

'The only thing it says about him is that he had a place in University of Wales Institute of Science and technology. It's now part of Cardiff University. Woods enrolled to the Biosciences department. It also says he joined Geographic after a brief stint working in...' He dithered. Shot a sheepish glance between Danskin and Parker. He decided against the facial contortions and settled for, 'Some other Welsh town.'

'Doesn't sound suspicious to me,' Danskin concluded.

'Unless he's got a Welsh accent,' Ravi Sangar interjected, remembering his theory about the McGuffie tape.

'Anyone know if he has?' Danskin barked. 'If not, find out. He must have done some piece to camera for the on-line content. Ball's in your court again, Todd.'

Lyall Parker, as ever the voice of reason, brought calm to the room. 'Let's think this through. The Mercury always covers the firework display. It makes sense they'd send a photographer like Woods to cover it. Vorster will want a news presence there, too, just in case. If we're thinking it could be targeted, so will he. So, I don't think we should get over-excited about Carpenter being there, either.'

Danskin, Robson and O'Hara nodded their agreement.

'Besides, there's no Florence Roadhouse connection. Exhibition Park will have Rick Kinnear and his Bishop laddies all over the place. I think we need to keep it in perspective. On balance, I'd say we're worrying about nothing.'

The DCI gritted his teeth. 'You're probably right, Lyall.' He looked around the bullpen. Picked out one of his detectives. 'What you got planned for tonight?'

'I was planning on doing a bit of,' the detective hesitated, 'Research.'

Danskin understood. 'Sorry, Hannah. Call off your 'research.' You can do that tomorrow. Get it?'

Hannah gave a resigned smile. 'I'll make some calls, sir.'

'Good. Because tonight, you and I are off to see some fireworks.'

**

Marcus Vorster spent the evening the way he'd spent every New Year's Eve for as long as he could remember. Dressed in tux, frill-fronted shirt and dicky-bow, he strode into the casino as if he were in Monte Carlo, not some anonymous franchise at the foot of St James' Boulevard.

He'd ignored the stares and sniggers as he took a stool at the roulette table. He'd played a reverse martingale all evening and it had proved unusually profitable. A crowd gathered around the table, watching as Vorster accumulated win after win.

Midnight approached. There were no clocks in the casino, but Vorster knew. A flotilla of waitresses had sailed out from an entrance marked Private and stood lined against a wall clutching silver trays laden with champagne flutes.

The croupier prepared for the final spin of the year; a year Vorster had grown to love. His book deal was signed and sealed, The Mercury was flourishing and, as a result, the stipend from his father's legacy would be bountiful.

The waitresses began to move amongst the guests as twelve o'clock approached. Vorster looked up. In the crowd around the table, he caught the eye of a blonde in short red dress.

'Ag, what the hell,' Vorster said. He pushed his chips – all of them – onto red twelve.

Even as the croupier spun the wheel one way and launched the ball in the opposite direction, Vorster left his seat and made for the bathroom.

**

During daylight hours, the Town Moor is a vast green ocean lapping against the concrete shores of Newcastle upon Tyne. At night, it appears as a giant black hole amidst a sky of twinkling stars of streetlight.

Tonight, its southernmost tip was a swathe of humanity huddled together for warmth. Stephen Danskin and Hannah Graves squeezed through the crowds in Exhibition Park; Hannah relaxed, Stephen less so.

'It's going to be ok. Look, we've uniforms all over the place. No-one's going to try anything,' she said.

'You're probably right, Hannah.' His eyes darted back and forth as if in REM sleep. 'But I have to be here, you know that.'

Hannah nodded in the darkness. 'I know.' After a delay, she asked, 'How are you? I mean, really.'

'If I'm honest, I feel like shite. I hate this time of year. Ever since you and your mam…' his voice trailed off as they passed a trio of uniform colleagues, relieved not to continue the sentence. 'And with all this going on, I don't know, Hannah. I feel everything's out of control. But I can't let it show.' He glanced at his stepdaughter. 'Except to you.'

She brushed her hand against his, the only display of affection they were allowed. A few more PCs passed. They acknowledged one another with imperceptible nods.

A sound system rigged over the arched entrance to the park played music from the year's blockbuster films. Almost imperceptibly, the score faded; the symphony replaced by a human voice counting down to the midnight hour.

'Ten, nine, eight.'

Danskin tensed. Not twenty yards in front of him, Raymond Carpenter stood, a microphone thrust under the nose of an exuberant child.

The crowd joined in the countdown.

'Seven, six.'

A sense of expectancy sucked oxygen from the air. Danskin held his breath, his hands bunched into fists deep within his coat pockets, his eyes fixed on the back of Raymond Carpenter.

'Five, four.'

Folk folded their arms in front of them. Grabbed the hands of strangers. Waited for Auld Lang Syne to strike up.

'Three, two.'

Danskin heard shouts. Children shrieked. The DCI tensed. Were they cries of excitement, or something more urgent?

'One.'

Danskin reflexively screwed his eyes tight shut. A loud eruption rent the air. The DCI jumped. Hannah sensed the movement alongside her and reached out to him.

The explosions multiplied. The sky lit fiery red. Golden yellow freckles sprayed outwards. Shouts drowned out the thunderous blasts.

Danskin swayed, wreathed in sweat. He forced open his eyes. Azure bows spread over the horizon, a rat-a-tat machine gun fire of white stars detonating within them.

'Happy New Year,' Hannah whispered.

As the fireworks reached their crescendo, Danskin muttered 'Happy New Year my arse.'

**

In a cubicle in the Gents toilets of the Grosvenor Casino, Marcus Vorster spread a line along the cistern; his first line of the year.

He heard the bathroom door open at the same moment he inhaled. He listened, glassy-eyed, as footsteps approached the cubicle. It didn't matter. The door was locked.

Wasn't it?

It wasn't.

'Shit, shit, shit.' Vorster hurriedly swept up his kit as the door swung open, the way a gunslinger enters a saloon.

He turned. Framed in the doorway stood a blonde in a short red dress. She was older than he'd thought. Much older.

'You just hit the jackpot,' she leered.

Vorster didn't know if she referred to the spin or to her. With the cocaine fresh within him, he didn't really care. Especially when she pushed him down onto the seat, hitched her dress above her waist, and straddled him.

In an office two miles to the east, the feed from the camera hidden in a brooch pinned to a red dress went dead.

The voyeur scratched at a Hopi sun tattoo.

'Gotcha.'

Megan Wolfe punched the air.

CHAPTER TWENTY-FIVE

The worst part of being alone is that nothing ever happens. And, when it does, there's no-one to tell.

Florence Roadhouse put down her telephone convinced it was a scam. The caller had left a number and asked her to call back so she could confirm his identity. Florence had read about such things in her newspapers; how dialing the number sent you half-way around the world and charged an exorbitant connection fee.

Yet, the number provided began with the local 0191 code. She thought for a moment, then went for it.

'Ah, Miss Roadhouse. I'm so pleased you called.' It was the voice she'd spoken to a few moments earlier.

Still suspicious, she asked, 'And you are?'

The voice laughed. 'I'm still Luke Padwell, same as I was two minutes ago. And I still work for The Mercury, and yes – I know it's New Year's Day and I should be on holiday.'

Florence relaxed the grip on the handset. Felt blood flow to her fingers. 'Mr Padwell, you've convinced me.'

Padwell's voice crackled up the line. 'I'm pleased. So, Miss Roadhouse, do I have your permission to use your letters as the basis of a full page-spread in tomorrow's edition? It would, of course, appear under your name, as if you'd written it. You'd get full credit for it, and you'd be paid our standard fee.'

Florence wasn't interested in the money, but she did have a question. 'Mr Padwell, you have my permission on one condition. I don't like the way you said it would appear as if I'd written it. I DID write it, young man. You do not change a word of what I wrote. Not a single syllable; do you understand?'

Padwell laughed heartily. 'You're no-one's mug, are you? Yes, of course, Miss Roadhouse. The article will be entirely your work. I may edit it, but I won't change any of it. You have my word.'

Florence smiled. 'In that case, I look forward to seeing it. Tomorrow, you say?'

Padwell confirmed the agreement, they exchanged pleasantries, and he ended the call leaving her alone once more. Florence Roadhouse sighed. She had no-one to share in her excitement.

Her eyes lit up. 'Yes, I have.'

It was only a short walk, but she wrapped up for it as if she were Captain Oates stepping out for some time.

**

Ryan hooked his coat off the back of the door at the same moment the bell rang.

'Hi. Sorry about cancelling yesterday. Work stuff.' The voice muffled by a thick black scarf was that of Hannah Graves. 'Thought I'd pop round to apologise. It happens all the time in our work but it's never nice.'

'There is such a thing as a telephone, you know. You didn't have to come all the way over here to say sorry. A quick call would've done, man.'

'Confession time. I'm really here to chat to Florence Roadhouse but she's not in. You're second choice, I'm afraid.' She stamped her feet. 'Anyway, aren't you going to invite me in? It's Baltic out here.'

Ryan hesitated. His father was in the lounge, stretched out on the sofa clad only in a dressing gown and yesterday's boxers while Jam Jar picked his nose in front of Clubland TV. Even Spud was less than welcoming, slurping noisily at his bits.

Ryan thrust his arms into his coat. 'I'm on my way out. Howay, come with me.'

She linked his arm. 'Where we going?'

'Not far. I need to visit Gran. She's got dementia,' he explained matter-of-factly.

They made innocuous small talk as they walked. 'I'm off duty tomorrow if you'd like to spend some time together. I'd like to make up for yesterday,' Hannah finally asked.

Ryan shook his head. 'No can do. I've got an appointment at the hospital to see about my hands.' A slight pause. 'And things.' He was grateful she didn't pick up on it.

'Some other time, then?'

He nodded; the silence awkward. He was pleased when they arrived at 122 The Drive. 'Just a word,' he said as he knocked on the door. 'Gran can be a bit funny at times. Don't correct her, please. Just go along with it.'

When the door opened, Hannah's jaw lolled open. She eyed Ryan with suspicion. 'Your Gran? You said you didn't know her. What's going on, Ryan?'

Before he could reply, Hannah flashed her warrant card. 'I'm Detective Constable Hannah Graves. I wonder if I could have a quick word with you, Miss Roadhouse?'

It was Ryan's turn to wear the astonished look. 'Seriously? This is Florence Roadhouse? Bugger me. She's my gran's friend. I didn't know.'

It felt odd, to be outside his own grandmother's house yet feel the need to be welcomed inside. As if reading his mind, Florence Roadhouse stood aside. 'You'd better come in.' Then, as an afterthought, 'This about your brother again, is it?'

Hannah gave Ryan another look. 'No, Miss Roadhouse. It's about you.'

Once inside, Ryan introduced Hannah to Doris Jarrod as 'his friend'. Nothing registered with her. He sat alongside his grandmother and took her hand in a silence broken by Florence.

'Are you going to tell me why you're here, Miss Graves?'

'Ryan,' Hannah said. 'Make a cup of tea for your grandmother and her friend, please.'

He looked at her, eyes wide. 'What?'

She smiled, but there was no dimple. 'Remember what the DCI said. You're not to get involved.'

'But this is different. This is my gran's.'

'Then, make her some tea. Now. Then, tidy up. Wash the dishes. Go to the loo. Just keep out the way.'

Florence Roadhouse watched the exchange. 'I'd do what she says, if I were you. Your lady friend isn't one to mess with, are you sweetheart?'

Ryan made his way to the kitchen, tail between his legs.

Hannah felt blindsided by the old woman's candour and perception, instinct telling her to be wary. 'Miss Roadhouse, you'll be aware of the incidents in and around the city which have caught everyone's attention.'

'Of course.'

'Have you ever been to any of the places affected? Recently, I mean.'

Florence Roadhouse laughed. 'I'm a bit old for student life, dear. And while I do like a spot of Wimbledon, you don't really think I'd follow football, do you?'

'Yet, you do write about them.'

Florence's reply was drowned out by a rattle of teacups and the sound of a boiling kettle.

'Sorry, I didn't catch that.'

'I said, I'm not sure I do write about them. What are you getting at, young lady?'

Hannah changed tack. 'Do you know anyone who works for The Mercury news corporation?'

'Good heavens, no. I like the newspaper. It makes me feel like I belong to the community. I correspond with them, and they're good enough to..' she stopped as Ryan emerged from the kitchen carrying a tea cup in his better hand. He repeated the act twice more. The interruption gave Florence time to think.

'As I was saying, they're good enough to publish some of my letters. Is that you meant by writing, Miss Graves?'

Ryan lurked by the doorway. Hannah shooed him away and drew an eye-roll in response.

'Please, carry on, Miss Roadhouse.'

'So, to that extent, yes I do 'know' them. But, I've never spoken to anyone. At least, not until this morning.'

Hannah tried not to let her voice show emotion. 'This morning?'

'Yes. Someone called me this morning.'

'Who? Who called you?' She prayed she'd here the name 'Vorster', or 'Milton', or one of the others she was familiar with. This, she thought, was the breakthrough.

'Luke Padwell.'

Hannah Graves let out the breath she'd been holding. 'Who?'

'Luke Padwell. At least, that's what he said.' She straightened herself in her chair, shook with pride. 'He wants me to write a column for the newspaper. In fact, I've already written it. They're going to print it tomorrow.'

Hannah no longer cared that Ryan had returned to the room, pretending to administer medication to his grandmother. Hannah closed her eyes as she asked the next question.

'Miss Roadhouse, this is really important. What did you write about?'

**

'He's gone missing, Sir.'

Danskin fixed Nigel Trebilcock with a glacial stare. 'No he hasn't. You just haven't found him yet.'

'Sir, Padwell's mobile's switched off. He hasn't been seen since this morning. The last call to his office phone came from Florence Roadhouse; exactly as Hannah reported. No-one's seen him since. Unless you want us to bring everyone from The Mercury in for interrogation, it's a loose lead.'

'You know we haven't got enough manpower for that. Plus, it would alert them. Get Sangar onto it. As soon as The Mercury even thinks about downloading Roadhouse's burblings, I want to know what it is. I don't want Connor's profiler to spread her runes over it and come up with a load of crap. This is our case. We'll crack it.'

Trebilcock went off in search of Sangar.

'This is it, Lyall. Shit or bust.'

Parker agreed. 'Dangerous game, Stephen. For what it's worth, I agree with you. We need to get the bugger red-handed. Catch him at the scene, at least.'

'Thanks, Lyall. It means a lot. Let's hope Connor feels the same way.'

Danskin took a second to absorb what had to be done. 'I need you and Sue to find out where Milton and Vorster have been in the last twenty-four hours. Get the lads doing the same for their watches. I want to know what they had for breakfast and how long it took to shit it out.'

Almost to himself, he said, 'We can't afford to bollocks this up, mate. We really can't.'

**

Ryan called in a favour from an old schoolfriend. Ashok worked in the Jamdani restaurant on Whickham's Front Street and said he'd squeeze them in around seven. Any later was impossible, he'd told him. When she'd rang to cancel, Ryan was disappointed but not surprised. Work, as always, took precedence. Especially at this stage of the investigation.

To his surprise and delight, he answered the doorbell's chime at nine thirty to find Hannah on his doorstep, a takeaway bag from the Moti Jheel held aloft in one hand, a four-pack of Cobra in the other.

'You're not angry at me, are you? For cancelling, I mean?'

He smiled. 'Of course not. I thought you might at least have got the carry-out from the Jamdani, mind, but I'm touched you've come all this way at this time. Besides, didn't you know, Ryan Jarrod doesn't get angry.'

She brushed past him, dimple puckering her cheek.

By the time he'd devoured a chicken dupiaza, her a vegetable balti, and Spud a spare popadom, it neared midnight. He told her he'd take the sofa and offered her his bed. Hannah let her eyes linger on him in an unspoken invitation.

'Honestly, Hannah. I'll be fine down here,' he mumbled.

Disappointment showed in her face. 'The perfect gentleman,' she whispered.

Time to come clean. 'It's not that I don't want to, you know. But,' he held up his hands, 'Thing is, it's not just these.'

She put a finger to his lips, mistaking the cause of his embarrassed blush. 'I know. Your dad and brother are in the house. It's fine. I have to be at the station early anyway. Goodnight, Ryan.'

Ryan silently cursed the superficial burns to his groin when they kissed a little too long and a lot too passionately.

**

'I didn't think you meant this early.' Ryan sat up and struggled to focus sleep-stuck eyes.

'MetroCentre. That's the next target. Today,' Hannah explained breathlessly as she hopped on one foot while pulling on her shoes.

'What? How?'

'I need your car. I won't get a cab in time. Give me the keys.'

'I'm coming, too.'

'No chance. You know what Danskin said.'

'I don't care what he said. It's virtually on my doorstep. I'm coming with you.'

She didn't have time to argue. The Uno chugged reluctantly into life after weeks of inactivity. The journey downhill was short and quick, but not fast enough for Hannah Graves. On the way, she barely had time to tell Ryan that Danskin had called her to say there were a string of targets but Imogen Markham, the profiler, was certain the prime target was the MetroCentre.

'Surely it won't be today? There's always a few days before he strikes,' Ryan asked as they clambered from the vehicle.

'Markham thinks not. She fears he'll up his game. Says he'll know it's only a matter of time before he's caught so he'll wreak as much havoc as he can.'

Hannah flashed her ID at a security guard who forced open the sealed automatic doors for them. They raced through the deserted mall, their footsteps echoing around the cavernous interior. Hannah took a sharp right at the Muffin Break coffee shop, and spotted Stephen Danskin ahead of her.

The DCI heard them coming. Urged them to hurry. Todd Robson and Nigel Trebilcock were already there, along with a woman Hannah didn't recognise.

Danskin glowered at Ryan. 'What's he doing here?' He didn't wait for a response. 'Ok. This is what we know. For reasons best known to himself, Vorster's handed over a whole page of The Mercury to Florence Roadhouse.'

Hannah and Ryan already knew. They guessed Todd, Trebilcock and the woman did, too, so Hannah urged Stephen to cut to the chase.

'Historically, the bomber seems to act on one out of three or four of Roadhouse's letters. In today's paper, she rants about commercialism, housing, immigration, and Social Services. Four subjects. One will be hit next.'

He looked at the woman. 'Ms Markham here suspects the MetroCentre is the primary target.'

The woman, tall, late thirties, long fair hair, jumped in. 'It was the lead subject in the article and hitting this place has the biggest impact, capture the public's fears and, more importantly, offers maximum publicity coverage. If you're right about it being part of The Mercury's rise, this is the place he'll go for.'

The impromptu conference paused while the attendees took in the information before Danskin continued.

'I'm not putting all our eggs in one basket.' He shot Markham a look of contempt. 'We've got the firearms squad at the airport with sniffers, and helicopters buzzing the ferry port in case he follows the immigration line. Lyall Parker's heading them up with support from HMRC and security services.'

He licked spittle from his lips. Checked his watch. 'Sue Nairn's increased security levels at and around both the Civic Centre and Gateshead Toon Hall. Gavin's with her along with a load of uniforms at both locations. We've dog patrols making sure no-one gets in.'

'And we're here,' Todd Robson stated the obvious. 'What are we gannin to do?'

'We get the place locked down for the day, that's what we do. And wait for the bomb squad to get here from Catterick Garrison.'

Todd's eyebrows arched. Hannah's jaw fell open. Ryan though he'd stepped onto the set of 24.

'And,' Danskin continued, seeing a figure approach, 'We talk to this bloke.'

A man in his mid-forties approached, running his hand through bed-hair. He wore a dapper suit but his off-centre tie looked as if it had been hurriedly fastened on route from PE to double Physics.

'I'm Graeme Foster, Duty Centre Manager. What's going on?'

He rubbed his forehead while Danskin recounted the bare minimum of detail. Only when Danskin instructed the man to lockdown the mall did Foster react.

'No way, Jose. Nope. Not happening.'

'Listen, pal. There's no way you're opening this place today.'

'And I'm telling you, Inspector, this our second biggest day of the year. I'm not shutting this place based on some cock and bull theory.'

Stephen looked away for a split second then spun back, his hand grasping Foster around the throat. 'Listen to yourself, man,' he hissed. 'You sound like the fucking Mayor of Amity.'

'Let me go. Please.'

'I will. But this place isn't opening until it's been searched.'

Foster massaged his throat. 'Who's doing the search?'

'We are. There's a couple of dozen PCs on their way to assist, and a trio of sniffer dogs.'

The man laughed incredulously. 'A couple of dozen?'

'And three dogs.'

'Have you the slightest idea how long it will take to search the second biggest mall in Europe? Almost two hundred thousand square metres with a couple of dozen men. Oh, I forgot. And three beagles.'

Danskin's face told Foster he'd never considered it. The Duty Manager spread out his arms. Pirouetted three hundred and sixty degrees. 'DCI Danskin,' he said, 'You're gonna need a bigger boat.'

Todd Robson massaged his knuckles whilst Foster picked himself up from the floor and held his jaw. 'I'll sue you for that.'

'You slipped,' Danskin said. 'One of the perils of your cleaners doing such a good job on the floor. I bet you don't pay them enough. Cheap labour, I bet. In fact, are you sure they're all legal?'

'You can't hang that one on me. I've nothing to do with recruitment. Look, DCI Danskin, I can't do what you ask. It's too late to stop people travelling. The A1's clogged at the best of times on our busy days. It'll be gridlock – quite literally – if you shut this place down.'

Danskin was about to speak again but Ryan interrupted him. 'Sir. He has a point. I don't mean we should let it open. Definitely not. But he's right about the roads. It'll be carnage. You mentioned the bomb disposal team. The lads will never get through the traffic; not in time. It'll be solid from Washington services.'

'Fuck.' Danskin sagged back against the Disney Store windows. 'Shit, fuck, bollocks.' He closed his eyes. Took several deep breaths.

When he opened his lids, he looked upwards. Giant-sized portraits of historic local figures looked down at him from their position on the Platinum Mall balcony.

George Stephenson: *'Father of the Railways'*, the banner alongside proclaimed.

Danskin's brow furrowed as he tried to unscramble his thoughts.

Grace Darling: *'Heroine of the Farne Isles'*.

Something he'd said lurked like a rat in the shadows of his mind.

Joseph W Swan: *'Let there be light.'*

He scrambled to his feet.

'You're fucking wrong,' he screamed at Imogen Markham. 'We're in the wrong place.'

CHAPTER TWENTY-SIX

Derwent Tower, a twenty-nine story edifice of brutalist concrete, dominated the Tyne Valley skyline. Built over poor ground on a sunken caisson foundation, it required the support of four external flying buttresses rising from ground level to the fifth floor.

Its resemblance to an Apollo spacecraft tethered to its launchpad meant the tower was universally known as the Dunston Rocket.

The Rocket had seen better days. Consistent lift failures, the cost of maintenance to its crumbling exterior and vandal-plagued interior meant only five of its floors remained occupied; a council-funded haven for refugees the world over.

From his position not two miles away in the MetroCentre car park, Stephen Danskin stared at The Rocket's looming menace. Behind him, Ryan Jarrod, Hannah Graves, Robson and Trebilcock followed his gaze. Imogen Markham steadfastly refused to lift her eyes from the tarmac.

'We need to get there. He's going for The Rocket,' Danskin urged.

'What? How do you make that one out?' Hannah asked.

'It's obvious. I should have got it as soon as I wound up Foster about his cleaning staff.'

Hannah moved a hand above her head. 'You've lost me.'

Imogen Markham provided the response. 'I believe the DCI's right. Don't you see? It ticks all the boxes in Roadhouse's article. It's used to house refugees; the immigrants she writes about. A number of them work here, which hits the commercialism button.'

'The cleaners. Immigrants who work here,' Danskin said by way of explanation.

'And,' Markham continued, 'it stood virtually empty for years when it could have offered social housing. I was wrong about Social Services. I was wrong about most things.'

Nigel Trebilcock began to speak but was cut short. They experienced a sensation, as if they were in a moving elevator. The sensation increased. Became a tremor which ran through their core; a deep bass thud in their chest. Then, they heard it. A rumble. Faint at first, it grew in intensity like the approach of stampeding buffalo.

Ryan was the first to recognise it. 'Oh my God. We're too late. The Rocket's going.'

They watched, transfixed, as a plume of dust and rubble rose in a grim cloud. It shrouded the lower floors, swirling and growing in density until The Rocket appeared to have lift-off.

Except The Rocket didn't rise. Instead, it folded in on itself as the explosion ripped out the loadbearing capacity of the tower's ground floor. The levels above – still intact - collapsed with an apocalyptic thunder, gaining downward velocity until they met resistance from the floors below.

The entire structure collapsed in a series of pancake-like layers.

Todd Robson spoke first. 'Shit the bed.'

Nigel Trebilcock swallowed hard. Pale-faced, he opened his mouth to speak. No words came. He cleared his throat. 'Sir,' he said, 'We've men in there.'

It took Danskin a moment to process the words. 'We've what?'

Tears welled in Trebilcock's eyes. 'I commandeered a couple of PCs from the duty roster to do some door to door. They'll be in there now.'

Danskin spoke slowly. Quietly. 'What the fuck for?'

'The McGuffie case. I had a tip-off someone who worked in the taxi office the night he went missing might have lived in The Rocket.'

'Ilona Popescu,' Ryan whispered.

Trebilcock gave a look of astonishment. 'How do you know?'

'Never mind that,' Danskin snapped. 'Who were they? Ours or the Bishops?'

'I don't know. I just picked a couple of names. Does it matter?'

Through gritted teeth, Danskin hissed, 'It matters to me. Names.'

Trebilcock tried to clear his mind. Eventually, he came up with, 'Keith Dyson.'

Stephen Danskin closed his eyes. 'One of ours. I'm sure he's just become a father.' They took a moment to reflect. 'And the other?'

When Trebilcock said the name, Ryan felt a knife plunge bowel-deep.

'A Frank Burrows, sir.'

**

The moment David Woods pressed the shutter, he knew he had an award winner.

Woods lay flat on his back, caked in grime like a commando on a night reconnaissance mission. His camera pointed skywards. Framed In the lower left third of shot, a mountain of rubble represented the remnants of Derwent Tower.

Through a comet trail of falling debris, a sleek navy blue and yellow police helicopter hovered against a battleship grey sky. The Eurocopter E-165 formed the centrepiece of Woods' image.

In the distance, deliberately out of focus, his shot captured the approach of two more helicopters. They, too, had been deployed from the Port of Tyne terminal where they'd been stationed. Top right of frame, a vibrant orange air ambulance approached at an angle.

It had to be the best image he'd ever taken, and he was so self-absorbed in his work he didn't notice a fleet of vehicles screech to a halt on Ravensworth Road.

DCI Stephen Danskin leapt from the first, followed by Todd Robson and Nigel Trebilcock. They barrelled their way through a crowd of stunned locals. Hannah Graves and an ashen-faced Ryan Jarrod emerged from a dirty white Fiat Uno. Imogen Markham remained in the back seat of the Uno, face pressed against the window in the style of Spud the pug.

Fire, ambulance and police vehicles hurtled towards the scene in a kaleidoscope of flashing lights and cacophonous sirens. A cavalcade of other vehicles arrived.

'Get a cordon set up,' Danskin ordered. 'This is a SOC. No-one gets in unless wearing uniform or with ID.'

Todd Robson saw him first. 'We're too late. Look.'

Danskin followed the line of Robson's arm. Saw a prostrate figure. 'We haven't got time to tend to casualties. Leave that to the paramedics.'

'It's not a casualty, man. It's a frigging journalist. It's my man. That's David Woods.'

'How the hell's he here already? We were only a couple of miles away,' Danskin said, immediately promoting Woods to the upper echelons of his imaginary league table of suspects. 'Get him away from there. Now.'

Todd sprang into action. He sprinted towards the prone figure, hurdling chunks of masonry, dodging the boulders which littered his path. Robson clambered up a four-foot cement hillock, prepared to leap from its summit, then stumbled as his weight precipitated a mini-avalanche. Robson's leg gave way beneath him with a sickening crack.

'Fuuuck.' He glanced down. His foot had turned one-hundred-and-eighty degrees and faced the direction he'd come from. He swallowed down bile. 'Jesus Christ, man.'

A figure hurdled him. Nigel Trebilcock. 'Stay down. He's mine.'

'Leave him, Treblecock. Let him be.' Danskin shouted the words to ensure he was heard above the backdrop of wailing sirens and the whump-whump of chopper blades.

Trebilcock skidded to a halt like Scooby Doo confronted by the phantom Black Knight. He turned to face Danskin and instantly understood the order.

A fleet of vans had arrived on the scene. Press vans. Men and women climbed from them, cameras attached to headbands. Megan Wolfe instantly made for the prone Woods, caught on camera in the role of the heroic pressman risking life and limb to bring his story to his audience.

Mike Cash strolled to Danskin. 'A wise decision. Wouldn't go down too well if one of your men was seen to interfere with press freedom.'

'Press freedom my hairy backside. How the hell did you get here so quickly? How did Woods get here even quicker? He was on the scene before us yet we were only a couple of miles away.'

'We have our sources,' Cash replied. 'They're obviously better than your own informers.'

Danskin clenched both fists by his sides. 'Strange how you lot are always first on the scene, though.'

Cash looked affronted. 'I hope you're not insinuating anything, Detective Chief Inspector.'

A car swerved onto the pavement in front of them, its approach masked by the sound of the descending air ambulance. Lyall Parker heard enough of the exchange. 'Press or nae press, you need to get your folk behind the cordon. This is a crime scene. Move it.'

Mike Cash withdrew and beckoned Megan Wolfe to follow. Wolfe shook her head, a wild look in her eyes. Carpenter stood alongside her like a faithful puppy, studying her with his eyes.

'I know who's doing this,' she said, her words tumbling from her; hoarse, breathless, and sexy. 'Raymond, I know who it is. And, when I've got the evidence, I'm going to screw him over with the greatest of pleasure.'

'You do? Who is it?' Carpenter asked.

Wolfe shook her head. 'It's my story. No-one's getting in on it, least of all you.' She pulled her hair in her hands, fighting against the chopper blade's downdraft. 'Once it breaks, not only have I the story of the millennium, but I've also got him by the balls so tight they're squeaking. I've film of him up to all sorts.'

Carpenter smiled. 'Up to your old tricks again?'

'You bet I am. And I tell you something else. When it's done, I'm going to need to unwind. Big style.'

Raymond Carpenter knew what that meant. He looked like the cat who'd got the entire dairy.

**

In the first-floor breakout area of the Forth Banks police HQ, Ryan sat head bowed, staring into the swirls of curdled coffee. He clasped his hands together, his better hand toying with a strand of bandage which hung loose from the other.

Alongside him, Hannah's silence offered support.

A sound, more than a sigh but not quite a sob, escaped Ryan's lips. 'I liked the miserable old sod. I mean, I really liked him. And you know what, I didn't even tell him.'

Hannah laid a hand on his forearm. 'I'm sure he knew, Ryan. I didn't have much to do with Frank but I reckon he'd be really proud of you.'

'You really think so? I'd like that.'

He retreated to the silence of the cocoon he'd built around himself.

Hannah looked up as Stephen Danskin made a tentative approach. He raised a questioning eyebrow. She shook her head.

Danskin placed a hand on Ryan's shoulder as he spoke to Hannah, his tone gentle. 'I need you upstairs. The rest are waiting for you.'

Hannah studied Ryan. 'Will you be ok?'

He gave a snort. It might have been an ironic laugh. 'Got to be, haven't I?'

Danskin scratched his jaw. 'Look, do you want to listen in?' he asked.

Ryan glanced up with doleful eyes. 'I don't need your sympathy, sir.'

'Son, I don't do sympathy. What, with Robson doing his leg in and all, I reckon we could do with a spare pair of hands.' He glanced at Ryan's bandages. 'Even if they are pretty useless, by the looks of 'em.'

The bad-taste joke drew a wan smile. 'That reminds me. I've missed my out-patient's appointment now. I've got nowt else on, so why not?'

'A word of warning. You need to keep a check on your emotions. Can't let emotions get in the way in this job. Understand?'

Ryan met Danskin's stare. Kept eye-contact with the DCI. 'I promise you, sir. Nothing's going to get in the way; not until Frank's killer's locked up.'

He stood as he continued talking. 'I'm not emotional. At least, not in the way you mean.'

Ryan's chair screeched as he pulled it away.

'Ryan Jarrod's just got angry.'

CHAPTER TWENTY-SEVEN

The Mercury On-Line coverage of the Derwent Tower incident played in a continuous loop on a wall-mounted plasma screen. A dozen or more detectives clustered around it in a horseshoe.

DCI Danskin watched from the back of the group for a couple of minutes before taking command. 'What does this coverage tell us about The Mercury's staff?'

Lyall Parker answered the question. 'Once again, they're first on the scene. Quicker than humanly possible without prior knowledge.'

Danskin agreed. 'We already knew that, even before Cash admitted they'd had a so-called tip-off. I never expected him to reveal how they came across the information and he didn't disappoint. Media men won't reveal a source even as you clamp the electrodes to their gonads. Especially if the source came from within their own ranks.'

On screen, the videographers captured the aftermath of the building's collapse in close-up glory, never missing an opportunity to include shots of their own in action. It left no-one in any doubt: this is The Mercury's baby. As good as any copyright.

'No sign of Vorster,' someone commented.

'Nah. Not significant. He's not a field reporter. Never has been. But, unless the device was detonated on-site, it doesn't necessarily put him in the clear,' Danskin explained. 'Sue, he's your man. What you got on him over the last couple of days?'

The group dragged their attention from the screen towards DS Nairn. 'As you instructed, sir, we haven't tailed him. What we do know, though, is that he spent New Year's Eve at the Grosvenor Casino. Seems he was on a winning streak. He was well up, and I mean massively so, until just before midnight when he staked his entire pot on a straight-up bet.'

Danskin interrupted. 'For the uninitiated, that's a bet on a single number, right?'

'Yes, sir. Odds are 37-1 against. Vorster made his bet, then walked away from the table as the ball rolled. Never gave it a second glance. He lost, of course.'

Someone let out a low whistle. 'Sounds like he knew he was on a winner anyway.'

'I think it's fair to say, he was,' Danskin remarked. 'Look.'

He pointed a finger towards the bottom right of the screen. A legend sat over the newsreel footage. It was a ticker, and it read: '397k are viewing this page.'

'I know plenty who'd think a hundred-thousand hits a month was good traffic. Vorster's had four times that in a matter of hours. Advertisers will be falling over themselves to get their product placed on here. His casino loss is nowt but loose change, even before he syndicates his footage to other media corporations.'

He looked back at the screen. 'What else do we see?'

'The photographer, Woods. He was there before we arrived,' Nigel Trebilcock offered.

'He was. What's he been up to in the last forty-eight hours?' The DCI waited for an answer. None came.

Eventually, Gavin O'Hara spoke. 'Todd was looking into him, sir.'

'Shit. So he was. And now he's in traction in the RVI. Brilliant.' Danskin scratched his nose. 'Ok, Hannah. You're off the subs bench. I want you on Woods while Todd's indisposed. You've got some catching up to do. We need more than the vague shite Robson came up with.'

Hannah Graves beamed. Ryan Jarrod, next to her at the very back of the group, noticed a PC booted-up and unlocked. 'No time like the present,' he whispered to Hannah.

Danskin fell silent. Concentrated on the footage. He walked back and forth at the rear of the group. On screen, he watched as the videographer zoomed in on Woods lying amongst the debris, his camera pointing skywards.

The DCI saw Trebilcock race into shot then shudder to a halt in response to Danskin's warning cry. In the distance, helicopters circled, part-hidden behind a man-made dust cloud.

The angle of shot changed. Another camera. It showed patrol cars arriving, men scurrying from them. It picked out the stunned expressions on the faces of those in the crowd; faces caked in white dust like the make-up of melancholy clowns.

Or the inhabitants of Lower Manhattan in the aftermath of 9/11.

Quietly, Stephen Danskin asked, 'Where's Milton?'

He repeated the question more loudly. 'Did anyone see Leeward Milton there?' Blank looks. 'Just about everyone else was there. Now, why would Milton want to miss out?'

Lyall Parker moved away from the group. 'I'm on it, sir.' He booted up a PC alongside Ryan.

Back on the plasma screen, Danskin saw himself appear in close-up. Not a pretty sight, but he didn't care. The SOC cordon had been enforced so there were no signs of The Mercury's staff. Instead the stream returned to the carnage of what was once the Dunston Rocket.

'Sir, I've got something on Leeward Milton. He's in London meeting with prospective investors.'

'Any idea how long he's been there? Can't have been long, surely. He could have planted something before he went.'

'We don't know it was a timer device yet,' a lanky detective said. 'If it wasn't, Milton's in the clear.'

Danskin gave it a moment's thought. 'Possible, but unlikely. The bomber might use different devices, but all have been a timer of sorts.'

On screen, The Mercury personnel were shown interviewing witnesses who were in no condition to answer the brutal line of questioning, yet not strong enough to push away the microphone under their nose.

An elderly couple spoke to a cold and detached Mike Cash, comparing the decimation to the blitz. Megan Wolfe gathered soundbites as she weaved through the masses as if she were Martin Brundle on the Silverstone grid. Raymond Carpenter, nominally directing affairs, did very little.

'Anything show up on Carpenter yet?'

'Negative, sir,' Gavin O'Hara declared. 'Nearest we've got is an Uncle's cousin who once worked on a TV documentary with Fred Dibnah, a steeplejack known for cocking-up chimney demolitions.'

Danskin managed to snort a laugh before refocusing on the plasma images. 'It's got to be one of them. I know it is.'

At the workstation opposite Lyall Parker, Ryan Jarrod searched information on David Woods. Like Todd Robson before him, he found very little beyond his brief National Geographic one paragraph bio. Yet, Gavin's throwaway comment sparked something.

Ryan kneaded the pad on his left hand, deep in thought, before taking advantage of a momentary silence. 'DCI Danskin,' he said. 'You know about Woods background?'

The DCI took a moment to respond to the unfamiliar voice. 'He was found as a baby in Mold. Went to University in Wales. You found something else, lad?'

Ryan shook his head. 'You'll know about his gap year, then?'

Danskin tried to think what Todd Robson had said. Something about working in some unpronounceable one-horse town. 'Where's this leading to, son?'

'It's probably nothing, but the town he worked in's called Blaenau Ffestiniog. It's…'

A light came on behind Stephen Danskin's eyes. 'I know what it is. I've been there. It's like the surface of Mars. The whole place is one giant slate quarry. It's been blasted to hell.'

Danskin's jaw moved left and right, like a ruminating cow. 'We discounted Woods because he had no connection to explosives. If he's worked in Blaenau, there's nowt else he could do except blow things up.'

The DCI grabbed a notepad. Scribbled down a few lines. He tossed the book at Hannah. 'Find out more.'

The newsreel showed the arrival of BBC and ITN news crews dwarfed by the skeletal remains of Derwent Tower. The message was clear: 'we got here before you, yah-boo sucks'; but The Mercury's period of exclusivity was at an end. The footage loop began to play again.

'Ok, guys,' Danskin announced. 'We'll watch it through one more time. See if there's anything we've missed. Then, I think it's time to rattle a few cages in Vorster's sordid little enterprise.'

Lyall Parker spun his chair around. 'Eureka. You've nae need. At least, not until you've spoken to Milton first. His credit card was used at Beaverbrook's in the Metrocentre the day before New Year's Eve. Not only that,' he pointed at his monitor, 'Look at this. This is Milton's car.'

Danskin dashed to Parker's side. The monitor showed CCTV footage of a vehicle leaving the MetroCentre; not by the main exit onto the A1, but by a back road.

The grainy image showed the car indicate a right. It pulled out and disappeared from shot.

'Where does that go; anyone know?'

Ryan recognised it immediately. 'I do. It'll lead him past the Royal Hotel and the Tudor Rose. Into Dunston. To be exact, right past the bottom of Ravensworth Road.'

The DCI smiled. 'And that's where Derwent Tower stood until a few hours ago.'

Stephen Danskin reeled in an imaginary fishing line.

**

The hefty Floridian was a relative newcomer to the withering cold of a Tyneside winter, but he'd heard of the phenomena in front of his eyes.

'Paradoxical undressing', that's what experts call it; the obtuse compulsion of those beyond hyperthermia to rip off their clothing as they experience a sensation of extreme heat caused by the constriction and dilation of blood vessels.

As he exited Newcastle Central Station onto Neville Street, Leeward Milton was convinced the affliction affected the whole of Tyneside.

Swarms of scantily clad girls wearing mini-skirts and blouses made from fairy wings laughed and danced their way from bar to bar, while their male counterparts staggered by dressed in shirt sleeves as if it were high-summer.

Milton drew the fur-lined Parka hood tight around his ears, slapped his snow mittens against his sleeves, and headed towards the meeting point in a cloud of frost-puffed breath.

It might only be a KFC but its interior was as welcoming as a Yuletide log fire. He stuffed the mittens in his coat pocket and made his way upstairs where Megan Wolfe waited.

'You made it back,' she said, stating the obvious.

'Figured there was no need to stay down there. I've seen our web traffic. Mercury don't need no investment for as long as this goes on.'

After a beat, Megan smiled. 'I got him, Lee.'

'You got proof it's Vorster?'

'I will have. Soon.'

'So, what's this all about, if you've nothing to hang on him?'

Wolfe smiled. 'I've got something on him, alright. Just not the bombings. Not yet. But, what I have got; it's dynamite. And it's all on film.'

He loosened his coat. Frowned. 'What you bin' up to this time?'

She laughed. 'I've got footage of him. In a casino's toilet. Shagging and doing coke.'

'How the hell did you get that?'

She tapped the side of her nose. 'For me to know, you to find out.'

He looked around. 'Guess we should order something. I figure there's a long story coming. I could do with a coffee. You?'

'I'm fine. Can't stop long. It's late and I need file more copy from this morning.'

Milton shrugged. 'I don't get how this all fits with the bombs.'

'It doesn't. Not directly. But when I do prove it, it's another angle to go at. I told you I'd ruin him.'

He shifted in his seat. 'You're a bitch, Megan Wolfe, do you know that?'

She beamed. 'Thank you.'

He opened his mouth to speak but noticed her scowl. She glanced first over his left shoulder, then his right.

The voice came from his right.

'Leeward Milton?'

'Huh?'

'I'm sure you know me. I know for a fact your colleague does. I'm DCI Stephen Danskin and this is Detective Sergeant Susan Nairn. We'd like a word with you, sir. Not here, though.'

**

'I've been in London, seeking investment for The Mercury. But I figure you already knew that.'

Across the table from Milton, Stephen Danskin offered no comment. 'And when did you leave for London?'

'Got first train down this morning. Intended staying overnight but when I heard the news, I got back as soon as I could. It is my job, you know; both reporting and seeking to broaden our reach.'

Danskin clicked the retract button of his pen-top over and over. 'Do you seek to gain financially from The Mercury's success?'

'Stupid question. Of course, I do. We all do. Look, Detective Sergeant…'

'Chief Inspector.'

'Ok. Chief inspector. Where are you going with this? I've got work to do. We are kinda' busy at the moment.'

'It might have escaped your notice, but I'm not in this for the shit and giggles, either.' He leant forward in his chair. 'Where were you on 30th December?'

Leeward Milton sat back. Regained his personal space. 'I went to the MetroCentre.'

'Any reason?'

Milton snapped out a laugh. 'Same as most folk. To do some shopping.'

Sue Nairn spoke for the first time since they entered the interview room. 'Where did you go next?'

'I headed home, got changed, and went to work.'

'Which way home?'

Something clicked. 'Whoa. I get it. Yeah, I took the quiet route. The one that goes by The Rocket. But that was days ago. And, besides, it might be a quiet road compared to the A1 but hundreds of others went that way.'

Danskin and Nairn remained silent. Waited until Milton squirmed in his seat. The DCI resumed the conversation. 'Tell me about your time in the Gulf.'

Milton slumped in his seat. Gave the detectives a potted history. His 'accident', as he called it. The vlog diary. Nothing they didn't already know.

'Is it fair to say you know a good deal about explosives?'

Wearily, Milton replied, 'Sure I do. You don't get to disarm devices without knowing them better than you do your woman.'

'You see, Mr Milton, it seems to me you have more than enough knowledge to be able to rig a device that would bring down Dunston Rocket.'

'I do. And, before you suggest it, all the others, too, for that matter. Nuthin' to it.'

The detectives didn't know what disarmed them most; Milton's frankness or the hearty laugh that accompanied it.

'Thing is,' Milton continued, 'Not only was I not present when The Rocket went up, I was out the country for days before the HMRC fire. And that's without checking my diary for the other incidents. Detectives, you're barking up the wrong tree, as I believe you guys say over here.'

Danskin signalled to Nairn. They left Leeward Milton in the interview room, a uniformed constable keeping watch.

'He's right, you know, sir. We know he went home a couple of days before the HMRC incident. We've a record of the ticket purchase. We know the bomber used a fused timing device but the earliest it could have been pre-set for is a couple of hours, at most. Connor won't give us the time of day if we take what we've got to him. We need more. We could release him under investigation, I guess'

Danskin expelled air until his lips vibrated. 'Thing is, if we impose a RUI, it'll reveal we know more about The Mercury connection than we've let on. It'll risk driving whoever it is – and my money's still on Milton – underground. Can we risk it? I don't think we can. We either come up with a fresh approach, or we let him off the hook. Release without charge. For now, at least.'

Ten minutes later, Leeward Milton zipped up his Parka, pulled on his ski gloves, and stepped out into a freezing Tyneside evening.

**

While Norman and James Jarrod slipped into the arms of Morpheus, Ryan sat alert and engrossed in the half dozen windows open on his laptop computer.

Yes, Hannah was the one detailed to keep tabs on Woods but she couldn't do it all by herself. Besides, this was personal now and, if he was to play a part in bringing Frank's killer to justice, he had to rule them out, one-by-one. May as well start with Woods.

In his naivety, he began by repeating tasks previously undertaken by Todd Robson and Ravi Sangar. He checked social media profiles, Linked-in, Wiki entries. He learnt nothing beyond what he already knew from the brief National Geographic bio.

He took out a month's free trial subscription to the Geographic's on-line content. Searched for articles written by David Woods. He trawled through them. Saved a montage of Woods photographs. Visited them time and time again. He found nothing suspicious.

Ryan's eyelids drooped. He jerked himself awake as his head fell towards his chest. He resolved to make a coffee but couldn't bring himself to leave his seat.

Ninety minutes later, he woke with a start and a pug whining at his feet. 'Okay, Spud. Let's go walkies.' He leashed the dog and stepped into air so frigid it would have woken Rip Van Winkle.

Ryan wandered the empty streets. Bare-branched trees lined his route like skeletal spectres. His thoughts turned to Frank Burrows, the old-timer he'd barely come to know yet whose memory now provided him with his raison d'etre.

Spud drew Ryan to a halt as the dog snuffled at a discarded fast-food carton. The pug emptied his bladder over a gatepost. Ryan let the dog's leader extend as Spud went in search of something hidden beneath a hedgerow.

A breeze rustled Ryan's strawberry-blond hair. He threw back his head and caught sight of the city of Newcastle across the Tyne Valley. Even at this time of night, or morning, lights still twinkled in the tower blocks as if they were concrete Christmas trees.

A snail's trail of streetlights revealed the city's thoroughfares, apart from a deep black pool where the University bomb had decimated the central motorway on the fateful night he and Frank found Teddy McGuffie.

Thoughts of the University gave him an idea. He remembered Lyall Parker's address to the detectives, and the confirmation in Woods' bio; something about Woods attending UWIST. It was now part of Cardiff University. Perhaps the University records held more information about David Woods' past.

He vowed to make it his last throw of the dice before shifting attention elsewhere; to Marcus Vorster.

Ryan ordered Spud to heel and set off for home.

CHAPTER TWENTY-EIGHT

'No, Stephen. Absolutely not. There's not a cat in Hell's chance of me sanctioning it.'

Superintendent Connor had adopted his favourite pose; face to window, back to room, hands clasped behind him.

'Sir, with respect, you might think it's a long-shot but it's a sure-fire way to smoke him out.'

Connor turned. 'Stephen, the answer is 'no.' In case it had escaped your attention, we've had four major incidents, catastrophic incidents, in as many weeks. That's as many as this force has had to deal with in forty years. If you think we're going to invite the perpetrator to commit a fifth act, then you're as mad as he is. Good lord, man. What if he didn't respond? Worse, what if he did and it went wrong?'

Danskin felt the energy drain from him, but he pressed on. 'Yes, there's a risk. Of course there is. But there's a risk he'll commit more acts anyway. At least this way, we're in control.'

Connor shook his head. Before he could speak, Danskin rolled the dice one last time.

'We tell Roadhouse to stop sending letters. We continue our normal investigations. If we haven't got the evidence to charge, we fabricate a letter. Set our own target so he comes to us. Make it somewhere out of town. Away from people and communities. Then, we lie in wait. We get him red-handed.'

'Stephen. Listen to yourself. The bomber doesn't react to every letter. How do we know he'll respond to this one? How much time, energy and funds do we exhaust in the vain hope he'll fall for it?'

'He'll respond, if we wait. Your own Imogen Markham said the killer's urge would grow. If he gets no bait for a while, he'll be gagging by the time our fake letter goes to print.'

Connor scowled at DCI Danskin. 'For your information, Miss Markham is an eminent criminal psychologist. She isn't 'my' Imogen Markham.'

'Sorry, sir.'

'But,' Connor conceded, 'You do have something.'

'I do?'

'Yes. We make sure Roadhouse doesn't send any more bloody letters. But that's as far as it goes. We catch this bugger by tried and tested methods, not by risking all on the roll of a roulette wheel like Marcus-sodding-Vorster, Leeward Milton or any of the other Mercury inbreds.'

**

Stephen Danskin stared at the plasma screen. He sat with feet on his desk, and fingers interlocked over his stomach. All that was missing was a bucket of popcorn.

He watched a montage of The Mercury coverage of the incidents. All of them. Scenes of desolation lifted from Armageddon or a Mad Max movie. He studied the images intently.

His gaze took in the awe-struck rubberneckers at each location as he sought out anything unusual in their behaviour, someone out of place, anyone without angst or incredulity etched on their face. He found nothing.

His attention switched to the journalists. Danskin focussed on Milton whenever he entered shot, Woods, Cash and Carpenter when he wasn't. Did any of them give anything away? Say something they couldn't possibly know? Go anywhere they wouldn't be aware of?

A detective approached Danskin with an armful of files. The DCI raised a palm in rebuttal.

Danskin stopped watching the video content. It continued to play but he closed his eyes. Concentrated on the commentary of The Mercury crew.

Still nothing.

He reran the footage once more, this time with subtitles but no sound. Might he pick up something from the words they used, rather than their speech?

Zilch. Nada. Sod all.

The room around him was filled with the noise and chatter of an investigation in full swing but he was cocooned in his own bubble.

At length, he wandered to the crime board. Stood with hands on hips. The board was divided into sections; one for each crime scene. Listed alongside each were details of The Mercury staff in attendance.

University: Woods, Cash, Milton, Wolfe, Carpenter.
HMRC: Carpenter, Milton, Woods, Wolfe.
St James': None.
Rocket: Woods, Carpenter, Wolfe, Cash.

He tapped a fingernail against his teeth. 'The features editor; the guy who invited Roadhouse to take over half the paper. Padwell, isn't it? Any sign of him turning up yet?'

'No, sir. Hasn't been seen this year so far as we can tell,' Nigel Trebilcock advised.

'Hmmm.'

Danskin shifted attention to the upper portion of the board. Above the scene of crime photographs, legends described the key facts.

University: Early hours. Explosive. Timer device. 9th floor.
HMRC: Late morning. Incendiary. Timer device (query). Storage hall.
St James': Target 3-5pm (query). Timer device (faulty). Intended location (query).
Rocket: Early morning. Explosive. Timer device. Ground floor.

'Lyall, here a moment, please.'

The Scotsman hurried to Danskin's side. 'Yes, Sir?'

'Humour me here, will you? Are we sure we're on the right track? I mean, this is the work of one guy, right?'

'Och, sure to be. There cannae be more than one madman out there.'

Danskin exhaled noisily through his nose. 'How many madmen have we come across in our time? Every murder, every rape, every kiddie-fiddling pervert; they're all madmen, to one extent or another, man.'

Parker saw where his boss was coming from. 'There's differences to each incident, I admit. But the similarities outweigh the variations. And there's The Mercury connection. It's too much of a coincidence for it to be more than perp.'

'Thanks for the confirmation.' He pinched the bridge of his nose. 'Doesn't help us though. As long as he's on the loose, the more chance there is he'll do it again.'

He caught sight of Hannah Graves. 'I need you to have a word with Roadhouse,' he instructed her. 'Tell her not to write any more letters. Under any circumstances. Tell her I'll lock her up if she does. Tell her anything, just make sure she doesn't give him a chance to strike again.'

'Yes, sir. I'll call her now.'

'No, Hannah. Pay her a visit. She needs to know we mean it. And, while you're there, check in on our mutual friend, will you?' He gave her the merest of winks, a mannerism an onlooker would mistake for nothing more than a twitch.

Hannah's dimple creased her cheek. 'I understand. I'm on my way.'

**

Detective Graves nursed a cup of milky tea between her knees. 'So, Miss Roadhouse, although I can't tell you why, it's really, really important you don't send any more letters to The Mercury. At least, not for the time being, anyway.'

Florence looked at her with one eye closed. 'This all most curious, I must say. But, I'll do as you say. Now, onto the important things. How are you and Doris's grandson coming along?'

Hannah was genuinely puzzled. 'Who?'

'Come, come. I know when a couple have a twinkle in their eye for one another. Ryan. Ryan Jarrod.'

Hannah grinned. 'He's a friend. Well, almost a colleague, really?'

'I see. A colleague, you call it now, is it? Used to call them a beau, in my day. Or a chaperone. A sweetheart, or a date. Even, 'my man'. I liked that one best, calling someone my man.'

Hannah caught Florence Roadhouse's eyes flicker to the photograph a soldier in uniform. 'He's very handsome,' Graves said. 'Where was that taken?'

The old woman gave a dismissive wave. 'Oh, that was a long time ago. All ancient history now. I forget where it was taken. I've been to sooo many places, dah-ling,' she said with mock grandeur.

'I bet you're a dark horse. Got some tales to tell, haven't you?'

Florence Roadhouse face changed. 'I have. And not all of them pleasant, I tell you. I've seen some dreadful things in my time. Inhumane things. Things you wouldn't believe. Vietnam was the worst...' she broke off. 'Still, I don't suppose it's all sweetness and light in your world, either, dear, is it?'

Hannah had warmed to the old lady. She hadn't expected to, but she had. 'You're right again, Miss Roadhouse.' She set down her teacup. 'And, I suppose, I'd best be off to those things. It's been lovely meeting you again. And, please, no more letters, yeah?'

Florence smiled. 'I promise you, there won't be any.' Then, with a twinkle, 'Be sure to give my regards to young Ryan when you get there, won't you?'

**

Hannah took a seat vacated by Ryan, who lowered himself gingerly to the floor.

Opposite, on the sofa, Jam Jar and Norman Jarrod sat transfixed in front of the TV. They barely acknowledged Hannah's arrival as Jam Jar's fingers blurred over the console and guided an Anthony Martial avatar past the despairing lunge of Norman's David Luiz.

Next to the radiator, Doris Jarrod lounged in an armchair, a vapid expression on her face.

'Welcome to my world,' Ryan said. Hannah ruffled his hair as if he were a retriever at her feet.

'Florence sends her love.'

'Gran's not having a good day again today. She hasn't heard you,' Ryan explained.

'I'm not talking to your Gran, silly. I'm talking to you. She was asking after you. I think she suspects we're an item.'

Ryan stiffened ever so slightly. 'And are we not?'

Hannah raised her shoulders. 'Let's see, shall we?'

Ryan exhaled. 'Because, I was wondering, well… do you fancy a little break? Just a couple of days away.'

Norman glanced towards his son; just long enough for Jesse Lingard to slide the ball past a stationary Bernd Leno. 'Ah, bugger, man,' he exclaimed amid Jam Jar's celebratory whoops.

'Ryan, that's not possible. Seriously, it's not. Not at this stage of the investigation. Perhaps later, if things are still good between us, I'd love to. But, I can't walk away from the case.'

'What if I said it's about the investigation?'

She raised an eyebrow. 'Go on.'

'I've discovered something,' he searched for the right word; 'Odd.'

Hannah looked at Jam Jar and Norman, engrossed in their game, oblivious to the conversation. She gestured Ryan to continue.

'I thought you might want to come to Wales with me.'

CHAPTER TWENTY-NINE

For three days, DCI Stephen Danskin followed Superintendent Connor's advice. He cancelled leave, even ordered Todd Robson's return to desk duties, and engaged with DCI Kinnear's uniform squad. They double-checked statements and re-interviewed witnesses while Ravi Sangar's crew trawled through telephone records and bank statements for the umpteenth time.

They came up with interesting snippets but nothing of substance. Danskin learned that Marcus Vorster had negotiated an increased advance for his biography in the wake of the Derwent Tower incident. Discovered he'd called his publisher only hours after the event. The conversation was lengthy, and the contract change significant.

The team unearthed a raft of background information on Leeward Milton, who Danskin still had down as the prime suspect. It added weight to the file but remained circumstantial at best, inadmissible at worst. There was no smoking gun.

Carpenter's frequent presence at the scene troubled Danskin. Something didn't stack up, but the man had neither means nor motive. Same for Woods. Apart from the failed St James' Park bomb, he was at every incident, often first there. Arguably, he had the means - Blaenau Ffestiniog - but he had nothing to gain. There was no motive.

So, after three days of what Connor would describe as diligent policing, the investigation had moved forward not an inch.

Then, just as Tesco's stock of Corsodyl became endangered, the breakthrough came.

On the fourth day, light formed in the firmament.

'Sir?'

'What is it, Graves?' Danskin growled.

'Ryan's got something to tell you. Might be something or nothing, but he thinks you should know.'

Danskin pinched the bridge of his nose. 'Spit it out man, woman.'

'I'll let him tell you himself.'

Ryan Jarrod's face filled the porthole window. She beckoned him into Danskin's office. He approached sheepishly; papers clutched in gloved hand.

'Sir, I've been helping Hannah look into David Wood's background. She couldn't take time out but I've been to Wales looking into a couple of things.' Ryan used the word again. 'It's odd.'

'I was hoping for something a bit better than 'odd', but howay – what you found?'

'Well, you know National Geographic claim Woods has a degree in bioscience from UWIST? Turns out he hasn't. He didn't go. Woods had a place, but never attended.'

'What did he do? Unless we've something concrete, like he joined an IRA cell or something, or he's related to Guy Fawkes, Ted Kaczynski or Bomber Harris, it doesn't add much. It certainly doesn't give a motive.'

'I agree. That's why I said it was odd. Even more strange, the University archives say he turned them down in favour of a degree at the School of Ocean Sciences, Bangor. Again, he accepted a place. Records show he enrolled, and then he disappeared.'

'In what way?'

'Well, I've trawled through the records at the University library. Spoke to the admissions clerk. Personally inspected the honours board. And each and every source comes up with the same answer. At the time Woods should have graduated, four Davids did so.' He lay a sheet of paper on the desk in front of Danskin. 'None of them were David Woods. There's a David Griffiths, David Patterson, David Tyfford and a David Yelland. There was a Dafydd, but he isn't Woods either. Dafydd Bellamy.'

Danskin stretched. 'Son, I admire your tenacity. Your enthusiasm. The fact you went all the way down to Wales: it's great. But it doesn't tell us much.'

'No. Except he's a liar. And, he's forged qualifications. What else might he have done?'

Stephen tried not to laugh. 'Lying isn't a crime. And it's a huge leap from forgery to cold-blooded terrorist. Seriously, though, Ryan. Keep at it. You might find something worthwhile next time.'

Ryan flushed. Opened his mouth to protest. 'Ah, that's not fair, man.'

The office door flung open. Ravi Sangar entered without apology. 'Sir, you got to see this. We've CCTV footage that blows the door wide open for us.'

Danskin's chair was still revolving minutes after he'd shot from it like a pilot ejecting from a cockpit.

A frozen image filled the plasma screen on the bullpen wall. Grainy, blurred and distant, the picture appeared to show a busy car park and access road.

Danskin squinted at the screen. 'What we got here?'

'I'll boost the image quality.' Sangar clicked a button. The screen pixelated. Reappeared brighter; clearer.

Danskin recognised the setting.

Sangar moved the jerky images forward. Three vehicles pulled to a halt in front of the camera. A family emerged from the first, unloaded the trunk, and waved as the car pulled away. From the second, a young couple emerged. They held hands and walked out of shot beneath the camera.

The third vehicle captured Danskin's attention. Captured it because of who emerged from the car.

Leeward Milton.

Milton delved into a pocket, tendered the fare to the cab driver, and wheeled his carry-on bag out of sight, into Newcastle International Airport.

'When is this?' Danskin asked.

'The day Milton left for his home visit.'

Danskin pulled at an ear lobe. 'We already knew this, Ravi.'

'Yes. But let's move on.' Sangar clicked his mouse and the camera angle changed.

Milton was inside the departure lounge. He stared up at the departures board and at a long line of check-in desks. He veered right. Another camera picked him up taking a seat at a table outside an Upper Crust outlet. He pulled out a phone and began tapping on it.

As Ryan stood watching alongside Danskin and Hannah, a thought struck him. 'The cab Milton came to the airport in – it was one of Charlie Charlton's.'

Danskin was only half listening. 'Mmm?'

'Charlton's. The same company Teddie McGuffie worked for.'

The words resonated with the DCI. 'Interesting. Something else to link Milton to the crimes. But not if he's out the country. It's back to the drawing board.'

'That's just it, sir,' Sangar said. 'Look.'

Milton stood and walked away from the café. The camera angle changed once more. It picked up Leeward Milton as he exited the revolving doors. He stepped into the cold of an early winter on Tyneside, rather than the temperate climes of Tampa.

'What the fuck?'

'My thoughts exactly, sir,' Ravi Sangar agreed.

'Jeezus,' Danskin exclaimed. 'We saw what we expected to see. We knew Milton was booked on an outbound flight but no-one bothered to check if he actually boarded the frigging plane. He didn't. It's him. It's Leeward-fucking-Milton.'

**

In Connor's office, Danskin paced the floor and spoke with the gunfire rapidity of a talk radio host on speed. 'I believe we've got enough to charge a suspect for the bombings. It's Leeward Milton.'

'Slow down, Stephen. You had Milton in only a few days ago and had nothing on him. What's changed?'

Stephen wrung his hands. 'Because he had an alibi at the time, and he hasn't any longer. We've proof he wasn't where he said he was at the time of the HMRC incident. If we can nail him on this, it's only a matter of time before we have proof he was responsible for the others.'

Hannah Graves was in the room with them, Ryan left outside with Nigel Trebilcock and Todd Robson. 'We've learnt a lot more about Milton's background too, sir. All the pieces fit.'

Connor looked her up and down. 'I'll hear this from the DCI, Graves. You're dismissed.'

Hannah's face flushed. She made a fist by her side. Danskin noticed. 'Leave it to me, Hannah,' he said quietly. 'You go see to Ryan.'

When the door closed behind her, Danskin confronted Connor. 'That was out of order. We're a team here and Hannah's an integral part of it.'

'There's a reason I sent her out, Stephen. We'll come to that later. For now, tell me what you got on Milton. It had better be good, because if it's not enough to stick, you can bet your bottom dollar Mike Cash will plaster 'police harassment' bullshit all over The Mercury. We've had enough bad press already.'

Stephen toyed with a marker pen as he took up position next to a whiteboard opposite Connor's desk.

'Leeward Milton is an ex-serviceman, employed on bomb disposal. He has a self-confessed and wide-ranging knowledge of a whole range of explosive devices. In his own words, he knows the devices used in our incidents better than his woman. 'Nuthin to it' were his exact words.'

He jotted bullet-points on the whiteboard as he spoke.

'Also by his own admission, he stands to gain financially from an increase in The Mercury's circulation figures.'

'Don't they all?' Connor asked.

'They do sir, yes. But other than Vorster himself, Milton has most to gain. He has responsibility for raising investment, and his contract includes a healthy commission bonus.'

The DCI wrote the figures on the board and noticed Connor's eyes widen at the numbers.

'We also need to take into account Milton's state of mind,' Danskin continued. 'As you know, he experienced a significant trauma whilst serving in the Gulf. As a consequence, he was discharged on medical grounds suffering from acute post-traumatic stress disorder.'

Connor raised a hand to halt Danskin while he digested the new information. After a while, he asked, 'And do we know what affect the condition would have on his actions?'

'It's a moot point, sir. Many experts believe someone suffering from PTSD will shy away from conflict. They'll do anything to avoid memories of the trauma recurring. There are others, though, who believe the opposite; that direct exposure helps the victim come to terms with what happened. They believe the victim is better off normalising the event.'

'The 'get back on your bike' approach.'

'Exactly. And guess what? Milton's therapist is one of the latter.'

Connor rose and adopted his window-gazing pose. 'If it comes to court, Milton's team will bring a whole string of experts spouting the alternative theory, though. They'll also argue the financial gain,' he pointed blindly behind his back in the rough direction of the whiteboard, 'Could never outweigh the personal risk.'

Danskin smiled inwardly. Time to play his trump card.

'And that's where we counter with more of Milton's own words. In one of his very last vlogs filed after his discharge, this is what he said, directly to camera.'

DCI Danskin recited from a pre-printed document:

'I will never be the same. For me, there is no safe place in the world. Every time I close my eyes, I replay the events of that day. I see the dust, the blood, the limbs. The bodies of my friends and brothers. I suffer horrific flashbacks and nightmares. I obsessively study all those around me. Anyone with a suitcase, or a parcel, I abhor. I see them as the enemy. I imagine what they might be carrying. And you know the worse thing? I want them dead. It's as if I've completely lost my mind. I feel I'll be forever seeking vengeance. What hurts most of all, though, is that I sure wish my father had never been patched up in Vietnam. I wish he'd died in the jungle. That way, I'd never have been born, and I'd never have to live through the hell I experience every day of my life.'

Danskin took in a deep breath. Tried hard not to sound self-satisfied.

'So, sir, he may have said it a number of years ago, but Leeward Milton has admitted he doesn't give a toss what happens to him. Or, for that matter, anyone else.'

Connor turned to face him. 'And you're absolutely sure his alibi is shot to pieces?'

'Without a doubt. We released him last time on the basis he couldn't possibly have carried out the HMRC incident because he was in the States at the time. We were wrong. He didn't catch the flight. We have him on CCTV entering the airport. Coincidentally, he arrived courtesy of a cab from the same fleet as Teddy McGuffie's. Once inside the airport, he spent some time on the telephone. Nothing show's up in his own phone records so it must have been a burner, which in itself is suspicious. Then, less than fifteen minutes after getting to the airport, we see him leave.'

Stephen paused. 'It mightn't be watertight yet, sir, but it's more than enough for an arrest. I just need your say-so.'

He stood back, waiting for Connor's praise. Instead, he received a kick up the backside.

'You've made a complete arse of this investigation, you do realise that, don't you? You should have discovered the hole in his alibi weeks ago. If you'd done your job, everything after the HMRC fire in Longbenton would never have happened. You've cost lives, man. Once the dust's settled, we're going to get crucified over this.'

Stephen looked aghast as Connor railed into him.

'Get out of here, Danskin, and don't come back until you've got Milton under lock and key. And I won't be taking your word for it. I want to see him in the custody suite for myself. Then, I'll start thinking about what I'm going to do with you. Go get him. Now!'

CHAPTER THIRTY

A crystal decanter sat in the centre of a table, one-quarter full with the barely-golden tints of an Islay malt. The remainder of the contents filled a dozen glasses spread evenly around the ovoid table.

The Mercury staff seated behind the whisky tumblers could almost see the pound signs glow in Marcus Vorster's eyes as he lounged in his chair, hands behind his head.

'I think this calls for a toast,' he said, reaching for his glass.

The others, with the exception of Megan Wolfe, raised their glasses to their lips.

'Megan, please, join us.'

'I don't drink,' she said coldly.

'Ag, of course you don't.' He revolved his glass at eye-level, squinting through the crystal at the smooth liquid. 'I forgot. You have no vices, do you?'

Megan felt Leeward Milton's hand grab her knee in a 'don't take the bait' gesture. She closed her mouth without speaking.

'To The Mercury,' he announced. 'And all those who sail in her.'

A few of the others repeated the toast with an embarrassed mumble. Most sipped in silence. Leeward Milton drained his glass.

'I feel in my water this is the year we reach new heights,' Vorster continued. 'The year we go global. Where we achieve our zenith.' He tossed his head back to free his eyes from the errant fringe. He looked at each in turn. 'And it's all thanks to the Tyneside Tyrant.' He raised his glass once more. 'To the Tyneside Tyrant.'

No-one followed his gesture.

'Please yourselves.' He refilled his tumbler. Savoured a nip. 'So, to business. What have you for me today?'

The assembled editorial team ran through their proposals. Jostled and bartered and pitched for column inches and on-line space. The bombings once more took precedence, Vorster eager to maintain momentum on what he viewed as his story; the strapline which had turned his fortunes full-circle.

As the meeting drew towards its conclusion, Vorster prepared to dismiss the team when he remembered something.

'Look; one more thing. While our news output has been unrivalled over recent weeks, among our core readership, our locals, if you like; we've had an astonishing response to a recent innovation. Luke Padwell, if anyone remembers who the hell he is, came up with the idea of introducing a guest columnist. That old bird who keeps writing to me. What's her name?' he asked.

'Florence Roadhouse, you mean?' David Woods suggested.

'Yes, that's her. Unbelievably, they want more from her. So, I want someone to do a piece on her. Encourage her to come up with some more of her drivel. Not that she needs much encouragement, though. Anyway, in the absence of Padwell, I need someone to talk to her. Any volunteers?'

The request was met with silence.

'Anyone?'

After a moment that seemed to last forever, someone broke the silence. 'I'll do it.'

All eyes turned to the speaker, surprise etched across every face.

'Good. That's sorted, then. Okay, guys. That's us done for the day. Leave your glasses behind, won't you? They cost a bloody fortune. A bomb, you might say.'

The editorial team stood to leave.

'Oh,' Marcus added. 'Leeward, Megan, Mike: can you news guys stay behind for a moment?'

'Don't you need me, Marcus?' Raymond Carpenter asked.

Vorster had completely forgotten Carpenter was, in theory, Wolfe's superior.

'What? Oh, yes. You stay behind, too.'

He made it sound like detention. Perhaps it was.

**

The revolving door spun like a child's top, such was the force of Danskin's entry. Lyall Parker dodged and weaved and finally plunged into a gap as the doors sped by.

Outside, a band of burly uniformed officers unpacked themselves from a van. They wore stab vests and riot helmets, complete with body cams. The irony wasn't lost on Danskin as they followed him into the lobby of The Mercury building.

'Milton: where is he?' Danskin snapped at a girl behind the reception desk; Moira, her name-tag said.

'You can't just barge in here like this,' a single security guard protested.

Danskin flashed his ID. 'I can and I have. Now, where can I find Milton?'

A clerk checked a PC. 'He's in a meeting with Mr Vorster at the moment.'

'Where?'

'Fifth floor conference room.'

'Is there another way out of here?'

The security guard spoke. 'Fire exit at rear. Loading dock in the alleyway.'

Danskin snapped his fingers. Three of the uniforms dashed outside and disappeared out of sight.

Danskin and Parker slipped into the elevator with a tooled-up copper while two of the remaining uniformed constables took the stairs. The final couple loitered by the lobby doors.

The elevator doors whooshed open, the DCI squeezing between them as they did so. He moved from room to room, checking the nameplates on the doors.

When he found one marked 'Quicksilver Conference Suite', he and Parker waited until the constables declared the staircase clear.

Danskin gathered his thoughts and waited for his breathing to settle. He lay a hand on the door lever, checked with his comrades, nodded, and flung open the door.

Bedlam ensued.

While Danskin and Parker stood back, the three fully-armoured officers burst through, shouting orders and commands.

Marcus Vorster reeled back in shock, his chair toppling over as he fell to the ground. He flung out an arm, caught the decanter, and sent it crashing to the floor. Raymond Carpenter hurled himself beneath the table. Wolfe grabbed Mike Cash's arm and tried to shield herself behind him at the same time as he attempted to duck behind her in a panic-stricken game of Twister.

They reacted the way they did, in shock, because they were in an office block in Newcastle upon Tyne. Things like this didn't happen.

Leeward Milton didn't react because he wasn't in Newcastle. The moment the door burst open, he was transported to another world; a world of stupefying heat, dust-storms, and mindless depravity.

Two of the officer's raced towards Milton, ordering him to the floor. But Milton didn't see police officers in protective clothing. He saw the chocolate chip uniform of Iraqi combatants. On their heads, they wore ballistic helmets, not polycarbonate visors. When they drew their batons, they raised Type 56 assault rifles. And their bodies bore suicide belts, not stab vests.

Instinct took over. Milton threw himself to the floor. He rolled away from the shouts of the aggressors. Rolled towards the broken decanter. He grabbed a six-inch shard, whipped it back and forth in front of him at arm's length.

The insurgents hesitated. It bought Milton enough time to spring to his feet. He moved towards his assailants in a crouch. They separated. One moved to his left, the other his right. Thought the pincer movement would trap him. They were wrong.

With the force of a bull elephant, Milton charged the rebels. He grabbed one round the neck with his left arm, the other the right. He squeezed. Tight. Forced them to drop their weapons. Milton spun around and ran towards the office window with the Iraqis still in neckhold. He rammed their heads against the plate-glass window so hard it rattled in its frame. Again. And again.

The enemy wilted, sagged in his arms. Milton retrieved the decanter shard. Raised it above his head. Brought it towards the jugular of the nearest assailant.

It never reached its target. The third officer raised his baton and crashed it down onto the back of Milton's head. He froze, staggered a pace or two, then crumpled to the floor.

Danskin had summoned the constables in the lobby. They sprinted into the room, hurled themselves onto the prostate Milton, and cuffed him in a single movement.

Slowly, Marcus Vorster pulled himself to his feet. He gripped the tabletop in a white-knuckled embrace. The face of Raymond Carpenter appeared above the table, wide-eyed and sallow. Mike Cash and Megan Wolfe disentangled themselves and looked at the wreckage around them.

'That's one sure-fire way of making sure you make the headlines, Danskin,' Cash said.

'I think you'll find you'll be making the headlines yourself. All of you.' He signalled for the cops on top of Milton to get to their feet. They hauled Milton with them, his head hanging lamely. 'The Tyneside Tyrant, as you call him.' He motioned with his head. 'It's him. One of your own.'

Megan snorted. 'Don't be so ridiculous. It's not Lee, it's...' her eyes flitted subconsciously towards Vorster, 'Not Lee,' she settled for.

Mike Cash waded into the argument. 'Detective Chief Inspector. You have just signalled the end of your career, you do realise that, don't you? This is police harassment of the highest order. The press will eat you up and spit out the pips. Won't we, Marcus?'

Vorster was grinning inanely. He held up his hands. 'I really don't care. This is win-win for me. Either The Mercury gets the exclusive on your appalling mismanagement of the case, or my publisher adds another zero to the end of my autobiography contract. Happy days.' He clapped his hands together.

'Fucking snake,' Megan Wolfe said.

'Ever the lady, Ms Wolfe,' Vorster responded.

'Sorry to interrupt your wee tiff,' Parker said, 'But we're taking this bastard downtown.'

'Aye,' Danskin confirmed. 'And you lot are coming with us.'

Mike Cash protested. 'You can't do that. Besides, you released Mr Milton without charge. You've no grounds to re-arrest him without new evidence.'

'Don't try to tell me my job, Cash. And we do have new evidence. Like, his alibi about being out the country at the time HMRC went up. That's the only reason Milton wasn't locked up. But, you know what? It was a load of bollocks. He didn't get a flight to Tampa. He was here all the time.'

The room fell silent. 'Ok, get him out of here,' Danskin said.

'Wait. I know he wasn't out the country. But he's not the man,' Megan Wolfe said. 'He can't be.'

'And you know that, how?'

'Because he was with me.'

Danskin and Parker exchanged looks. Once he'd gathered his composure, Danskin spoke. 'Howay, Miss Wolfe. Loyalty's one's thing. Perjury is another.'

Wolfe straightened herself. 'I can prove it.'

Milton raised his head. 'Megan. No.'

Danskin's head spun towards Parker again. 'Carry on,' his voice less confident.

'No, Megan.'

She turned to Leeward Milton. 'Yes, Lee. We have to.'

'Cut the shit, Wolfe. Can you prove Leeward Milton was with you or not?'

'Yes.'

'How?'

She hesitated. 'I have a video.'

'Whoa, whoa. Now why on earth would you take a video of you talking to Leeward Milton?'

Megan stared directly at Stephen Danskin. 'We weren't doing much talking, Detective Chief Inspector. We recorded it for our own private entertainment, as they say.'

Danskin's jaw hit the floor.

'Leeward and I, we're an item.' She waved her left hand towards Stephen, revealing a ring bought from Beaverbrook's. 'We'll be married as soon as his divorce comes through.'

Megan caught sight of Raymond Carpenter. He looked like he was about to cry.

**

They continued staring at the screen long after the show was over. When the static settled and the screen shone a deep ocean-blue, they saw their own reflection: a wide-eyed Nigel Trebilcock, slack jawed Lyall Parker and a leery Todd Robson.

'I think we should watch it again. Just in case we missed summat, like,' Todd proposed.

Trebilcock nodded. 'Good idea.'

'How about we put it up on the plasma this time?'

'Even better idea.'

Lyall looked around. 'Hannah and Sue are here.'

Robson shrugged. 'We're just reviewing the evidence. I'm sure that's what Foreskin would want.'

'I would indeed,' Danskin said from behind them. 'Put it up.'

While Todd Robson connected the PC to the plasma, Danskin sent Hannah out the room on some unnecessary chore. The DCI turned his attention to the screen.

The camera was set-up at ground level. It captured the lower portion of a fully clothed, bulky male. The man swept away a pile of magazines from a sofa. He rearranged the tendrils of a spider plant standing on top of a TV so they cascaded over the upper half of the screen.

A hand picked up the TV remote. A black hand, Danskin noted. The TV came alive with some ridiculously moustachioed man laying flagstones outside a castle.

'What's he doing?' Danskin asked.

'Laying a patio,' Todd replied.

'Not the bloke on the telly, stupid-arse. Milton. Why's he put the TV on if he's about to shag Megan Wolfe's brains out?'

His question remained unanswered. A female appeared. At least, the lower half of a female. A naked lower half. Danskin glanced at Sue Nairn and shifted uncomfortably in his seat.

The man on screen snaked his arm around the woman's waist. Pulled her towards him. Her hands went to his belt. She slid it from its catches and tossed it aside. The man began to wriggle himself out of his pants.

'Faces,' Danskin said. 'Without faces, this could be anybody. It doesn't clear him.'

The man's trousers fell to the floor, revealing a fleshy black rear. Black, apart from a slash of vivid pink in the shape of a figure seven.

'A scar. Find out if Milton has a scar.'

'Already have, sir,' Nairn piped up. 'He does. Got it in the Gulf.'

'Fuck,' Danskin said. 'Still, doesn't prove he's with her. This could be any random female, at any time. This proves nowt.'

The couple on screen rolled onto the sofa, the man's bulk covering the petite woman. Her arm wound over his shoulder. An arm which bore a unique tattoo of a Hopi sun.

'Double fuck.' Then, 'The TV. Check the schedules.'

He continued to watch as the body of the man rose and fell, at first rhythmically, then more urgent.

'Got it, sir,' Trebilcock said. 'It's called Escape to the Chateau.' He paused. 'It clears him, sir. Given the time it was transmitted, there's no way he could have got from there to the crime scene in time. The timings are at least thirty-five to forty minutes out.'

Danskin roared in anguish. 'I've seen enough. Switch it off.'

'Aw, sir,' Robson protested.

'Off. Now.' Danskin let out a groan like a creaking floorboard. 'I need to tell Connor.'

Inside the Super's office, Danskin gave a nervous cough. 'There's some news, sir. We've managed to rule out one of the suspects. Narrows the field down a little.' He hoped against hope Connor bought the positive spin.

'It's not Milton, is it?'

'No, sir. It's not.'

Danskin felt the silence ingest him. He wondered if Connor had heard him. In time, the Superintendent spoke.

'Stephen, we need an arrest. Desperate times require desperate measures. I've given some thought to your proposal to set a trap for the Tyrant. I've consulted Imogen Markham, and she believes there might be a chance we can lure him to us, if we tread with caution.'

Danskin exhaled in relief. 'Thank you, Superintendent. You won't regret this. DC Graves is in regular contact with Florence Roadhouse. The old bird trusts her. I'll get Hannah to encourage her to write to The Mercury. We'll work on the wording. I'll bring Markham in to approve it, to make sure we get the tone and content right.' He stood to leave. 'I'll get onto it straight away.'

'No, you won't. Sit down, Stephen.'

'I don't understand. You said…'

'I'm standing you down from the enquiry.'

It took a moment or two for the words to register. 'You're joking me, right?'

Connor avoided Danskin's eye. 'From now on, DCI Kinnear's leading the investigation.'

'You can't do that, man. Why?'

Connor picked up a remote. Flicked on the Smart TV in the corner of his office. The Mercury channel streamed live. Danskin saw himself in close-up at the scene of the Dunston Rocket, a gormless expression on his face. The picture changed. It re-ran his confrontation with Megan Wolfe following the ill-fated press conference after the first incident.

The next image caused Danskin to emit a high-pitched whinny. The scene was captured from a camera mounted high up on a wall. It showed a room strewn with wreckage. An officer in combat gear raised a baton above the head of a man already being assailed by two other officers.

Towards the rear of the room where the confrontation took place, Lyall Parker stood alongside a clearly smiling Stephen Danskin.

'They've used their security camera footage. Shit.'

'Shit indeed. Very deep shit. That's a man being assaulted by three officers. A man you've only recently released without charge.'

Connor put his signature on a sheet of paper on his desk.

'DCI Danskin, I'm suspending you from duty. Immediately and indefinitely.'

CHAPTER THIRTY-ONE

Hannah used her key to let herself in. The smell hit her straight away. She grimaced, pinched her nose, and held the door open for Ryan to follow.

'Hello. Anyone home?' Hannah's question was rhetorical. She knew the answer.

She edged into the passageway. Lingered there for a while. Took a deep breath. Stepped into the compact lounge.

He lay half on, half off the sofa. Strings of vomit clung to his chin; the rest congealed in a vile-smelling pool on the carpet. He clutched a vodka bottle in one hand. Another lay empty on the floor.

'I knew this would happen.' The matter-of-fact way she said it resonated with Ryan.

'I didn't know he had a problem.'

'He hasn't. Not for the last eight or nine years. Not since Mum left. Not until today.' Hannah tenderly wiped drool from Stephen's mouth. 'Get me some water, will you? It's through there.'

Ryan did as asked. He found the kitchen easily. Finding a clean glass was something else. He settled on one which didn't appear to cultivate Gruyere.

It hardly mattered. It wasn't for Stephen to drink. Instead, Hannah tipped it over his head.

Danskin spluttered awake amid a stream of curses.

'Come on, dad,' she said. 'Sort yourself out for me, will you?'

Ryan had never heard her refer to him as anything but the DCI, Danskin or Stephen. The tenderness in her voice surprised him.

Danskin offered an embarrassed smile. 'Hannah. I'm sorry. I love you, you know that, don't you?'

'I do. But right now, you need to love yourself more, ok? Here – I'll help you up. Take a shower while I clean up in here. And don't lock the door, right? I've seen people drown in a shower tray before.'

'Now there's a thought,' Stephen said as he clung to the edge of the sofa for stability. 'Don't look at me like that. I was only joking. I think.' He stood, contemplated where he'd find the shower, and unsteadily made off into the corridor.

Stephen Danskin re-emerged twenty minutes later, bleary-eyed but pink-skinned and shaven, into a lounge smelling of Febreeze and Dettol carpet cleaner. 'Right. This is what's going to happen,' he began, as if what went before had never occurred. 'I want you to keep me in touch with the investigation. Rick Kinnear's a steady hand but he'll never solve this. I will, if it's the last thing I do.'

'I can't do that. You know I can't.'

'You can, love. And I know you will. I want you to work with Ryan. If you keep me in the picture, I can guide you. If you need another pair of hands, use Treblecock.'

Hannah snickered. 'What, the same Nigel Trebilcock you can't stand?'

'He's a canny lad, is Treblecock. A bit of a lummox, but he means well. Besides, I can't compromise Lyall or Sue's careers, and Todd'll never keep his mouth shut.'

'Sir,' Ryan said, 'You can't put Hannah in that position. Let me work with you. I'd like nothing better. Remember, this bloke killed Frank Burrows and I'll do anything it takes to see him behind bars.'

'Son, you can't do it on your own. I admire your principles, but you'll soon learn to lose them in this job. No, you and Hannah work together.'

Hannah shook her head. 'He's made his mind up, Ry. Nowt's going to change it now.'

'That's ma girl. Ok, listen. Listen to me. All you have to do is use your powers of persuasion. Once Kinnear's agreed, it's in your hands.'

'What's in my hands?'

A broad grin stretched across Stephen Danskin's face. 'You'll see.'

**

'You've got me all confused, young lady. It's no time since you told me I had to stop writing. I've been going out of my mind with boredom. Yet, now, you're telling me you want me to start again. Which is it to be?'

Hannah took her time explaining. 'We want you to write, Miss Roadhouse. But I'm going to tell you what to say.'

Florence tisked. 'Preposterous. Why don't you just write it yourself?'

'Because, it needs to be in your words. Exactly as you would choose to write it. It's important you do this for me, Miss Roadhouse. I wish I could tell you why, but I can't. Not yet. I promise I'll explain as soon as I can.'

Florence shook her head. 'I don't know. All very secretive.' She addressed Ryan. 'What about you? What do you think?'

'I think you'll be doing your community a great service if you do as DC Graves asks.'

That did the trick. 'You do? Well, I'm sure you know me well enough to realise I like to do my bit for our community. You're positive your Superior agrees to this?'

'He does.'

Florence paused for thought. 'And you promise me it's not that dreadful Danskin man?'

Hannah suppressed a laugh. 'No. We're asking on behalf of Detective Chief Inspector Kinnear.'

'Good. I saw that other fellow on TV. Awful what he did. Just awful.'

Ryan stepped in to protect Hannah's feelings. 'Ok, Miss Roadhouse. What we want you to write about is something iconic to our region.'

'Happy with that so far. I'm always keen to promote our heritage.'

'Thing is, we don't want you to promote it, as such. In fact, we need you to have a little rant about it. You do that very well.'

'Is that meant as a compliment?'

Ryan ignored her. 'What we're after is a piece about something that's been part of the region for longer than I've been alive. Something first installed on a hill outside Gateshead over twenty years ago. Are you with me?'

'I think so. You're talking about the Angel of the North statue, aren't you?'

'I am.'

'I have to say, I quite like the rusty old thing.'

Hannah interrupted. 'For us, though, we need you to pretend you hate it. Really hate it.'

'In fact,' Ryan said, 'In your own words we'd like you to explain why you think it's a monstrosity. A waste of money. How it cost £800,000 which, back then, could build three or more hospitals. Or over eighteen nursing homes for the elderly and infirm.'

A glint appeared in Florence's eyes. 'That would mean a lot to you, Mr Jarrod, wouldn't it?'

Ryan thought of his grandmother. Nodded his agreement.

Florence's pensive look evaporated. 'I have to say, The Angel's supposed to protect and defend us. He hasn't done much of that these last few weeks. I suppose I could mention that, if you want.'

Ryan and Hannah shared a glance. 'I think that's a really good idea.'

'Anything else you want me to include?'

Hannah wanted to make sure the location piqued the bomber's interest. That it was significant enough to target. 'I read the Angel's seen by one person every second, either by those travelling on the main northern rail line or driving by on the A1. It's probably the world's most viewed art installation. You could weave facts like this into your letter.'

'You don't ask for much,' the old lady laughed. 'Any other demands?'

'Yes,' said Hannah. 'Don't, under any circumstances, send it until we tell you. DCI Kinnear needs to approve it.'

'And one more thing,' Ryan concluded. 'Don't post it. Deliver it by hand so The Mercury believe its authentic. Give them no reason to believe it's anything but your own genuine work.'

Florence narrowed her eyes. 'You make it sound like a James Bond film. I'll do it. Just tell me when.'

**

Rain fell solidly for two days, hampering Kinnear's attempts to ringfence the scene. He'd listened to Hannah Graves, unaware he was being played by Danskin. On her suggestion, he reached an agreement with the local authorities and began fake restoration work on The Angel.

Scaffolding appeared around the sculpture. Floodlights were installed. Men in hard hats and coveralls seemed to work feverishly on their cleansing work while actually fitting cameras and motion sensors.

In the trees alongside The Angel, faux forestry commission workers trimmed branches whilst also assembling hides and look-out posts.

Officers disguised as council workers placed pressure pads on footpaths and approach roads. Still more men donned hi-viz jackets and pretended to carry out remedial work on the railway lines running above The Angel, and parallel to the A1 below. In reality, the men observed potential entrance and egress routes available to the Tyrant. They also scrutinised the scene for blind spots and weaknesses.

On the third day, the scaffolding disappeared. Work came to a halt. Except for those officers, including DCI Kinnear, holed out in the nearby Angel public house observing the cameras. And those who'd taken up refuge in the hides. And the Armed Response Unit positioned in the woods, in a railway signal box, up telegraph poles, and down drainage ditches.

Earlier the same day, Florence Roadhouse greeted Virginia and Moira on The Mercury reception staff in her usual formal manner as she handed over her Letter to the Editor.

**

Ryan and Hannah sat alongside each other in Stephen Danskin's apartment while Hannah updated the DCI on the investigation.

'Everything's in place. The site's secured and we've men monitoring it twenty-four seven on CCTV, people in situ on the ground, and firearms officers on the scene.'

'I can't see him planting anything in broad daylight,' Stephen said. 'The Angel's too exposed; completely different to his other targets. I take it Kinnear's using thermal imaging cameras?'

'He is. And the men are equipped with night vision goggles, too.'

'Good. You seem confident we've got all basis covered but if this goes belly-up, we'll never have another chance.'

Ryan spoke. 'Can I help? I feel like a spare part. I've done virtually nowt so far.'

'You can't really, Ryan,' Hannah said. 'Kinnear won't take as kindly to your involvement as Stephen does.'

Stephen Danskin checked through his notes. He looked towards the ceiling.

'You've thought of something,' Ryan observed.

'Son, you need to be honest with me. Are you up for this?'

Ryan tried to play down his eagerness. 'Tell me what you're thinking, and I'll say whether I'm capable or not. I won't agree out of bravado. I'll be truthful because this is for Frank. I won't do it if I think I'm likely to foul it up.'

Danskin cast a glance at Hannah. 'You've got a good 'un here,' he said.

Hannah smiled. 'I know.'

Ryan blushed. 'What do you want me to do?'

'Well, Kinnear's calling the shots now so Hannah will have to follow his lead, or at least let him think she is. You can pick up where Hannah left off with David Woods.'

Hannah squinted. 'What have you got in mind?'

'We know less about him than the others. If form's anything to go by, Woods is almost certain to be at the scene when the shit hits the fan. He's never missed one yet. I'm thinking it'll be an ideal opportunity to have a look around Woods' place.'

'We haven't a warrant for it.'

'Which is why it's risky. If you're discovered, Ryan, you'll go down for breaking and entering. Neither Hannah nor I will be able to help you. You'll have a record, which will rule you out of ever joining the force.'

'I'll just have to make sure I'm not found then, won't I?'

'Good lad. So, as soon as Imogen Markham does her witch doctor bit and predicts when the bomber's going to hit, Ryan will take himself on a jaunt to the seaside while everyone else concentrates on the Tyrant.'

Hannah checked her watch. 'I need to get away shortly. I'm on duty soon.'

'Wish I could say the same,' Stephen said, with feeling. 'We're just about done here. For the time being, at least.'

They sensed it was now or never. If the case was ever going to be cracked, everything rested on the trap they'd laid. The three of them sat without words, listening to the wind work itself into a ferment over the eaves of the building and rain rap against the windowpane like an unwelcome visitor.

Slowly, Stephen reached behind his chair. Produced a bottle of clear liquid. Hannah's face contorted in anger and disbelief. Before she could protest, Stephen handed it to her.

'I'm done with this. Get rid of it for me, will you kidda?'

Ryan had never seen Hannah's dimple dig so deep into her face.

**

In a claustrophobic room in the Angel public house, Rick Kinnear sat in front of a bank of monitors, waiting for a signal. Lyall Parker's voice crackled over the radio. 'It's driech out here, sir. Can hardly see ma hand in front of ma face. Are the monitor's picking anything up?'

'Negative, Lyall. Seems the cameras might work in the dark but don't cope too well with Jack the Ripper weather. I've got Ravi back at base looking into it but we're relying on the sensors for now.'

Lyall expelled air. 'What's Markham got to say for herself?'

Rick Kinnear clicked off the handset. Thought about his words. Clicked it back on. 'She's sure it's tonight. The letter's been published. She's gone over every word of it and she's confident it'll provoke an urgent response. We just need to be patient.'

Parker screwed up his face against the driving rain. Water dripped from his nose. Mud squelched over his shoes and caked his ankles in clay-cold filth. 'Easy to patient in a warm hotel room, sir.' As an afterthought he added, 'With respect.'

'He'll turn up. Trust me.'

'In that case, we could really do with those cameras.'

'I get it, Lyall. Just hang in there.'

Lyall Parker thrust his hands deep into his pockets and bunkered down beneath a bare-branched thorn bush next to Hannah Graves. The Angel of the North was barely visible through a haze of low-slung cloud and mizzle, yet its presence loomed over them like a tyrannosaur.

The silence was eerie. Kinnear had taken DC Graves advice and diverted northbound traffic off the A1 via Birtley, while the southbound route took drivers away at the Team Valley interchange. The perpetually busy A1 sat as desolate as a jilted bride at the feet of The Angel.

Parker jumped at a burst of static in his earpiece. Kinnear's whispered voice screamed in the silence.

'We got something on the sensors.'

CHAPTER THIRTY-TWO

The fourth flight of the night made its final approach towards Nigel Trebilcock's desk.

Todd Robson immediately reached for a new sheet of paper and began folding the fifth. 'Christ, I'm bored.'

'I'd never have guessed.'

'Remind me never to do a Foreskin. Desk duties would kill me.'

Trebilcock nodded towards the cast on Robson's leg. 'Teach you to be more careful in future, so it will.'

'Aye.'

They were the only two in the bullpen and silence settled, save for Treblecock's repetitive drumming on his desk. 'Like a morgue in here.'

'Thought you'd be used to it. Can't be much goes on in Pastyland.'

'There's not. That's why I wanted out.'

Silence resumed, broken by Todd Robson's sigh. 'I wish I was out there with them.'

'Me too. I blame your bloody leg. I know someone has to man the station but if you could get around better it wouldn't need the two of us.'

'Listen, pal, if I could get around more there's no sodding way I'd be stuck here. Especially with you.' Flight Five morphed into a meteor as Robson launched the scrunched-up paper at the Cornishman, who deftly deflected it into the wastepaper bin with his head.

'One-nil.'

'Divvent try to pretend you know owt about football.'

Before Trebilcock could respond, Ravi Sangar entered the bullpen.

Robson chuckled. 'Forgot you were locked away in your tech room. Feel free to join the party.'

'No thanks. I'm trying to get some sort of tune out of the cameras at the Angel. It's a pea-souper up there and the lads are working blind. I just found out something Treblecock'll be interested in, though.'

Nigel raised an eyebrow. 'Such as?'

'You're still on the McGuffie case, aren't you?'

'I'm working on it in the background, yes.'

'Thought so. I've finally got some sense out of the voice recordings from the back of McGuffie's cab. Pity the DCIs on gardening leave. He didn't think I'd do it.'

Trebilcock had to agree. 'Neither did I. You took your time.'

'I know. Thing is, the vocal patterns weren't what we expected. The voice wasn't English.'

Robson sat upright. 'South African? Is it Vorster?'

Sangar shook his head. 'Try again.'

'American. If it's Milton, Foreskin's been right all along.'

'No,' Sangar said. 'I don't mean it's not an English accent. I mean the language isn't English.'

Trebilcock and Robson looked at one-another. 'Well?'

'I've just alerted DCI Kinnear. The man in McGuffie's cab was speaking Welsh.'

**

Ryan popped a couple of painkillers from their packaging and thrust them down his throat. He wiggled his fingers. They ached almost as much as the burns on his palms. He shouldn't be driving, but how else was he to get to Newbiggin?

The Fiat Uno sat alone in the deserted car park of The Point. Buffeted by gales whipping in from the North Sea, the car rocked and bucked as if occupied by eager lovers. Within minutes of arriving, the windows fogged up adding to the illusion. Ryan swiped at the glass with a tissue, just enough to reveal total and absolute blackness outside.

Silver nails of rain hammered against the glass. Merged with the banshee screech of the wind in a crescendo of white noise. For the first time, Ryan doubted Danskin's certainty. No-one would set foot outside in this. Yet, Ryan had. And, so might David Woods.

Ryan grabbed the catch and pushed against the door. It didn't open, his efforts beaten back by the force of the wind. Even with his shoulder against it, the door wouldn't budge. He shuffled to the passenger seat. Tried the door. It ripped from his hands and flung itself back against the car chassis.

Ryan grabbed the door frame with both hands and jettisoned himself into a wind tunnel which swept him away in whatever direction it chose.

**

Hannah Graves felt the phone vibrate in her pocket. Instinctively, her hand went to it. She fumbled for the power-off button and the throbbing stopped.

Thirty seconds earlier, Kinnear had ordered radio silence for all but essential contact. Hannah felt the blood pound at her temples; not only because someone had entered the cordon around The Angel, but also because the unanswered call meant Nigel Trebilcock had information relevant to Ryan's mission. Information she couldn't access. Information which set her imagination running free.

Lyall's tap on her shoulder brought her focus back. He signalled for her to crawl to the next line of trees. Bog brown sludge clung to Hannah. She lay there, isolated and blinded by the shavings of mist which rolled over her.

An explosion of static in her ear caused her to gasp out loud. Kinnear's whispered voice followed.

'There's more than one of them. We've three motion sensor alerts now. Two to the east of the site. Looks like the other one is making his way towards them.'

Rick Kinnear spoke the words Hannah, Lyall, and the rest of the crew were thinking. 'Jesus. It seems the whole of The Mercury lot are involved.'

The volume of Kinnear's voice lowered still further as he read the signals from the motion trackers. 'Hannah,' he whispered, 'You've one of them right behind you.'

She rolled over as a screen of thorns moved aside.

**

'It sounds like you're in the shithouse.'

'I am,' Nigel Trebilcock asserted. 'Todd's hanging around like a bad smell. Look, I can't get hold of Hannah. She's not picking up.'

Danskin took time to absorb the words. 'Means nothing. Kinnear might have ordered silence. Have you got something?'

'I think so. Ravi's interpreted the speech patterns from the back of McGuffie's cab. The speaker's Welsh.'

'Woods! Does Ryan know?'

'Not yet. I didn't want to scare him unnecessarily. Besides, if it is Woods, he'll be at The Angel. Ryan's on safe ground.'

'True. But he needs to know. You get back to your station. I'll call him.'

Stephen pinched his lower lip. He'd been wrong all along. It wasn't Milton. Connor was within his rights to kick arse.

He dialled Ryan's number.

**

Ryan battled his way to St Bartholomew's church. Into a headwind, it was tough going. Breathless, he took shelter behind an ancient gravestone. The wind battered his jacket. Tore at his hair. Scrambled his thoughts. Icy rain seeped through his clothing. Penetrated to the skin. He shivered convulsively.

The North Sea raged malevolently at his back; dark, brooding and thunderous. Above his head, the flag at the end of its horizontal flagpole whipped and snapped and cracked loud as a thousand Jumping Jacks.

So loud, it was impossible to hear the Blaydon Races ringtone play from his cellphone.

Bent double as an aged crone, Ryan emerged from his worthless shelter and made for the row of fishermen's cottages, thankful for the knowledge the storm would mask the sound of breaking glass as he gained entry.

The caravan park adjacent to St Bartholomew's church shielded him from view of anyone foolish enough to venture out. He emerged from his cover a hundred yards from David Woods' cottage.

Ryan froze. Lights shone from every window.

David Woods was home.

**

Hannah's heart pounded in her chest, adrenalin coursed through her veins, heightened her senses; gave her the high needed to confront the Tyrant. She crouched, positioned herself to pounce as he emerged from the thorns ahead of her.

Then, she heard the squelch of footsteps behind. Felt raspy breath, almost snorts, on the back of her neck.

They were here, all of them. Right on top of her.

Three shadowy figures stared down at her.

She switched on her microphone.

'False alarm,' she said. 'Repeat; it's a false alarm.'

Three roe deer turned tail and scampered back into the bushes.

**

Imogen Markham prowled the hotel room like a caged tiger. Rick Kinnear sat back in his chair, relieved and frustrated at the same time.

'He's still out there, somewhere,' he said. 'We just need to hold our nerve. He'll come to us.' He looked at Markham. 'You are sure it'll be tonight?'

Markham spoke as she wore another furrow in the carpet. 'I am. It's tonight. Everything in his make-up tells me it's tonight.'

Kinnear spoke into his mic. 'Maintain position and maintain silence. We're still good-to-go.'

Lyall Parker's hushed voice crackled back. 'We're working blind here, sir. Has Ravi got anything on those monitors yet?'

Kinnear stared at a grey haze. 'That's negative, Lyall. Keep your cover. Leave the rest to me.'

Lyall switched off his mic. 'Och, that's what I was feart of,' he said to himself before resuming position alongside a bedraggled and shaken Hannah Graves. 'You look like you've seen a ghost,' he said.

'We'd better be right about this. There's too much at stake here,' she said, her thoughts on a windswept promontory twenty-five miles north.

'Markham's sure it's tonight.'

Hannah clicked on her mic. 'Sir, how sure are we about this? It's nearly five a.m. If this weather ever lifts, it'll be light in little more than three hours.'

Kinnear's voice hissed back. 'We're on silent here, Hannah, man. But, yes; it's tonight.' He ended the communication with a glance towards Imogen Markham. 'You look worried,' he said. 'Everything ok?'

Markham didn't reply. Not at first. She stopped stalking. Stood stock still. 'She's right, you know. He's leaving it late.'

'What?'

'I need to feel it.'

'What?' Kinnear repeated.

'I need to be with The Angel.'

CHAPTER THIRTY-THREE

Ryan ducked back into shadow. Rested with his back against the rain-slick carcass of a Willerby caravan. It shook and swayed in the gale, but no more than Ryan trembled. How was he to enter Woods' property when the Welshman was still at home?

But, was he at home? Perhaps Ryan had checked the wrong house. In the darkness, he may have miscalculated.

Rain turned to sleet turned to hail, peppered his face with lateral volleys of icy gunshot. He wiped crystals of ice from his forehead and peeked out. The row of houses presented itself as a shadowy monolith. It was impossible to identify which one belonged to Woods from this distance.

The Blaydon Races went unanswered for the third time.

Ryan clambered over the golf club fence and trekked towards the houses. In the exposed openness of the golf course, the wind made his progress even more tenuous. Eyes fixed on the cottages, the wind caused him to lose balance. His foot disappeared from view beneath him. The rest of his body followed as he tumbled into a bunker. Sodden sand clung to him. Seeped beneath his gloved and bandaged hands.

He clambered out. As his head emerged above the lip of the sand trap, lightning flashed as a muted glow deep within the darkened heavens. Muted, but sufficient for Ryan to make sense of what he saw.

Woods' cottage was the illuminated one. But it wasn't lit by lamps. The light in the windows flickered red. The house was ablaze.

He sprinted as best he could into the gale, ignoring the friction burns to his lower stomach. Ryan disregarded the warning thoughts of the last time he confronted fire. Cast them to the back of his mind.

He charged towards the door, turning sideways, braced for impact. He hit it with all his might.

The door was unlocked and off the latch. Ryan was pitched forward into a nightmare world, greeted by a haunting, otherworldly cry.

It froze him to the marrow.

**

Rick Kinnear leapt from the unmarked car. Imogen Markham followed, tentatively placing a stiletto into a quagmire.

'Okay – where do you need to be? Remember, he could still be out there. You have to maintain cover.'

She picked her away across a slime-infested field. 'I don't. He's not here.'

'Well, where the fuck is he?'

'That's why I had to come to the site. See if I could sense anything.'

Kinnear gauped at her. 'Are you a criminal profiler or a fucking medium? Christ, what's Connor thinking of?'

'Sshh.' Imogen Markham closed her eyes. She felt the rain wash over her. Absorbed it. Her nostrils flared.

A disheveled Lyall Parker made his way towards them. Kinnear shrugged and rolled his eyes, but he put his finger to his lips all the same.

Markham took a step forward. Left a shoe stuck in the mud. She limped a few more paces. Opened her eyes. Stared in the direction where The Angel of the North stood shrouded in its cloak of mizzle. Lightning flared. Three armed officers dropped to the ground as they were silhouetted against the light.

Neon blue lightning smote the sky again, casting a halo over The Angel. The giant structure looked down on them, almost pleading Markham to make the connection.

'It's too easy,' Markham said. 'Way too obvious for him.'

'And you realise that now. Fan-bloody-tastic.'

'He's used all the other letters cryptically. Hasn't gone for the correspondence's main subject. I should have realised.'

Kinnear raised his face skywards. 'Yes. You should.'

Imogen Markham turned towards Kinnear and Parker. A smile creased her face.

'Got it,' she said.

**

The first thing Ryan Jarrod noticed was the fact that David Woods cottage wasn't on fire.

Candles, scores of them, stood on every available surface. A sickly cocktail of scented aromas flooded the air. A plethora of dreamcatchers purloined from far-flung lands hung from the ceilings like alien spider-webs.

Ryan jumped as the eerie wailing sound resonated through the cottage, again, and again. A sporadic, high-pitched, ethereal moan.

'Who's there?' he asked, realising how stupid he sounded. He inched forward. Pushed open the living room door.

'What the…?'

Ryan's gaze was drawn to an array of display cabinets affixed to the walls. Each contained some exotic species, mainly sea creatures.

On a glass coffee table, a copy of National Geographic sat open at one of Woods own set of photographs. Alongside it, an empty bowl and teacup. Ryan touched it. Hard to tell through his dressings, but he sensed it retained a slight warmth.

On the shelf below the table, a pair of old loafers stuffed with socks gave further credence to recent occupation.

A different sound emerged above the moans. A shrill cry. A series of staccato clicks followed. Realisation dawned. The cry of dolphins; the other, whale song. Ryan shuddered. Woods' cottage was creepy beyond compare.

Ryan studied the display cabinets. He recognised a species of squid, piranha, lionfish. The jawbone of a juvenile tiger shark sat bathed in candlelight. Examined a horrific-looking deep sea creature with bulbous eyes and huge, gaping mouth. The last cabinet stood empty.

He edged towards the kitchen. Gently pushed on the kitchen door. It opened with a creak. He peered around it, and cried out in shock.

**

In the near-deserted bullpen of the Forth Street Police HQ, Nigel Trebilcock paced the floor. The DCI, the proper DCI, not Kinnear, hadn't got back to him. He had no way of knowing whether Ryan had received the message.

'Howay, man, Treblecock. Sit doon, will you?' Todd Robson asserted. 'You're making me nervous.'

'You mean you're not already?' Trebilcock said, continuing on his road to nowhere.

'Nah. Why should I be? It's out of our hands. Leave it to Lyall and Hannah and co. They'll sort it, if anyone can.'

Nigel Trebilcock didn't seem convinced. He walked to a vending machine. Deposited some coins. The bottle of water landed in the dispensing tray with a thud. Nigel took a swig, then another.

He wandered to the crime boards. Looked them over.

'Think you'll see something no-one else has?' Robson asked with a hint of sarcasm.

Trebilcock shrugged. 'You never know.'

But Robson was right. Nothing leapt out at him. Nigel took another drink. Drummed his fingers on the board. 'Foreskin was convinced it was Milton.'

'And I don't blame him. I think we all did. But hey, that's what happens if you get it wrong at his rank.'

Trebilcock dispensed air with bloated cheeks. 'Does the Super never get involved?'

Todd barked out a laugh. 'He'll make an appearance once we've got our man. Take all the plaudits. Probably head up the news conference. He'll keep his head down until then, though, mark my words.'

Nigel idly leafed through some papers on Hannah's desk. Replaced them where they came from. He picked up another pile. Four sheets down, he came across Ryan's list of graduates from Bangor Uni.

Dafydd Bellamy. David Griffiths. David Patterson. David Tyfford. David Yelland.

Trebilcock did a double take. Dropped the sports bottle. Reached for his phone. Dropped it, too. Picked it up again.

Finally, he succeeded in dialing Danskin's number.

**

Ryan gave a nervous laugh. It was the cottage, he decided. The damn creepy cottage had got under his skin.

When 'The Blaydon Races' played out loud in his pocket, he'd jumped with fear in the doorway of David Woods kitchen. He'd heard the ringtone a hundred times. It was as familiar as his grandmother's voice. Yet, in the setting of the eerie cottage, with its whale songs, its candles, and its weird creatures, the tune had scared the shit out of him.

He retrieved his phone from the pocket. Looked at the screen. He'd heard the tone a hundred times, but not the last three.

Three missed calls.

'Shit.'

He swiped the green button. 'Sir, sorry. It's blowing a hooley out there…'

'Shut up and listen, Ryan. Don't go into Woods cottage.'

'Too late,' he said with pride. 'I'm already in.'

'Then, get out. Now. This minute. It's definitely Woods, and he's not at the Angel. If he's not already home, he will be. Soon.'

'But I haven't found any evidence yet. Plenty of weird shit but no evidence.'

'Just go, will you?', Danskin pleaded. 'I'll explain on the way.'

'Okay, but I don't understand. How do you know it's him?'

Ryan opened the front door to be met with a white wall of snow. Cyclonic funnels spiraled furiously in the wind. The blizzard rained down; frosting his hair, smothering his jacket.

'Ravi Sangar's worked out the voice from McGuffie's cab,' Danskin informed him. 'The occupant's speaking Welsh.'

The gale ripped half of Danskin's words from the earpiece of Ryan's phone. 'I didn't get that. I'm going back inside.'

'Don't!'

He did.

'What was that about Ravi?'

'The person in the back of McGuffie's cab was Welsh.'

Ryan took a moment to absorb the words. 'So, that ties Woods to McGuffie but it's not enough to convict, surely, or prove he's the Tyrant?'

'That's not all.'

'Go on.'

'Treblecock's looked over your list of graduates from Bangor University. Woods did attend.'

'No, he didn't. I've got the names. All of them. Woods wasn't one of them. And, it still proves nothing.'

'Trust me. He's on there. And it proves everything.'

Ryan twisted his face. 'I'm not following.'

'Treblecock's Cornish. Their traditional Celtic language has similarities to Welsh. You remember a David Tyfford being on the University register?'

'Yes.'

Danskin paused for a second.

'The English translation of Tyfford is Roadhouse.'

CHAPTER THIRTY-FOUR

Ryan slipped and skidded over virgin snow which creaked under his feet. His breath condensed in a plume the same dull silver as the skies as he scurried back to the Uno.

Woods, or Tyfford, or Roadhouse, had been home. Recently. The teacup still warm, the bowl unwashed. Perhaps he was still nearby. A door banged open and closed several times in the wind. The church door. The church which offered sweeping views over Newbiggin bay and the approaches to the village.

Ryan ducked into St Barthelomew's. The silence inside hit him like an uppercut. Stopped him in his tracks. He looked around. Through an archway at the northern transept, Ryan saw a narrow, stone staircase spiraling upwards. Up, towards the fortified church roof.

He took the stairs two at a time, his footsteps echoing on stonework bent and beveled by centuries of tread. He scurried onwards, the staircase becoming ever steeper, ever narrower.

In the darkness, a light glowed bright in his brain.

Florence Roadhouse. A nurse. An angel of mercy. The Angel.

If Danskin feared Woods was on his way home to discover Ryan in his property, it meant the DCI hadn't made the connection. Ryan withdrew his phone from his pocket. Dialed Danskin. Nothing. The thick stone walls blocked all signal.

He reached the top of the staircase. Flung open the dwarf-sized door. Snow and wind and bitter cold engulfed him even before he stepped out onto the church ramparts surrounding its tower. He circumnavigated the turret-like enclosure seeking any sign of Woods in the streets below, the faintest pre-dawn light insufficient assistance to his search.

He made out a couple of sets of recent tyre tracks in the snowy roads. Other than that, the streets were as deserted as the surface of the moon.

Ryan reached again for his phone. He had to alert Danskin of the threat to Florence. The tide raged against the rocks below and the Northumbrian flag slapped thunderously against its horizontal flagpole. Would Danskin hear him above the riot of noise? He'd know soon enough.

As he dialed, the wind caught the door behind him. It slammed shut. Ryan jumped. Swiveled on one foot towards the sound. His foot slid from beneath him. His cellphone slipped from his grasp as his hands scrabbled for purchase on the rough stone.

A gust of wind hit him head-on. Drove him back against the fortified parapet; a parapet no more than knee-high. Ryan already knew what would happen next.

He arched backwards. His arms windmilled, and gravity did the rest.

Ryan tumbled towards the jagged rocks and frigid waters below.

**

The man shrugged off his backpack and set it at his feet as he lowered himself onto a floral decorated chair.

'Thank you for agreeing to see me at such an early hour. I really appreciate it,' he said.

Florence Roadhouse sat opposite him, straight-backed, hands clenched in her lap. Alert. Wary. 'It is early. Very early.' She tightened her tartan robe.

The man smiled apologetically. 'And it's an entirely selfish motive, I'm afraid. I've been working through the night. Thought if I could see you now, I could get home and get some shut-eye. I can go, though, if it's inconvenient.'

She raised a hand from her lap. Gave a dismissive wave. 'You're here now,' she said, the swollen hand immediately resuming its place in her lap.

'Thank you, Miss Roadhouse. It is Miss, isn't it?'

She nodded.

'Good. Wouldn't want to get off on the wrong foot,' the man said. He showed her his credentials for the second time.

'There's no need for that. You wouldn't have got through the door if I hadn't recognised them first time.'

'Of course.' The man smiled, as cold as the morning air. 'I suppose you'll want to know why I'm here?'

'That would be a start, yes.' She remained aloof. Distant. Inside, all her senses told her this wasn't right.

'Well, as you know, I'm David Woods, and I'm from The Mercury,' he resisted the temptation to flash his press card a third time, 'And we've all been most impressed by the response to your spread. You have a serious following out there. We'd like you to do more.' The man beamed at her.

'Where's Mr Padwell?'

'I'm sorry?'

'Mr Padwell. The man who asked my permission to do the piece.'

A look passed across the face of the man called Woods. 'Mr Padwell covers a different field to me and, if I'm honest, I'm here to interview you; to find the real person behind our new columnist. Mr Vorster himself suggested our readers might like to hear about you; what your background is, where you get your ideas from.'

Florence continued to look at Woods, and he her. A silence, filled by the ticking of the mantlepiece clock, dragged by. Abruptly, Florence rose.

'Where's my manners? I'll make us a cup of tea. Milk and sugar?'

'Just milk, please.'

She felt her way into the kitchen, closed her eyes, and breathed deeply. Whatever it was the police had asked her help for, this was part of it. She felt it in her bones. She moved towards the wall-mounted telephone. The number of Hannah Graves lay scribbled on a notepad close by. She reached up to the cradle.

'I'll have a sugar after all,' the voice behind her said.

Florence lowered her hand and donned her impassive face. 'Of course. That's no problem at all.'

Back in the sitting room, David Woods looked around, drinking in the surroundings. 'So, Florence, we understand you were a nurse. Is that right?'

'I was. For more years than I care to remember. Would you like to hear about it?' Please say yes, she thought. Buy me some time.

'Very much. I want to learn all about you, Florence.'

For the next twenty minutes, she filled his head and his notebook with her memoirs. Finally, she had no more stories to tell. A tense quietness overtook them, much like the seconds before a cheetah breaks cover and embarks on her thirty-second kill chase.

'What of brothers and sisters?' Woods asked. 'Tell me about them.'

'Would that I could. I don't have any. I'm an only child so there's nothing to tell there.'

He looked at his notes. 'And, you never married?'

'No, I didn't. Neither the time nor inclination for any of it.'

'Children?'

Florence bristled. 'I beg your pardon?'

'Just because you didn't marry doesn't mean you don't have children.' He glanced at a photograph of a man in uniform. 'Tell me about him, if you don't mind.'

She did mind, but she needed the man there until daylight broke. If it ever did. 'If I was going to marry anyone, it would have been Samuel,' she said, rising to pick up the photograph more so Woods didn't sully it with his eyes than anything.

Woods looked up from his notes. 'Samuel?'

'Yes. We met when I was in the forces. He, too. I treated him for a while.'

'What happened to him?'

'He died, Mr Woods. That's what happened to him. Died in action.' Her eyes misted over. 'I was going to tell him something, that very day. But, I never got the chance.'

'What were you going to tell him? Something important?'

She snapped out a laugh. 'No. Not really.' She rose spritely. 'I'll make us some more tea.'

When she returned, daylight less than an hour away, the man's rucksack lay open. He cradled something in his lap. Rubbed it, almost caressed it, with his sleeve. It looked, to Florence, like half a giant easter egg. She adjusted her glasses and saw it wasn't.

'We have a lot in common, you and I,' Woods said. 'Never married. No siblings. Live for our work because we've little else to live for.'

'Speak for yourself, Mr Woods. I'm perfectly happy with my lot.'

'Are you? Are you, really?' Woods asked rhetorically. He stopped polishing the object in his lap. 'Do you know what this is?'

She set down the cups. 'Tell me.'

'This is a carapace from a loggerhead turtle. I keep it with me at home. It's very precious to me. Remarkable creature, the loggerhead.'

Florence shot a glance at the clock. The paperboy would be here soon. 'You've piqued my interest. Tell me all about them.'

'A female loggerhead can weigh as much as three-hundred pounds yet, during nesting season, she leaves the sea at night and lumbers her weight over dry sand. There, perhaps a hundred yards or more from the shoreline, she digs a pit with her flippers. It must be quite an effort, yet she does all that to make sure her eggs are protected.'

He began rubbing the shell again. 'And do you know the saddest thing of all? That same night, she'll lay her eggs and heave her way back to the sea and swim off, knowing she'll never get to see her offspring.' He locked eyes with Florence. 'Can you imagine how awful that must be?'

Florence maintained eye contact, though she felt her soul being sucked from her.

'Few of her young survive, you know. Only the strongest do. Only the very strongest. And her young are equally remarkable. They navigate by using oceanic magnetic fields in a migration covering thousands of miles. And they always find their way back to the very same breeding grounds where they were conceived. Where their mother left them. Remarkable indeed, don't you think?'

Florence's eyes darted over Woods face, taking in every line, every fold of flesh. Instinctively, her gaze flashed to the photograph.

'You know, don't you?' Woods said, his smile reaching his eyes for the first time. 'Finally, after all this time, you know who I am.'

Florence swallowed hard. Tried to speak. No words came.

'Why did you do it?' Woods voice was hard.

'How did you find me?'

Woods laughed. 'It's not the most common of names, is it? And once I found your name in the Northumberland archives, it was easy to trace you. Now, I ask again: why did you do it, mother?'

It was the word 'mother' that broke her. She reached into the pocket of her robe for a handkerchief. Blew her nose. 'It was different back then. So very, very different. I had no-one to turn to. All I had was my career.'

'No, you didn't. You had me. Or, you could have had me. But you chose not to. In fact, you've just said what you were going to tell my father the day he passed away 'wasn't important.' You were going to tell him you were going to have his baby, weren't you? But that, in your own words, wasn't important.'

He thumped his fist against his chest. 'I wasn't important. Have you any idea how that makes me feel? Have you?'

Florence shook her head. 'No,' was her pathetic response.

'I didn't even have a name. You couldn't be bothered to leave a note on the doorstep of that bloody pub telling them to look after 'Mark', or 'David', or 'Samuel Junior', or whatever name you had in mind. Did you have one in mind, honestly?'

Florence looked at the floor. Shook her head. 'But I did want you to have a family. That's why I left you on the doorstep where Mrs Denby could look after you.'

Woods spat out a cruel laugh. 'You couldn't even get that right, could you? Mrs Denby sold up weeks before you dumped me. I grew up with a complete stranger to both of us.'

Woods was stalking the floor now, back and forth. 'I honestly wondered what this day would be like. How I'd feel. What I'd want to say.' He walked around the sofa. Stood behind Florence Roadhouse. 'And you know what? I feel nothing. Absolutely nothing.'

He held the carapace aloft in both hands, above the head of Florence Roadhouse.

And brought it crashing down.

**

Ryan felt at peace as he tumbled silently through the snowy skies. An odd acceptance settled over him. No fear, no panic, no regrets. Just a clear sense of order.

Until the clatter of the flag slapping against its flagpole, closer and closer, filled his senses and brought him back to reality.

He knew where he was, and he acted on instinct. His spatial awareness honed through a decade or more of gymnastics sessions remained with him. At the same time as plummeted downwards, Ryan reached out, opened his fingers and felt them close around the flagpole.

Gravity forced his entire body to loop around the pole as he hung on grimly. The friction burned intensely on his damaged palms. The padding on his left hand acted like handguards in a manoeuvre he'd practised countless times before in the gymnasium. But the newly grown pink flesh on his lesser-protected hand shredded like grated cheese.

He let go of the bar with one hand. The strain on his left shoulder became unbearable. He grasped the bar again with his right hand and released a scream to relieve his burden.

As he swung away from the flagpole, he locked out his arms, arched his back, and kicked with his legs. He even remembered to point his toes as he circled the flagpole in the drifting snow and the darkness and the wind as if it were a high-bar; the turbulent seas below his only crashmat.

On the fourth circuit, his momentum slowed. He adjusted his grip. Hung from the flagpole with stinging palms, aching groin and, now, intense fear. Cold sweat doused his brow.

The flagpole began to sag under his weight. It creaked and groaned. He heard a popping noise. Then, another. A rivet bounced off his head as the mountings began to give.

With a monumental effort, Ryan muscled-up on his arms until his torso hovered over the flagpole. Gently; ever-so-gently, he lowered himself onto it, releasing the burden from his burning biceps.

Ryan edged along the flagpole until he sat at its strongest point and rested against the stonework of the church tower. Another rivet popped. The strongest point, but not strong enough.

Gingerly, he stood on the pole, the wind tearing at him like a rabid hound. He reached up. Inserted the fingers of his right hand into a crevice. Raised his left foot chest-high. Put it against the stonework. And hoisted himself from the flagpole.

He felt for another handhole. Found one. Raised his other foot. Inch-by-inch, he winched himself skywards. Finally, one hand looped over the rooftop crenalations. The other followed. And he pulled himself upwards before toppling headfirst into three inches of soft snow on the church roof.

He lay there, crying. Great, fathomless heaves as the pains in his hands, his memories of Teddy McGuffie, and the loss of dear old Frank overwhelmed him.

Something glistened in the snow alongside his tears. He felt for it, the cold wetness soothing his fingers. He touched the object. His phone. With trembling fingers, he dusted off a covering of snow.

Would it work? He had no way of knowing. Not until Stephen Danskin answered.

'Sir, you're never going to believe this...'

CHAPTER THIRTY-FIVE

It was Jam Jar who found her.

The front door was pulled to, but not on the catch. When he pushed the newspapers through the letterbox, the door inched open. Light shone through.

'Hello, missus. Your door's open.'

Jam Jar pushed it a little wider. Stepped into the passageway.

'Hello?' he said again.   He coughed loudly. 'Don't be frightened. It's me, James Jarrod. I've brought your papers.'

He knocked on the living room door. No answer, but a light shone round the frame like a halo. Jam Jar shoved on the door. It swung open. And that's when he found her.

She lay on the sofa, body twisted, face contorted, eyes wide.

Everything happened at once.

The front door was thrust open. Smashed against its joists. Light and noise and bodies stormed in, crowded the tiny room, squeezed the air out of it.

Wet and bedraggled faces, anxious, serious faces, took in the scene. Hands reached for him as more people filled the confined space. Jam Jar felt himself forced sideways. Strong arms engulfed him. Held him in a bear hug

'I didn't do anything. Honest. She was like this when I found her.'

'I know, James. I know.'

He recognised the voice. 'Hannah?'

'It's okay, James. It's all over now.' She took over from the detective who'd held him.

'I want my brother,' Jam Jar sobbed, tears streaming down his cheeks.

Hannah hugged him, caking him in clay and mud. 'He's on his way.'

A voice broke over the hubbub. Urgent. Commanding. 'In here. Quick.'

Hannah turned her head in the direction of the voice. The kitchen door stood open. David Woods hung from the ceiling beams, his legs dangling eighteen inches from the floor.

Hannah turned Jam Jar's head into her and cradled it against her chest.

'It really is all over,' she repeated.

**

All the usual suspects inhabited the bullpen, the mood sombre yet relaxed. In Superintendent Connor's office, Stephen Danskin prepared to hear his fate.

'Stephen, I can't condone the mistakes you made. You left the force wide open to criticism. Your actions were naïve, prejudicial and, if I'm honest, not what I'd expect from an officer of your standing or experience.'

Danskin remained silent yet didn't avoid eye contact. A nerve twitched in his cheek, the only indication of the tension he felt.

'But, at the end of the day, I can't deny that it was your plan to set a trap for the Tyrant, and that's how we solved this. You were right about Imogen Markham, too. She got it wrong. Again. And it nearly cost us. Again.'

'Sir,' Stephen said, 'In fairness to Miss Markham, she got it right in the end.' Discretion, not modesty, prevented him from revealing he'd already worked it out for himself, alerted Hannah, who set the ball rolling before Kinnear had put his arse into gear.

'That's very magnanimous of you, Stephen. So, all things considered, your suspension is lifted, as of now.'

'Thank you, sir,'

Connor raised a finger. 'Don't get ahead of yourself. There are conditions. One, you're station-based. Two, you do not speak about the case to anyone outside the force. In particular, anyone in the press. Do I make myself clear?'

'Crystal, sir.'

'And, three: you report to Kinnear.'

'What?'

'Don't push it, Stephen. You heard me. Finally: welcome back, DCI Danskin. You've been missed.'

Stephen took the Super's extended hand and fought back the urge to smile. He wasn't sure how he'd been missed when he'd never really been missing.

He'd worked with Hannah, Nigel Trebilcock and the remarkable Ryan Jarrod throughout the case. The four of them had solved it, not Kinnear, not Markham, not even Lyall Parker or Sue Nairn, and certainly not Superintendent Connor.

Stephen left Connor's room. His eyes searched out Hannah. With an incline of his head, he motioned for her to step outside. Once in the corridor, he said, 'There's someone here to see you.'

Stephen moved a discrete distance away as Ryan and Hannah embraced, awkwardly. Ryan stood with his arms extended, fresh bandages wound tightly and thickly around his hands. They hugged for a long time. Both wept. Neither spoke. They didn't need words.

Finally, they pulled apart. 'Sir,' Ryan said, 'We're going for a drink. We'd love it if you'd join us. For a Coke, that is,' he added hurriedly, blushing for the first time in a while.

'You don't want me hanging around you, man.'

'Yes, we do, dad,' Hannah said.

'Detective Graves. You do not call me 'dad.' He couldn't keep his false anger up for long. 'But I'm paying, okay?'

'Deal.'

'And, we're walking. I need some fresh air.' He looked through the window of the bullpen, at the self-congratulatory mob inside. 'Howay, let's get out of here.'

**

'I still don't get how anyone can do those things.' Ryan held his pint in two hands to make sure it didn't slip through the padding.

'Probably because you had a good, stable upbringing, lad. Who knows what growing up feeling abandoned and unwanted is like? It must do things to your psyche.'

Ryan shrugged. 'I guess so. But to kill dozens of innocent bystanders, and then specifically target your own mother.' He shook his head. 'I'll never understand.'

Hannah touched his leg. 'Then, don't change. Ever. Stay just the way you are.'

'He didn't go through with it, remember,' Danskin added. 'He didn't kill his mother.'

'Perhaps not, but only because she had a stroke before he had an opportunity to do it.'

Danskin contemplated for a moment. 'He had plenty of time, if he really wanted to. He didn't have it in him. All his anger, he let that out when he smashed the shell. No wonder the old dear got the fright of her life.'

Ryan felt his spirits rise. 'It's over now, anyway. He's not going to cause any more mayhem where he is.' He paused. 'Sir, if my hands ever heal properly, will I have a future in the force? I mean, not as an ordinary copper, but a proper detective?'

Stephen gave a rueful laugh. 'You mean you still want to, after all this? Yeah, 'course you do. We can fast-track you into CID these days.'

Ryan stiffened. 'I don't want your help. I want to make this on my own, the way Hannah has.'

'And how do you know I didn't help Hannah?'

'Because you wouldn't. I know you. Both of you.'

The three sat in silence, Ryan sipping beer, Hannah prosecco, and Stephen ice-laden Coke.

'Do you think they'll let me see her?' Ryan said at length. 'If she makes a recovery, that is.'

'Florence, you mean? I presume so. Dunno. Never thought about it,' Stephen said, thinking about it.

Hannah held his hand. 'You shouldn't get too involved in the case, Ryan. You can't do it. It'll kill you. Trust me.'

'I feel I owe it to her, though. She was good to my gran. Not every case I deal with will feature somebody I know. This is a one-off. I just feel, I can't explain. I guess it might let her know somebody still cares.'

Stephen Danskin steepled his fingers. 'You're a good lad, Ryan Jarrod. And, you know what, I owe it to her, too. If I'd been smarter, joined the dots earlier, hadn't be so focused on Leeward-sodding-Milton, her son would still be alive. Let's see what I can do,'

**

'I really can't allow you more than five minutes, you know.' The ward sister held a pained expression, a brow furrowed with tramlines of worry and stress.

'I promise you, we won't be more than that. We just thought it might help if she knew people cared about her.'

'Five minutes, that's all,' the sister said. 'It's been less than three days. She needs time and rest to make whatever recovery she's capable of.'

The medic held them back. 'And, before you go in, I must warn that you her body might be broken, but there's enough brain activity going on to confirm her mind is unaffected. She can hear everything you say. She can't show it, because she's locked-in, but she knows.'

Ryan shook his head. 'Must be awful for her.'

'It must,' the sister said. 'She's still very anxious, very restless.'

'How can you tell? I thought she couldn't speak?' Danskin queried, his detective instincts still at work.

'Oh, she can't. Not a word. Possibly never will again. But you mustn't tell her. She needs to keep believing.'

'So, do her brain patterns show she's anxious? I'm sorry. I'm a total newcomer to all this, as you might have guessed.'

The sister gave what passed for a smile. 'Much less scientific than that, I'm afraid. Miss Roadhouse is totally inert, completely paralysed, except for a little movement in her left wrist. She's never stopped tapping away since she came out of the immediate after-effects of the stroke. The poor dear's driving our nurses demented with it. That, Detective Chief Inspector, is how I know she's anxious.'

She swished the curtain aside. 'Now, five minutes.'

Florence Roadhouse lay inert, deathly pallid, older than time itself. She was connected to feeding tubes, drips, catheters; all manner of plastic piping snaked under her translucent skin.

Ryan swallowed hard. 'You ok, son?' Stephen asked.

'Hello, Florence,' Ryan said, trying not to do the stereotypical shouting thing. 'It's me. Ryan Jarrod. Do you remember? You know my grandmother, Doris Jarrod.'

The old woman lay silent as death.

Ryan and Stephen shared a glance. Stephen nodded, inviting Ryan to continue.

'I've got someone with me. His name's Stephen. He's Hannah's dad.' The phrase sounded odd. 'You remember Hannah, don't you? You and her hit it off.'

Silence. Stillness.

Ryan expelled air. Tried again.

'My, you've been through the wars, haven't you, Miss Roadhouse?'

The word 'wars' triggered something within Florence. Her wrist lifted a centimetre. Came down on the bedframe with a clang.

The noise made Ryan and Stephen jump. 'Jeez, you gave us a fright there. But that's a good sign. Do it again if you want.'

Florence Roadhouse did. Again, and again, a relentless tapping of boney wrist on metal bedframe.

'The sister wasn't wrong, was she?' Stephen commented.

'Ssshh. She's with us. Remember what the sister said.'

Stephen nodded. Ryan continued with banal chat. The remorseless tap-tap continued, too.

Stephen checked his watch. Ryan talked about the weather. His gran. James. Told her about Spud and his recent unrequited fondness for a neighbour's bull mastiff.

And still Florence tapped away, an anxious, heart-rending plea from another world.

After four minutes and twenty seconds, Stephen Danskin swore loudly.

'Sir, really. There's no need; not here.'

'Shut up and listen.'

Ryan listened. 'What am I listening to?'

'Listen to me, Florence. If you can hear me, tap once.'

The old woman's wrist rose and fell, and remained still.

'Good. Now, when you worked in the forces, did you spend time with the signaling corps? Tap just the once if you did.'

Her arm moved a fraction of an inch and fell. Once.

'Fucking hell, Ryan. Florence isn't anxious. That's Morse code. The wily old bird's sending us a message.'

CHAPTER THIRTY-SIX

Stephen Danskin, Nigel Trebilcock, Hannah and Ryan poured over files and evidence. They watched endless reels of footage. Danskin knew it had to be squeaky-clean this time; no base left uncovered. This was their last shot.

But, like the Boss in Level Ten of a game of Sonic, one obstacle stood in the way.

'Run it again,' Ryan asked.

Hannah clicked her tongue. 'Must we?'

'Just once more. Please. There's something we're missing, and I feel we're going to kick ourselves when we find it; it's going to be that obvious.'

They replayed the footage.

'Any the wiser?'

Ryan shook his head.

'Ok,' Stephen said. 'We'll have to go to the Super with what we have. If Florence survives long enough, we should be ok. If she doesn't, God bless her, it's anyone's guess.'

He prepared to face Connor one last time. 'I just wish we had a 'plus one' to corroborate Florence's story in case she doesn't pull through.'

Ryan slapped his padded hands on the desk. 'Eureka! That's it! That's exactly it!'

They looked at him, expectantly.

'Ouch,' he said, wringing his hands. 'That bloody hurt.'

**

'Sir, I have new information on the Tyneside Tyrant case. I need you to consider it as a matter of urgency.'

Connor didn't look up from the pile of papers on his desk. 'Closed case, Stephen. Surely it's not that urgent?'

'Well, that's just it, sir. The information blows the case wide open. We got the wrong man.'

Connor was sufficiently interested to set down his pen. 'You're telling me someone else was in on it? I don't think so, Stephen. It's an open and shut case. It's Woods, all right. You said so yourself.'

Stephen had prepared himself for this. 'Why would he do those things? It defies logic.'

'The man was off his trolley. He discovered the mother who'd abandoned him. Took his angst out on anything associated with her, or that she associated with. In other words, the crap she wrote about. Then, when he'd had enough, he killed her – or thought he had - and topped himself.'

'I don't think that's what happened, sir. I don't think Woods was involved at all. I believe the Tyneside Tyrant is alive and kicking.'

Connor let out a sigh which lingered for what seemed like minutes. 'I know I'm going to regret asking, but just who do you propose is the culprit?'

'Sir, I'm seeking a warrant for the arrest of Leeward Milton.'

Connor flopped back in the chair. Interlocked his fingers over his stomach. Shook his head. 'You need a holiday, Stephen. Or help. Or both. How many times do you want to arrest the poor bloke? You're obsessed, man.'

'Bear with me. Don't see what you expect to see, ok?'

'I haven't time for this.'

'Yes. You. Fucking. Well. Have.'

Danskin thought the Super was about to spontaneously combust so he ploughed on.

'We know Milton has the means. Much more so than David Woods. We also know he's skilled in arm-to-arm combat. Can you honestly see Woods being capable of inflicting those injuries on McGuffie? And, then, having the wherewithal to follow up to the hospital and see him off?'

'You're forgetting one rather important matter. Milton wasn't in McGuffie's cab. It was Woods, remember?'

Stephen smiled. Not quite triumphantly, but a smile nonetheless. 'I believe Milton was in Teddy McGuffie's cab. When Treblecock was investigating the assault, he set out to interview a Romanian lass who worked the switchboard the night McGuffie was attacked. He got nowhere with her, because Charlton sacked her. Why? Because she was about to spill the beans. That Charlton let his cabbies go rogue at the end of their shift. Switch off radios, the meter, everything. He let them charge what they liked for the last fare of a shift, and trouser the proceeds. You see, sir, Woods wasn't the last in the cab. Leeward Milton was.'

Connor rocked back and forth. 'And you have proof?'

'Not outright proof, no. But we know McGuffie dropped Woods at the Printer's Pie. Guess who used his bank card to buy a round of drinks not half an hour earlier? Leeward Milton, come on down.'

Connor rose from his chair. Paced the room. 'Understand I'm doing no more than humouring you here, Stephen, but suppose you're right: why would Milton kill McGuffie, let alone go on the rampage?'

'McGuffie, because he could ID him. Potentially, McGuffie was the only witness who could place Milton at the Uni. Why? Because he dropped him off there. As for the other atrocities, we've already gone over Milton's motives: his background, the trauma in the Gulf, and his reaction to it.'

'Ok. He's a madman. A nutter. Just supposing it is him – just supposing, mind – and Milton blows up all and sundry on a whim and a letter. Why go for Roadhouse? Why's she the catalyst?'

'That's what I couldn't figure, sir. But, remember last time I brought him in? We went through his vlog diary. The fact he wished he'd never been born. The fact he wouldn't have if his father had perished in Vietnam.'

Connor paused for thought. 'And you think, because Roadhouse served in 'Nam treating US troops, Milton somehow connected her to it?'

Stephen rubbed the crown of his head. 'That's about the size of it. The old bird's been writing to the paper for years but the attacks only started after Roadhouse first mentioned her Vietnam connections.'

'He has an alibi, Stephen. Signed, sealed, delivered and witnessed by every perv in the force. They've watched the video of him and Wolfe until it's as scratchy as a Laurel and Hardy flick. He was clearly otherwise engaged at the time of the only incident we thought we could pin on him.'

Stephen almost laughed. 'Ah, but he hasn't. Ryan says...'

Connor held his hands aloft. 'Whoa, whoa, whoa. This is the vastly experienced Detective Ryan Jarrod we're talking about here, is it?'

'I know, but he's good at it and he'll get a damn site better,' Danskin continued undaunted. 'What's more, he's uncovered the flaw in the alibi. Remember when Milton sets the camera up? He moves the plant on top of the TV. None of us understood why. We do now.'

Connor looked unimpressed. 'Enlighten me.'

'He moved the plant so it covered the TV channel logo. The channel he was watching wasn't Channel Five. It was Channel Five 'Plus One'; a catch-up channel. You see, that means his timings are out. By an hour. We've gone over the timescales. He had time to do the deed, get back home, set up the scene, and still bang Wolfe as an added bonus.'

'If you're right, she's implicated, too.'

'I wish she were after the way she screwed me over; I really do. But, sadly, I think she's made an innocent mistake. Genuinely lost track of time and saw what she expected to see once Milton had set it up as an alibi. She took what he said at face value. After all, in normal circumstances, half an hour here and there isn't significant. In terms of Milton's alibi, though, it's absolutely crucial.'

Danskin waited for Connor's verdict. Waited for praise, or the sack. He got neither. Not for a long while.

Finally, Connor shook his head. 'Too many holes, Stephen. You've almost convinced me, but a good lawyer would blast your theories to high-heaven. We need more.'

Danskin pulled his rabbit out the hat. 'Would an eyewitness help?'

Connor's jaw hit the floor.

**

Stephen collected Ryan from the cafeteria and wandered towards the bullpen.

'You should have seen Connor's face,' Stephen said. 'When I told him Florence Roadhouse would be more than happy to tell, in her own unconventional way, how a black American gate-crashed her reunion with her only child, and went on to leave her for dead after stringing David Woods to the cross-beams of her kitchen ceiling, he went an odd shade of puce. I thought he'd swallowed his tongue.'

Ryan laughed out loud. 'But he bought it. That's the main thing.'

'Aye, lad. It's the only thing that matters. We got him in the end. Come on, let's celebrate with the crew.' He led Ryan towards the swing doors with their porthole windows.

'Sir, if you don't mind, I'd rather not.'

'Come on, man. Divvent be shy.'

'No. This is your case. You've been through hell for it. You were right all along, but it nearly cost you your career. You take the plaudits. You deserve them.'

'Hadaway man. It was a team effort, and you were part of that team.'

'Sir, I'm not a Detective. Not yet. You can't order me to go in there with you.'

Danskin pulled away from Ryan. Looked at him at length. 'You, my lad, are one of the best.'

'Go on. Get in there. They're waiting for you.'

Stephen went to shake Ryan's hand. Remembered the wounds. Decided on a high-five. Changed his mind for the same reasons. Settled for a man hug. He pushed open the swing doors and walked into a silent bullpen.

Ryan watched as Stephen made his way through the squad, each head turning to follow him, not a word spoken.

Slowly, Todd Robson gathered his crutches under his armpits, struggled to his feet, and began to applaud. Nigel Trebilcock followed more enthusiastically, then Ravi Sangar. Soon, every man jack of the team was on their feet, applauding Stephen Danskin.

Rick Kinnear gave him a thumbs-up, Connor stood in the doorway to his office and gave an old-fashioned salute. The staid Sue Nairn offered Stephen an embarrassed air-kiss at the same moment Lyall Parker threw an arm over Danskin's shoulder.

As the door swung shut and Ryan continued watching the scene through the porthole window, Hannah Graves turned to face him.

Ryan raised his hands and tried to wiggle his fingers in a child-like wave. Nothing happened. He saw Hannah laugh, her dimple as cute as a puppy.

He blew her a kiss. She responded in kind before hugging her boss, colleague, step-dad; Stephen was all of those things, and more.

Ryan Jarrod stepped into the elevator. As the door slid shut, he took in the scene, the smells, the sounds of the station.

'I'll be back,' he said. 'Mark my words. Soon, and for keeps.'

****

Author's note:

Thank you for taking the time to read *The Angel Falls* - it means a lot to me.

If you did enjoy it, please tell your family, friends, and colleagues. Word of mouth is an author's best friend so the more people who know, the greater my appreciation.

Oh, and I love seeing your feedback so please leave a review of your experience reading the first Ryan Jarrod novel.

If you'd like news of the next book in the series, you can follow me on:

Twitter - @seewhy59
Facebook - @colin.youngman.author

Thanks again.
Colin

About the author:

Colin had his first written work published at the age of 9 when a contribution to children's comic *Sparky* brought him the rich rewards of a 10/- Postal Order and a transistor radio.

He was smitten by the writing bug and has gone on to have his work feature in publications for young adults, sports magazines, national newspapers and travel guides before he moved to his first love: fiction.

Colin previously worked as a senior executive in the public sector. He lives in Northumberland, north-east England, and is an avid supporter of Newcastle United (don't laugh), a keen follower of Durham County Cricket Club and has a family interest in the City of Newcastle Gymnastics Academy.

****

Coming Next

from

Colin Youngman:

The Girl on the Quay

A Ryan Jarrod Novel

Printed in Great Britain
by Amazon